PS 3563 .C261185 P58 1997
McClain-Watson, Teresa, 1960
-
Plenty good room

Plenty Good Room

Teresa McClain-Watson

Plenty Good Room

Fjord Discoveries No. 1

Fjord Press
Seattle

Copyright © 1997 Teresa McClain-Watson

All rights reserved. Without limiting the rights under copyright reserved above, no part of this book may be reproduced, stored in or introduced into a retrieval system, or transmitted, in any form or by any means (electronic, mechanical, photocopying, recording, or otherwise), except for the purposes of a review, without the prior written permission of both the copyright owner and the publisher of this book.

This is a work of fiction. Names, characters, places, and occurrences are either the product of the author's imagination or are used fictitiously. Any resemblance to actual persons, events, or locales is purely coincidental.

Published and distributed by:
Fjord Press, PO Box 16349, Seattle, WA 98116
tel (206) 935-7376 / fax (206) 938-1991
email: fjord@halcyon.com   www.fjordpress.com/fjord

Editor: Steven T. Murray
Cover design and illustration: Jane Fleming
Design & typography: Fjord Press
Author photo: Don Morris
Printed on acid-free paper by Versa Press, East Peoria, Illinois

Library of Congress Cataloging in Publication Data:

McClain-Watson, Teresa, 1960–
    Plenty good room / Teresa McClain-Watson.
        p.   cm — (Fjord discoveries ; no. 1)
    ISBN 0-940242-74-5
    I. Title. II. Series.
PS3563.C261185P58   1997
813′.54 — dc21   97-23995
                                          CIP

First edition

To
my husband Johnny,
my knight in shining armor

With special acknowledgements to:
Fred and Nancy McClain, Minnie Hogan, Elder James McClain, Marion McClain, Shameika, Sherronda, and Sherman McClain, Mae Ola Norton, Minnie Lee Jordan, Dolphus and Shirley Jordan, Judea Cooper Mikell, Marilyn Enos, Anthony Cobb, Elizabeth Hicks, Deborah Lee, Betty Gainous, Jimmy Tadlock, Canary Girardeau, Annette White, Gwendolyn Lee-Green, Annie R. Brookins, Amparo Santiago, Gloria N. Felder, Ida Reed, Tasker Hannon, Donna Buchanan, Jenetha Denmark, Pastor Charles West, Jr. and the Greggs Temple A.M.E. Church family, Lynn Skapyap, Bartholous G. Woodley, II, and numerous other family, friends, and supporters

There is plenty good room
Plenty good room
Plenty good room
In my Father's kingdom
Plenty good room
Plenty good room
Choose your seat and sit down

—*Traditional hymn*

Plenty Good Room

One

I don't care what Mama, Dr. Dan, or anybody else says about it, pain is too painful to just talk about. They say it's supposed to help, but I don't see where it helps anything at all. And Mama wants me to talk to Dr. Dan about it. Yeah, right. Like I wanna sit in that dusty little old office of his and tell him my life story like he gives a shit. He don't care nothin bout me. He's only seein me cause he wants my Mama, but my Mama ain't even thinkin bout that man. He looks like a basset hound to her. But they want me to talk about it. Everybody wants me to talk about it, as if I'm this little black boy with nothin else to do but tell people my business.

It's not like I know what happened. I don't know what happened no more than they do. I went to live with my daddy down south, it didn't work out, now I'm back home. What difference does the details make? I'm back home, what else they wanna know? But Mama don't give up. She thinks I'm a walkin basket case. She thinks I'm gonna just start screamin any minute now and snatch all my hair out. I think she thinks I'm crazy. She thinks because it didn't work out with Daddy I'm supposed to act like some heartbroken little boy with no sense. But she can forget that. It ain't worth it. Why should I waste my time bein all miserable and shit when he don't even care if I'm dead or alive? I'll look like a fool worryin about it. I tell Mama this but she still don't believe me. I heard her tell Dr. Dan she know I'm hurtin cause I'm still her baby and she want my pain to stop.

Mama, as usual, got it all wrong. Number one: I ain't no damn baby. Number two: I ain't hurtin no more than nobody else got to live in this world is. Number three: Dr. Dan, who I don't think even graduated high school, let alone doctor school, can't help himself, how the hell he gonna help me? He can't tie his shoes. I swear to God. The man don't know how to tie his own shoes. He likes to walk around smilin and actin like it don't matter, but man, that junk don't be lookin right. Mama says I be worryin about the wrong things. She says Dr. Dan's a genius, that's how come he can't tie his shoes. But that's crazy. How can he be a genius and can't do what I do every day? I don't think he's a genius at all. I think because he walks around with a pile of books in his arms all the time and likes to talk about all these people nobody never heard of, people figure he's real smart. That's why he likes kickin it with uneducated people. He can quote great sayings all day and not a one of them would know what he's talkin bout.

Like this dude Aristotle. He's always talkin bout this dude Aristotle. He says Aristotle would say it's not important why things didn't work out with my daddy, but what's important is what I'm gonna do next. Judge men by their actions, he says Aristotle says. Yeah, right. That boy Aristotle bout as crazy as Dr. Dan. How should I know what I'm gonna do next? If I knew what I was ever gonna do next I wouldn't of done what I did in the first place, and me talkin to Dr. Dan, Mama, or anybody else wouldn't matter cause there wouldn't be nothin to talk about.

But it ain't like my mama listenin to me. She got me goin to Dr. Dan every day almost. He sit me down in this tiny office of his and ask me all sorts of stupid questions. He says traumatic experiences must be dealt with or they'll come back to haunt you later. Then he has to spend another fifteen minutes tryin to explain to me what traumatic means. But he can save his breath. I know what it means. It means when bad things happen to you, that's what it means.

But how can I tell *him* about it? He's Mama's friend. There's nothin to stop him from runnin to Mama soon as I shut up and tellin her everything. Everything! But Mama just will not give up. She says I either tell Dr. Dan about it or tell those strangers on a funny farm somewhere. Either way, I'm sho gon tell it. Besides, she says, how do I know she don't already know about it? My daddy could of told her, she says. Don't even try that. Daddy don't tell her nothin and she knows it. He cares even less about her than he do about me.

Anyway, it was on a Saturday morning. I went downtown to Dr. Dan's office like I had to do every week since I got back in town. But this time I shocked the mess out of him. I laid down on his couch (he actually had an old raggedy couch in that dingy little office of his) and started talkin. He couldn't believe it. And man, he didn't know nothin. He didn't know why I left Harlem in the first place, he didn't even know that! I decided, what the hell. Maybe Mama's right. Maybe if I talk it all out and put it all back on my mind, then maybe I can stop actin like somebody who done been messed up and can go back to livin my life again.

Monroe Oliver died, that's why I left Harlem. Only Monroe didn't just die, he didn't have cancer or nothin, but his own daddy shot and killed him.

I saw the whole thing. I saw Mr. Oliver bust in the door all drunk and shit, tellin Roe he was gonna beat his ass for stealin some money he was claimin to have. Roe said he ain't stole nothin, but Mr. Oliver wasn't listenin to him. He jumped your boy like your boy was a feather, and took him down to the floor in a headlock. But Roe was big, almost big as his daddy, and before I knew it, Roe had Mr. Oliver pinned to the floor. He beat the stew out of him! I ain't never in all my life seen Roe that mad. It scared me, man. I guess I should of pushed Roe off of him, but I just couldn't see myself gettin involved in that shit. Roe and his daddy fought all the time. It was a family thing with them two, so I did like I usually did and started gettin the hell out of there. Besides, it was like two in the morning already and Mama thought I was home in bed anyway. So I turned to go home.

That's when I heard the gunshot. It was like a bang, like a toy pop sound goin off. I didn't know what it was. When I turned around, Roe was still on top of Mr. Oliver, but his back was arched. I didn't realize Mr. Oliver had a gun till I heard the second shot and Roe fell over. Mr. Oliver, he was like in a trance, man. He just laid there. I bet his ass got sober then! But Roe was already dead. He was my best friend. My only friend, really. And we were both thirteen.

Mama naturally took it hard. She wouldn't let me out the

house for days after that. She kept talkin about how insane everything was, how we couldn't trust nobody no more, how children weren't safe in the hands of their own parents no more. She even called over Reverend Ruby. Mama hated Reverend Ruby because she was one of those holy-rollin jack-leg preachers who talked about Jesus way too much. But Mama didn't know nothin bout no prayin, and Reverend Ruby did. She wanted her to pray for me. Chile see his best friend kilt like that, she said, he need prayer.

I'll never forget that day. It was one of those hot June days. Our two-bedroom apartment was on the fourth floor and with windows so small you could damn near suffocate in there. Me and Mama sometimes would sit out on the fire escape for hours just to cool off a little. It was hot enough. But big fat Reverend Ruby still came bustin through our apartment door. Mama used to say whenever Reverend Ruby showed up, it seemed like the little breeze we did have got all sucked up, but that still never stopped Mama from callin her. She told Mama that I needed more than just a prayer. I needed to be "prayed through," with the layin on of hands and junk. It sounded like somethin straight out of one of those tent revivals Reverend Ruby was always settin up in an empty lot by the night clubs, so I got scared. I told Mama I didn't need all that religious stuff, but Reverend Ruby, who probably thought a talkin child was a dangerous thing, told me to shut up.

"He need it," she told my mama, "just as sho as a drunk need wine."

And Mama, who was as scared as I was, who didn't have a clue what was gonna happen to me, smiled and told the Reverend to go right ahead.

She slapped her fat, cold hand across my forehead, and before I knew it she had flipped me down to the floor. "All right, Bay Dawson," she said. "Let's get it on!"

She leaned down on me and started sayin "yes, Jesus" this and "yes, Jesus" that so fast that she started soundin like she was speakin Chinese. Mama later said Reverend Ruby had caught the Holy Ghost and was speakin in tongues, but whatever it was it was weirdo stuff to me. She was talkin so fast she started spittin all in my face and was foamin at the mouth. I wanted to get up and run but Reverend Ruby had the weight of her whole body on me. I looked up at Mama and she was lookin terrified with her mouth wide open. I wanted to tell her to get this crazy woman off me, but every time I tried to say somethin Reverend Ruby screamed somethin else in my ear about Jesus.

And if all her yellin wasn't enough, she had the nerve to have bad breath too. I mean it stank. I would twitch my head from side to side like I was havin spasms every time she opened her mouth, but that only made it worse. She thought the Holy Ghost was makin me jerk my head like that. "Help him, Holy Ghost!" she'd scream every time I made any movement.

But I got smart in a hurry. I stopped movin. In fact, I acted like I was dead.

At first, Reverend Ruby didn't know if she should keep on praisin God for doin whatever it was He was supposed to do to me or call 911. But when I didn't move—even when Mama had slapped me on the cheeks and told me to wake up, baby—Reverend Ruby panicked. She didn't figure she had that much power, not enough to knock anybody out anyway. I could feel her roll her big body off me.

She looked at Mama. Mama was damn near crazy.

"What you did to my baby?" Mama said. She was cryin as she put me in her arms and kept slappin the fire out of me. "Wake up, baby. Please wake up! What'd that crazy woman do to you?"

I almost smiled when Mama said that, cause Reverend Ruby was known as a mean somebody before she found Jesus, and she didn't take nothin from nobody.

"Crazy?" she said. "Who you callin crazy, Juanita Dawson?"

"You!" Mama said quick, cause she was a mean somebody too.

"I may be a lot of things," Reverend Ruby said, "but I ain't crazy. I can't help it if the Holy Ghost knocked him out. He'll come to."

"He better come to. Or I'll be knockin *you* out."

"Oh now look here," Reverend Ruby said, but before she could gear up to cuss Mama out, I started wakin up. I figured they were probably gonna start fightin any minute, so I decided to quit playin.

"Oh Bay, are you all right?" Mama said as I opened my eyes.

"I'm all right, Mama," I said, tryin to act sleepy.

"The Holy Ghost got a hold of you, boy," Reverend Ruby said. "It was the Holy Ghost."

I wanted to tell her she was out of her stupid mind, but I figured that would bring on a sermon from her, so I said, "Yeah, I guess so," and didn't say another word. Reverend Ruby felt so good that I agreed with her that she started preachin anyhow.

"Oh don't you underestimate the power of God, honey, don't you dare. My God is a good God. My God is a merciful God. I was in the muck and the miry clay…"

"I'm sure you was," Mama said, standin to her feet. "But I got work to do right now."

Reverend Ruby got mad. "Oh," she said. "I pray your boy through like you wanted and now you wanna throw me out?"

"That's not it, Reverend Ruby, and you know it."

"That's sho what it look like. First you gonna call me crazy, now you wanna throw me out. I figure after what I done for you I'm entitled to leave when I feel like leavin."

"Oh, you gettin away from here," Mama said, gettin mad too. "I don't care if you feel like it or not. This my apartment. I pay rent here. If I don't want you in here, your ass gettin out."

Reverend Ruby didn't say nothin at first. She looked at Mama, then at me, like we was the devil or somethin. I felt bad for her. Mama was too hard. You shouldn't talk to no preacher the way Mama talked to her. I guess Reverend Ruby wasn't used to that. But I still say it was all her fault. She knew how every time the two of them started in on any kind of conversation about anything, Mama was gon end up bein Mama and her cussin nature would come out.

I remember the time my brother Joe Nathan had to go to court for beatin up a white boy, Mama called over Reverend Ruby the night before to pray for him. But naturally Reverend Ruby can't just pray and let well enough alone, she has to do some preachin too. For some reason that night, Mama wanted to prove to the Reverend that she was as sanctified as anybody else, so she started repeating everything Reverend Ruby said, the way those old ladies in church do when the preacher do his thing. It was so funny because Mama didn't know what she was talkin bout, and me and Joe Nathan knew it.

"Jesus saves, chile," Reverend Ruby said that night, when

her and Mama were sittin on the couch with me and Joe Nathan between them.

"Yes He does," Mama said, like she knew what she was talkin bout.

"Jesus saved a wretch like me."

"Like me too, Reverend Ruby. Me too."

"I was in the muck and the miry clay."

"The miry clay. Yes Lord. The muck and the miry clay."

"But Jesus…"

"Jesus!"

"I said Jesus, Sister Nita."

"Jesus, Reverend Ruby. I say Jesus!"

"Put my ole tired feet on the rock to stay."

"Yes He did. He put mine there too."

"He saved me."

"Saved me."

"Sanctified me."

"Sanctified me."

"Filled me with His Holy Ghost."

"Yes He did now."

"Not any ole Ghost, Sister Nita. His *Holy* Ghost!"

"His Holy Ghost! Yes Lord."

"And I'm gon tell it from the mountain top."

"Tell it, Reverend Ruby."

"I'm gon tell it in the valley low."

"Tell it, Reverend Ruby."

"I'm gon praise the savior."

"Praise that man!"

"Everywhere I go!"

"Oh hallelujah."

"Cause I been in that lion's den with Daniel."

"Daniel, yes sir!"

"I seen that wheel in the middle of the wheel with Ezekiel."

"Zekiel!"

"I been in that prison with Paul and Silas."

"Paul and Siren too!"

"I been in that grave with Lazarus, chile."

"Laz'us, yes Lord. Laz'us chile."

"And I done been burned in that fiery furnace with Shadrach, Meshach, and Abednego."

"A billy goat, Meshack, and all them!"

By now me and Joe Nathan were cuttin looks at each other with big smiles on our faces. We wanted to bust out laughin but we knew Reverend Ruby didn't play that. But to see our mama actin all religious like she was tryin to act just didn't look right. Reverend Ruby, though, didn't seem to care if Mama was for real or not. She rolled her fat self off the couch and pushed to her feet. Joe Nathan kicked my shoe when she did that and told me with his eyes to look at Reverend Ruby's big breasts, which almost was showin when she pushed to her feet. Mama jumped up too.

Only Mama jumped up smilin. She didn't have no clue who Paul and Silas and Meshack and all those people was no more than I did. But she was tryin to prove somethin that night. She wanted to prove that a big-time, big-talkin sinner like her could get off on religion too.

Reverend Ruby didn't waste no time. She started in on the preachin again as soon as she hit the floor.

"Nobody knows my troubles like Jesus," she said, bendin down.

"Nobody," Mama said, bendin down too.
"Nobody knows the pain I bear."
"Nobody."
"Nobody knows the hurt and sorrow."
"Nobody."
"Nobody knows the shame I bear."
"Nobody, Reverend Ruby, nobody."
"Nobody, I said, nobody."
"Nobody, Reverend Ruby, no goddamn body!"

Like all those other times, Mama's true self came out. I guess a sinner can't get off on religion after all. And Reverend Ruby, who always acted like she was so shocked by my mama, stood in the middle of our living room with her mouth wide open.

"What you said, chile?"

Mama played crazy. "Bout what?"

"You just blasphemed the Holy Ghost."

"I ain't black-sheem nothin. What you talkin bout?"

Reverend Ruby, her hog head hunched and confused, looked at me and Joe Nathan, then back at Mama. "You ain't just one minute ago blaspheme God, chile?"

"I didn't."

"Reverend Ruby ain't deef now. Reverend Ruby heard you."

"Well, Reverend Ruby heard wrong."

"Now you lyin. First you commit blasphemy with your spiteful tongue, now you're lyin. You better repent, chile. You better fall on your knees right here and now and give your life to Christ."

Of course Mama didn't even think about doin that. She got mad and started cussin out Reverend Ruby for claimin that she cussed. You'd think they would of known to stay away from each other by then. Yet every time somethin bad happens and Mama need to get a prayer through, she call on Reverend Ruby. And every time Reverend Ruby comes. Her prayin helped Joe Nathan that time, cause he only got probation. But that was four years ago. When she came over and prayed for me, it was a different story. Cause even after she did all that prayin and speakin in tongues and layin on of hands, I could still see Monroe Oliver archin his back like a cat, then fallin off his daddy.

The thing I remember most about that day when Reverend Ruby tried to pray me through was when she left. That was when Mama told me I was leavin Harlem.

"Leavin Harlem?" I asked as I followed her into the kitchen. Our kitchen has always been a small space, with a refrigerator we got from some lady that Mama's friend Miss Cency used to work for, and a stove that worked when it felt like it. Our kitchen was so small that the table we ate off of was jammed against the wall and only two chairs could get around it. I sat down in one of them.

"Leavin Harlem?" I said again, since Mama acted like she didn't hear me the first time.

"That's what I said," she said and pulled a pot of lima beans out of the refrigerator. "Looks like lima beans again. Damn."

"But why, Mama? I ain't done nothin."

"I ain't said you done somethin. I just wanna stop it before it happens."

"Before what happens?"

Mama put some water in the pot of beans and put them on the stove to warm up.

"Before what happens?"

"Stop askin so many questions."

"Ma-*ma*!"

She looked at me. She knew full well what I was gettin at. She sat down at the table with me and pulled out a pack of cigarettes.

"I don't want what happened to Monroe Oliver to happen to you," she said. "Folks too crazy nowadays."

"But where I'm gonna go, Mama?"

"Florida," she said like she had been waitin to say it for a long, long time.

"Florida?"

"Where yo daddy is."

She said it! I knew she was one day gonna say it, and she said it. But was it true? I wasn't about to get too excited. Not yet. "He don't want me there with him, Mama."

"You don't know what he want. Besides, he ain't got no choice, cause you sho gettin out of here. This so-called city done took one of my boys, it ain't takin my other one too."

Mama was talkin bout Joe Nathan, my older brother. He was fifteen when he got shot up in a store robbery. It happened three years ago. Mr. Peterson got tired of bein robbed. He told Willie Cooper's mama so, the day before he killed Joe Nathan. He was tired of those little smart-alecky black boys runnin in his store and robbin him blind day after day. The next one that tried it was gonna find themselves face down in the gutter, he told Miss Cooper. Joe Nathan was the next one.

I remember when the policeman came to our apartment and told Mama what had happened. He was real cool about it too, tellin Mama her son was dead like he was tellin her what time it was. He was one of those fat-faced, full-of-himself white policemen who acted like black boys dyin was nothin new to black mamas, but it was new to mine.

It was a Saturday night. Mama's best friend Miss Cency and Big Ike, a man who lived upstairs, was at our apartment laughin about old men. I was in me and Joe Nathan's bedroom, which was just off of the living room, laughin too cause Miss Cency had a way of makin me laugh.

"Ain't he crazy?" she said. "What I look like marryin him? He ain't old as Methuselah, he older than Methuselah! What can he possibly do for me?"

"Keep you down," Mama said.

"Damn straight. That's all. Keep me barefoot and pregnant and around the house gettin him all excited. But I am not the one. I told him too."

"And what he did?"

"Cried like a goddamn baby!"

"Cried?"

"Cried, girlfriend. I wanted to kick him out of my house so bad but I was scared I'd kick his crusty old skin in."

"Don't be too quick to give him up, Cency," Big Ike said. "A lot of women would love to have them a sugar daddy."

"Sugar daddy? That fool? He had two nickels back to back once in his whole miserable life and that was in 1969! What sugar he got? Never worked nowhere in his life. Can't even get social security. Now that's bad. And he want Cynthia Marie Brunswick? I don't think so!"

By the time the policeman came I was laughin so hard I like to peed in my pajamas. Not cause it was all that funny—it wasn't—but the way Miss Cency said it, that's what got me goin. But the laughin stopped real fast when the policeman came.

Mama couldn't take it. She tried to run out the door like she had to see it to believe it, and Big Ike and the policeman both had to wrestle her to the couch. By the time I jumped out of my bed and was in the living room, scared to death, Mama was kickin and scratchin the fire out of the policeman. He was gettin damn mad too. He ain't had no sympathy for her, none at all. He took her skinny arms and slung them from round him like he hated her touchin him. But why he wanna do that? Mama jumped up ready to fight, tellin that cop she was gonna beat his funky white ass if he didn't get out of her house. The cop cussed her back, sayin she was nothin but a trash-barrel hoe and it was amazing Joe Nathan lived to be fifteen with a mama like her. That hurt me to my heart when he said that. How could he say that? I felt like I had to do somethin, I don't know, cause it was like I didn't hear what he was sayin about Joe Nathan bein dead. All I heard was him callin my mama a hoe. That's why I jumped on his back and started punchin on him. I didn't do much damage though, cause he slung me from off him like I was a feather. I hit the floor hard.

That got Big Ike goin. Big Ike was a crazy somebody who was crazy for a lot of reasons, but mainly cause he liked to cut people. And he cut people for stupid stuff too, like if you looked at him wrong. Mama said he once stabbed up a girlfriend of his cause she cooked his pork chops too long. He grabbed the butcher knife, said, "Burn this, bitch," and stabbed her two or three times, Mama said.

Ain't no doubt about Big Ike bein crazy, but he also loved me and my mama. Nobody messed with us when Big Ike was around. Mama, though, didn't care that much for him. He was just too crazy, she told me. But when that cop finished slingin me off him and my little ass hit down hard, I could feel the craziness start to come out of him. He knocked that big cop to the floor so fast that even Mama jumped back. Mama started screamin, sayin that crazy nigga was gonna have us all put in jail, but Big Ike wasn't listenin no more. He started bangin the cop's head into the floor.

Miss Cency ran downstairs and got RayRay just in time. That cop could of been dead if Ray hadn't knocked Ike off him. Ike went to jail for that. He's still in jail for that. But I never bothered to care about it. Joe Nathan is dead. *Dead!* And all that cop ass-kickin we did or worryin about what became of Big Ike ain't gonna change that fact.

Miss Cency stayed a good part of the night with Mama. I laid on my bed and listened. I laid on my bed and listened to Mama cry and cry like couldn't nobody say nothin to slow her down. She kept yellin to God and sayin, "Not Joe Nathan, Lord! Not my Joe Nathan!" I don't know, but it seemed to me like she was sayin if she had a choice she would of let God take somebody else. Like me, for instance. I don't know. Mama loved me and all that, but when it came to Joe Nathan, well, you can forget it. Everybody loved Joe Nathan. I was short and redheaded and scary and kind of stupid when you came down to it, but everybody loved Joe Nathan. He was a rogue and cussed grown people out, but he was handsome and could run fast and was real mannerable when he wasn't cussin you out.

And Mr. Peterson shot and killed that perfect big brother of mine. It happened three years ago, but I remember that night like it was yesterday. I remember when I left the apartment, climbin down the fire escape so Mama wouldn't see me. I wanted to talk to Monroe, since he was my only friend, but it was nearly four in the morning and no way was I gonna knock on Mr. Oliver's door at that time of morning. I walked. I was only ten then and had to steer clear of the beat cops who would try to give me a hard time for bein out so late, but I didn't try very hard. I didn't really care if the cops beat me or put me in jail or took me down to children's shelter. Joe Nathan was dead. My oldest brother was dead, and gettin harassed by some cop wasn't somethin that mattered to me right then.

I walked to Mr. Peterson's store. It was a little blue-colored store on Eighth Avenue. They said Joe Nathan was shot inside so there was no trace of death outside that store. In fact, there was no trace of anything outside that store. It looked normal. It looked like Mr. Peterson opened his store, sold popcorn and candy, shot my brother, closed his store, and went home. I must of cried for a long time standin there lookin at that there store of Mr. Peterson's. I remembered the zillion times me and Joe Nathan went in there, buyin things for ourselves or Mama or Miss Cency to keep Mr. Peterson's business goin. Mr. Peterson liked me and Joe Nathan, he even said we were nice, clean boys, he could tell. And we liked Mr. Peterson because he was the nicest black store owner we knew. He wasn't like the Korean and Arab store owners, who were the worst, and he wasn't like the other black store owners who always watched you like a hawk when you walked in their stores, and even if you didn't want to buy anything you felt you had to just to prove you wasn't no rogue. At least *I* would buy somethin. Joe Nathan would ask them what they were lookin at, tell them to kiss his ass, and then leave.

Mr. Peterson wasn't like that. He was mostly nice, pattin us on our backs and rememberin our names, and sometimes he gave us free candy. But he must of been too nice because the word got around. And before you knew it, he was bein robbed every week. Joe Nathan and his gang didn't even think about robbin those other black store owners because they would of shot the fire out of Joe Nathan before he could think about stealin from them. But Mr. Peterson was different. He wouldn't shoot nobody. And for a long time he didn't. He took all them robberies by all them different gangs and kept on smilin and givin away free candy. But by the time Joe Nathan and his gang got up the nerve to do it, Mr. Peterson had changed. Willie Cooper's mama said he bought a gun and was gonna use it on the next rogue who stole from him. He couldn't afford to be nice anymore, he told Miss Cooper. It had to take a mighty slick thief to steal from a desperate man.

Joe Nathan and his gang weren't slick. They were just rogues. Miss Cooper said Mr. Peterson told the police there were four of them, and all four had on stocking caps. He didn't know their guns were water pistols and didn't ask. He pulled out his rifle and started shootin. Enough was enough, Miss Cooper said he said. Joe Nathan was the only one killed. Earl was hit but was all right. Fish and Iceberg dropped their guns and fell to the floor cryin. It was the biggest job they had ever done. Beatin up the mamas' boys or robbin the old ladies wasn't bad enough for them anymore. It was the stupidest thing they had ever tried. But it was like Joe Nathan to try it. That was why I cried long and loud that night. I was mad at Joe Nathan and I was mad at the world. I cried so loud in front of Mr. Peterson's little store that night that, at first, I didn't even hear Mr. Ruby call out my name.

"Bay? That you, Bay? Bay Dawson, that you?"

When I saw Mr. Ruby I got embarrassed and tried to hurry and wipe the tears with the back of my hand. Mr. Ruby was Reverend Ruby's husband.

"Yo mama worried sick about you, boy. She out of her mind wit worry."

"I'm all right."

"She figured you'd come here, lookin for the dead. She told me you gon be right here, she knew you was."

"I'm all right," I said again and inhaled the snot back up my nose. Mr. Ruby was what Mama called a henpecked man. His wife bein a jack-leg preacher and all, it made him kind of in her shadow. He wasn't bossy or ran things, and he always seemed excited, too excited about everything. Joe Nathan said Mr. Ruby was nothin but a lanky old F-boy and that was all there was to it, and Joe Nathan didn't like Mr. Ruby one bit. But I liked him. He was a jet-black, ugly, stupid-actin man who smiled a lot, but he was sad too, like he knew he was henpecked, and he knew he was an F-boy, and he was sorry. I remembered when I first saw his black self, when him and Reverend Ruby were comin up the stairs inside our apartment building and me, Mama, and Joe Nathan were goin downstairs.

"Mama," I said, pullin on her dress hem, "that black man blue!"

Mama hit me so hard upside my head that I fell down the stairs. Joe Nathan, who was always takin up for me and who Mama was always too scared to hit, looked at Mr. Ruby and then at Mama.

"Well he *is*!" he said, and Mama smiled and acted like she didn't hear him.

Mr. Ruby came and got me that night for Mama. We walked home together. He held my hand and didn't say a word to me, not even about me cryin, not even about my brother. I liked that blue-black henpecked man even more that night. Just because he didn't talk. Just because he didn't tell me everything was gonna be all right.

When we got home, Reverend Ruby was sittin at the kitchen table with her Bible wide open. Mama was sittin at the table too. She wasn't cryin anymore but she was still real sad. I wanted to run up to her and hug her and tell her everything was gonna be all right. But I was scared of Reverend Ruby. When she got that Bible in front of her she could go on for days talkin bout Jesus and hell's fire, and hell's fire scared me more than anything. Especially that night. Accordin to Reverend Ruby, hell was for bad people. And since Joe Nathan had tried to rob a store, he was a bad person and was probably in hell. That scared me more than anything. It was terrible enough that he had to get shot all up before he was even sixteen, but then to get knocked down in a pit in the middle of a fire too! That was too much to think about. There he was, all in pain from havin bullets all up his ass, and then, in all that pain, here comes a fire. Damn. It was too much to even think about.

I sat on the couch. Reverend Ruby told Mr. Ruby to make a pitcher of Kool-Aid for me to drink. Mr. Ruby, bein who he is, jumped up fast and hurried to the kitchen. Mama was about to say somethin to me, probably to cuss me out for leavin home late at night like that, but Reverend Ruby put her fat hand on Mama's little one and told her to hold her peace.

"The Lord is in His Holy Temple," she said. "Let all the earth keep silent before Him."

I couldn't believe Reverend Ruby was tellin people to keep silent, since she was always talkin loud and fast and always had somethin to say. Then I saw her standin up in her white sheet-lookin dress. I began to get scared. She moved over to me and sat next to me. She smelled kind of funky, like dried sweat or somethin. But that didn't stop her from puttin her arm around my shoulder.

"Chile," she said, her over-sized, hoggish head bent down to my little face, "let this be a lesson to you."

It didn't make sense what she was sayin, but I looked her in the eye anyway. She had been cryin too. Her eyes were red as fire. She had been cryin like a river or drinkin up a storm.

I didn't smell liquor, so I figured she had been cryin. At first I didn't know why. She hated Joe Nathan. She was always callin him a rogue and sayin he was goin to hell and threatenin to hit him with her pocketbook. She couldn't care that Joe Nathan was dead. I didn't know why she would be cryin. I wanted to ask her, but she was an old sanctified jack-leg preacher and she never said a sentence without addin twenty more.

"Yo brother was a devilish boy. He got in all kinds of trouble, always stealin from old people. He was gon die one way or the other. But he was young. And that just breaks my heart. He was strong. He could of been anything he wanted to be. But he wouldn't listen. Now he dead, chile. He dead at fifteen. You ten now. You mind yo mama. But you got the same way to go if you ain't careful. Yo brother broke yo mama's heart. He broke it, Bay! He split it sunder like he was cuttin it up! You all she got now. Don't go the way yo brother went. Or you gon wind up in hell too."

I stood up quick as a light and looked at Mama. "That ain't true," I said. "Is it, Mama?"

But Mama didn't look at me. She shook her head, covered her face with her hand, and started cryin. I looked at Reverend Ruby. She was tryin to work up tears herself.

"He can't go to no hell," I said. "He been shot up. He hurtin too much. He can't take no more, Mama! What he gon do if he can't take it?"

Reverend Ruby didn't miss a beat. "Unlessen he repented right there on the floor of Mr. Peterson's store, he in hell, chile. I ain't gon lie to you and tell you it ain't so. Cause it is. Yo brother knew right from wrong and he choosed wrong. Now he got to pay."

"Big Ike be cuttin people up," I said, "and he ain't in hell yet."

"Not yet. But he on his way."

Reverend Ruby looked so sure of what she was sayin, so determined to make me believe her, that it made me madder than I had ever been.

"You goin to hell too," I said to her, and Mama looked up at me so fast her hand knocked Reverend Ruby's Bible off the table. Mr. Ruby hurried in the living room with a pitcher of Kool-Aid in his hands.

"What you know about it?" I said with total hate for Reverend Ruby. "You ain't nothin but a jack-leg old ugly big fat preacher lady. You don't know shit about nothin! I'll beat yo ass you talk about my brother like that again! I'll tear that sheet off your black ass and kick you real hard you say somethin like that about my brother again!"

I was out of my mind, but I said it. Reverend Ruby didn't say a word. Mr. Ruby didn't say a word. And Mama kicked my ass. She kicked me, hit me, knocked me down. Then she sent me to bed. It was then that I knew how Joe Nathan must of been feelin, cause I was hurtin both ways too.

When I woke up, the Rubys were gone and Mama was callin Daddy. I remember hurryin to her. I remember throwin a big stack of old newspapers on the floor and jumpin up on the bed beside her.

I acted like I didn't want her callin him. I even put my hand on the phone dial to stop her, yet all the while I was prayin she would call him. We needed him. We needed somebody to handle things for us, to help us see that things were gonna be all right, because Joe Nathan's death was the only dyin we ever knew about. We were nervous wrecks. Sometimes we would just look at each other and start cryin or think about somethin funny, or stupid, or crazy that Joe Nathan did, and you could forget it. We were through dealin. I needed my daddy then. But I couldn't let Mama know I needed him. She was broke up enough. She didn't need to be worryin about how I was gonna take it if Daddy told us to get lost and quit botherin him.

I kept tellin her not to call him, but (thank God) she kept on dialin. Joe Nathan was his son too, she said, and kept on dialin.

The phone must of rang a long time because Mama waited and waited. But I could tell when Daddy answered. Mama got scared. Her eyes started battin like they were out of control and lines came across her forehead.

"Hello, Tom," she said and started puffin on her cigarette. "I know what you told me. I'm not just callin you. Yes, I have a reason. Well if you shut the hell up I'll tell you!"

Like always, Mama's fear turned to anger. But I was still scared. Take it easy, I wanted to tell her. Don't scare Daddy away!

I moved closer to where my cheek was touchin her cheek and I heard Daddy say, "Not another penny!" real spiteful like, like Mama was callin to blackmail him or somethin.

"Did I ask you for money, Tom Bach? When did I ever ask your tired butt for one red nickel? My mama told me you ain't changed. Damn!"

Then I heard Daddy's voice again, real smooth and proper like: "I'm busy, Juanita, all right? Now what is it?"

Mama began puttin out her cigarette on an old newspaper. She pushed down on it and twisted and turned until it was a nub. She tried with everything she had not to cry. "Joe Nathan got shot."

Daddy was quiet for a time. "Shot?"

"Uh-huh," Mama said as a long tear dropped down her face.

"Good Lord. How did he... is he... what happened?"

Mama closed her eyes. It made me sick too. "He died."

"Died? How? I mean, how?"

"He was with some good-for-nothin boys round here and they tried to rob a store."

"Rob a store? He was fourteen years old!"

"Fifteen."

"Rob a store? How can a fifteen-year-old rob a store? Where did he get the gun from? Who shot him? What about the others—what happened to them?"

Daddy wanted to know everything. Mama had to tell him the whole story, the way witnesses told her, and Daddy didn't say a word. We had him, I felt. He was probably cryin and thinkin about comin to get us for all we knew. But Mama blew it like she always did. The more she talked about Joe Nathan, the madder she was gettin with Daddy. Then she said, "If you had of been here for Joe Nathan, he'd be alive today!"

Why she wanna say that? How can anybody handle that? Daddy probably knew he should of been here, but Mama tellin him that had to hurt. I tried to calm her down, but she was out of her mind with anger. I even tried to take the phone from her, so I could tell Daddy that she didn't mean what she was sayin, but she kept knockin my hands away. She kept on killin Daddy with her words, blamin him for shit that happened years ago. He took it as long as he could, I guess, then he hung up in Mama's face. Just like that.

Mama stared at the phone at first, like she couldn't believe he hung up on her. Then she hung up too. We waited for him to call back. We didn't tell each other that, but that's what we were doin. We expected him to give Mama a chance to calm down then call us back. We waited all day, and the next day, and the day after that. Even on the day of the funeral, we sat in that big old church and kept takin turns lookin toward the entrance, expectin at any moment for a strange, beautiful man to come walkin in. It never happened. That was the first time in my life I knew what hate was. Because I hated him. *I hated him!* I couldn't cry, even when I saw my brother in that casket lookin like an angel, for hatin my own daddy.

Daddy is a man by the name of Tom Bach. He lives in Jacksonville, Florida and owns a lot of what Mama calls "rent houses." Compared to us, he's rich. Mama said I saw him one time, when

I was four, but I don't remember it. Mama wouldn't tell me more. She didn't like to talk about him. I asked Joe Nathan a few times about Daddy, but he didn't never say much more than Mama.

He's rich, Joe Nathan said one time. He's rich and was a full-grown man when he knocked up Mama. Mama was somethin like sixteen. Grandmama, Mama's mama, was rentin a house from him. He started foolin around with Mama, and Grandmama let him.

When Mama got pregnant, he left. Then Joe Nathan was born. Then he came back. Then Mama got pregnant again. And he left again. Then I was born. Joe Nathan said he was married and had a whole nother family, that's why he kept leavin Mama, but I knew that had to be a lie.

Accordin to Joe Nathan, we left Jacksonville when I was four years old. Miss Cency, Mama's friend since her childhood, moved to New York a couple of years before and had a good job in the uniform factory there. So we moved there too. Before we left, Mama took me and Joe Nathan to an office in the downtown to see Daddy. He wasn't glad to see us or anything, Joe Nathan said, because he hardly even looked at us, but he gave Mama a lot of money. The way Joe Nathan saw it, Daddy was payin Mama off because of this other family of his, but Mama heard him tell me that one day and said it was a bald-faced lie. Our daddy is a good man, Mama kept tellin us, and he loved us so much that he gave her all that money to take care of us. Joe Nathan really didn't believe it though. He said Daddy wasn't stuttin us, that he gave Mama all that money to get rid of us, that me and him was just a couple of poor little nigga boys Daddy didn't give shit about. Joe Nathan was very outspoken about it.

He hated callin Daddy "Daddy," but Mama made him. It was very confusing. Mama talked about Daddy like he was Jesus Christ, and Joe Nathan talked about him like he wasn't shit. I didn't know what to believe.

For years I wanted to ask Mama about it. I wanted her to tell me who Daddy really was and why he never called us or came to see us. I wanted to know why she made us call this stranger man from Jacksonville Daddy, when she didn't even have a picture of him so I could see what he looked like. But I didn't ask her. She thought too much of him. Sometimes at night she would get real desperate and call him on the telephone cryin. He would hang up in her face. Once I heard her tell Miss Cency she still loved him, that he was the only man she had ever loved. Naturally Miss Cency couldn't believe it.

"You got to be crazy!" she said.

"No, Cency, I mean it. When we was together, Tom Bach treated me better than any man ever treated me."

"And then he gave you two babies and said, 'Wham, bam, thank you ma'am!'"

"Don't try that, girlfriend, cause it ain't even like that. I don't care what you or nobody else say, Tom Bach treated me good."

"Nita, please! Treated you good? Every time you got pregnant he ran his tired butt on down the road, what kind of treatin good that is?"

"For yo information, even though it ain't none of yo business, I'm the one what discontinued the relationship. *I* discontinued it. Not Tommy."

"You sho did discontinue it. And I'm sho Doris Day."

"You might be."

"A tired old uppity nigga like Tommy Bach."

"Careful, Cency."

"I know Tom Bach. Can't nobody tell me nothin bout no Tom Bach!"

"All I know is he was good to me. Now I can't speak for nobody else. But me, he treated good. He bought me things. And he gave my mama that house too. She didn't have to pay rent no more and she still don't."

"Nita, who you think you foolin, girl? That old shack was a burden off his shoulders. That's how come he give it to yo mama. And I know what he gave you. He gave you a double knock-up and ran you out of town, that's what he gave you!"

Mama and Miss Cency stopped bein friends for a long time after that conversation. Mama said Miss Cency was just jealous, because me and Joe Nathan had the same daddy and her five children had five different daddies.

Mama was always seein things like that. No matter how clear people said what they said, Mama was always claimin they didn't mean what they said. They were just jealous, she would say, because she was pretty and they were ugly or because she graduated high school and they could barely read. When other women would call Mama a hoe and a junkie because she had a lot of boyfriends and got high sometimes, she would chase them down the street with a butcher knife. "Least I got sense to charge for it!" she would holler at them. Then she would tell me and Joe Nathan that the women were just jealous because men favored her over them. It didn't matter that it was true, that she was a hoe and she did get high sometimes.

But truth was always beside the point with my mama. She believed what she wanted to believe. That's probably why she kept tryin to call Daddy, even after he didn't show up for Joe Nathan's funeral. She tried to make excuses for him even after that. But those excuses didn't mean shit to me when he didn't show up. I didn't want to hear them no more. But Mama kept callin him. He would always hang up on her and she would act like he didn't, sayin bye to the dial tone just after goin into a long speech about how shameful it is that he treats her so bad.

That was three years ago. Monroe was still alive then and I was only ten. By the time I turned thirteen and saw Monroe get shot, Mama had forgot all about how Daddy didn't show up for his own son's funeral and she was talkin up a storm about him all over again.

She placed a plate of warmed-over beans on the table in front of me. Then she sat down and pulled out a cigarette. She was really a beautiful woman. She had long black hair that was always in a ponytail or just hangin down her back. Her skin was real dark brown and smooth, with arched-up eyebrows and small brown eyes. She smiled a lot and had a pretty white smile, and every time she smiled her little eyes danced up in the corners. She was almost built up like a model, except she wasn't as skinny as a model, and all the dudes at school used to always tell me and Joe Nathan that our mama was fly and fine as a Coca Cola bottle.

Men used to say it too, all those so-called friends of Mama's who came in and out of our apartment all times of the day and night, and they used to leave shakin their heads and sayin, "Lord ham mercy!" and "Jesus Christ that woman fine!" That made Joe Nathan proud. He hated the men, because he knew what their comin in and out meant, but he loved to hear them brag on Mama's beauty, as if they were braggin on him somehow. I felt a little differently about it. The way I liked Mama's beauty was real private. I never even told her I thought she was pretty, and I tried to criticize everything she would put on when she was goin out to party. I figured if everybody stopped tellin her how beautiful and fine she was then she'd slow down. I figured wrong.

Mama lit her cigarette and shook the fire off the match. She tossed the match on the table and took a hard puff, blowin the smoke out upwards. "This ain't no place for you to grow up in, Bay. Not when you don't have to be here."

"But Daddy don't want me."

"You don't know that."

"Mama, I do know it. And you know it too. I ain't even seen him but one time, and I don't even remember that. And what about Joe Nathan's funeral, Mama? We supposed to just forget about that? He ain't gon let me come down there with him."

"He ain't got no choice," she said and blew more smoke. "You just as much his responsibility as mine. That's why I called him."

I was scared Mama was lyin, that she was ignorin the truth again and tellin me what Joe Nathan called one of her ever-lovin lies. I wouldn't put it past her if she dumped me on a bus and sent me to Jacksonville without even tellin Daddy I was comin. That was the kind of mama I was dealin with. I loved her, but that was the kind of ever-lovin lyin mama I was dealin with.

"You lyin, Mama," I looked at her and said, and I waited for the slap. It didn't come. Mama didn't hardly look at me.

"You ain't gon live if you stay round here, Bay. I just know you ain't. Monroe own daddy kilt him. All them dope dealers runnin up and down the street shootin folks left and right and the police don't give a fuck. This ain't no place for no chile like you, Bay. You ain't gon survive it."

"Them drug dealers don't be botherin me, Mama. And as for Monroe gettin shot up—dog, Mama, I'm used to that."

She looked at me. Her small eyes were dancin, goin from right to left lookin at me. "Ain't no chile got no business bein used to shootin," she said. "You can't have no childhood here. Most of these folks round here can't help it cause they ain't got no place to send they boy. Yo daddy a big shot in Jacksonville. He can give you everything you pose to have. I can't give you shit, Bay, cept more death and hard livin. And I ain't gon do that to you."

I could feel I wanted to cry, because Mama was too serious, but I kept chokin the tears back. "I don't know nothin bout no Jacksonville, Mama. Them crazy people down there."

"You ain't gon be livin on no plantation, boy. Jacksonville a big city, but it ain't like New York. It's right on the tip of the south. It ain't deep down in there like Mississippi and Alabama and all them. It's practically northern."

I knew Mama didn't know what she was talkin bout, but I let her talk. I even got a little excited when she told me about how Daddy asked her if I could come down there with him and how he lived in a big house, but I was mad too because I knew Mama was probably lyin. After she went on for a long time about Daddy, I lost it and slammed my fist down on the table. As soon as my fist hit down, tears started runnin down my face. I looked at my mama. "Is it true, Mama?"

"What you mean, 'is it true'?"

"Is it true, Mama?"

She took her hand and started rubbin her neck. "He wants you to come, Bay."

"You talked to him?"

"I just said he wants you—"

"Did you talk to him, Mama?"

"Yes. All right?"

"When?"

"Now look—"

"When, Mama?"

"Bay!"

"When you talked to Daddy, Mama?"

My tears kind of touched her, I guess, and she pressed her warm finger to my face. She knew she had to tell me the truth. Lyin and double-talkin no longer was gonna work. It was my life and my future we were talkin bout now.

"I called him, and yes, at first he said no. He said it was my problem, I ain't gonna lie to you. But I spected him to say that. So I sent Mama over there. My mama. Now I don't know what all Mama told him and how she told him, but she persuaded him to change his mind."

"She blackmailed him?" I asked like I was shocked or somethin.

Mama smiled and then laughed, slappin me on the back. "You somethin else, Bay. Just like yo old daddy, just like him! Blackmailed him. What you know about blackmailin? Just know he changed his mind, Bay, and he called and told me to send you on down."

Mama had decided I had to go and I knew I couldn't change her mind. Then I thought about Grandmama Dawson. Since she wanted my daddy to take me in, maybe she could take me in instead. That way I'd be in Jacksonville but not livin with somebody who didn't really want me.

"What about Grandmama?" I asked. "She live in Jacksonville. Maybe I can stay with her at her house and Daddy can visit me there."

"No!" Mama said so loud that I jumped. "Hell no! Grandmama ain't got shit either! Stayin with her will be just like stayin in Harlem! And you gettin out, you hear me boy? Mr. Thomas Jeremiah Bach yo ticket out!"

One week later I was on a bus for Jacksonville. Mama packed me pork chop sandwiches and told me what town to eat one in. A man friend of hers gave her fifty dollars and she gave them all to me. She was as scared as I was. She told me how to say "yes sir" to everything Daddy said (Mama said he was a "yes sir" freak) and to never ask him a whole bunch of questions. She even told me to never talk about Joe Nathan around Daddy because he didn't know how to deal with that situation. She told me to be nice and friendly with all those high-class people I was gonna meet, but to stay away from Grandmama Dawson because she was poor. I told Mama not to worry about me, but she cried all the way to the bus station. I even tried to pretend that I was real happy about leavin home. I didn't have any friends, not since Roe died, and Mama was right: It was bad in Harlem.

But at least I knew Harlem. I didn't know nothin bout no Jacksonville or the south or my own daddy or even Grandmama Dawson that well. What if Daddy hated me? What if he thought I was too short or too stupid or too poor to be his son? What if he said I wasn't his son, that Mama was just as big a hoe in

Jacksonville too and I could be anybody's child? What if he already had children? What if he had a wife? What if they didn't like me and tried to kill me or somethin? What if Daddy was a madman and just wanted me down there to rape me or sell me to rich white people? *What if what if what if...*

    I tossed and turned through the entire bus ride and forgot all about those pork chop sandwiches. Daddy had wired the fare for me to make the trip, so at least he knew I was comin. But that didn't mean he wanted me, and it did nothin to calm my nerves. Because I knew like Joe Nathan knew and like Monroe probably knew when he felt that bullet rippin into his chest: That I was no more my daddy's son than he was a real daddy to me.

TWO

The bus ride to Florida took forever, seemed like. I thought I'd never get there. I slept and tossed and looked out the window (I had a window seat) and tossed some more. But mostly I slept. When I did wake up, I was usually groggy and out of my mind, like I thought goin to live with my daddy was a nightmare or somethin. And to make things worse, I was sittin next to this real old lady and every time I woke up she was like starin down my throat. She was real creepy too. But I liked her. I liked her because she told somebody off for me who I thought was my mama. It was crazy, I know, but I woke up from dreamin about my mama and as soon as I opened my eyes I thought this person sittin in front of me was my mama. I mean, the ponytail and all. So like a fool I say, "Mama?" like I want her to turn around and say, "Yes, baby," like she always did. She turned around all right.

"Who you callin Mama?" she said in a voice as heavy as Barry White's. Not only was she not my mama, she wasn't even a she! She was some big, black, juicy-lip man with a wig on his head. I like to died. Man, I was scared.

"I said, who you callin Mama?" he said again.

"Nobody, ma'am," I said. "I mean sir. I mean ma'am. I mean sir."

"Oh don't you be gettin all worked up, boy," the old lady sittin next to me said. "I thought he was a woman too with that old wig slapped on his head like that. He oughta not be lookin like no woman, then nobody won't be thinkin he they mama."

"Watch it, old lady," the man said. "I don't look like no woman."

"You's a lie. You look just like one from the back and you know it. Look just like J.J. mama from *Good Times*. Just like her. Gap teeth and all!"

The man-woman and the old lady went at it for a while, then he finally shut up and turned his big self around. The old lady kept talkin, mostly about how she was goin back home to Georgia and how her daughter didn't need her no more. I fell asleep. When I woke up, the bus driver said we were in Florida, the sunshine state. But only it was rainin when I got there.

Jacksonville looked nothin like I thought it would look. It wasn't wide open like New York, and most of the buildings the bus passed by weren't skyscrapers but no more than two or three stories tall. It was strange to see. Even the traffic was different. Some cars were fast and whipped right by but many moved slow, like they was sightseein or somethin. The faces in those slow cars were mostly old and white, and I could see why

Miss Cency kept tellin me that Florida was the retirement capital of the world. Must be nice to be retired, I thought, where all you had to do all day was drive around slow in your big Cadillac, nobody to tell you what to do or bother you bout all that junk that don't matter in the long run anyway. Must be nice. I guess that's why I ain't never met nobody in my life that done retired.

The bus drove straight down a freeway that acted like it didn't wanna end until a big green sign finally gave us a choice: Jacksonville Beaches one way, Downtown the other way. I remember wonderin why the sign said Beaches instead of Beach and how come a town most New Yorkers never heard of could have more than one beach. Then I thought about the retirees and figured that town probably had a lot of beaches. Old people with money love hangin out on a beach. I couldn't see myself on one though. Just my luck, I'd go out to one of those beaches and end up seasick or somethin, or drowned. But if my daddy turned out to be one of those beach freaks, then I'd take my chances. I was pretty much willin to do whatever it took to make my life with Daddy work, and if it meant drownin, I don't know, but it seemed at the time that it would be worth it.

The bus curved a little and we headed in the direction that pointed to downtown. Mama always said Jacksonville was nothin but a big country town, and when we drove through the downtown I saw what she meant. The streets were all narrow and closed-in-lookin, and for every building up and runnin there was a deserted one too. And talk about your shotgun houses! They were so tiny they looked like rows of wooden boxes stuck together. Our apartment in Harlem was twice the size of one of those jokers. I could only hope those weren't the rent houses Mama said Daddy owned, cause if they were, he couldn't be as rich as Mama claimed. People in houses like those were poorer than me. Who ever heard of poor people makin somebody rich?

And talk about people. The people of Jacksonville were a trip. Soon as I stepped off the bus I saw this really tall man sportin a big nappy afro, a polyester jump suit, and platform shoes. Swear to God, man! It was like the dude was trapped in the seventies or somethin. And this was the nineties! "Damn!" I said to myself.

Then I see these two funny-lookin hoes hangin round the front part of the bus station askin people to buy them bus tickets. What were they, nuts? Who the hell gonna buy them a ticket? They didn't even look all that good. And they had the nerve to be fat too? I mean, one of them was so chunky, when she stood up she looked like an elephant. I mean it! Ass one way, stomach the other! But that's life in big country towns, I guess. Looks don't matter. Clothes don't matter. Hoes don't turn tricks—they just want the money.

I told those bitches to get out of my face and hurried to get my suitcases. Mama told me what to do: get my suitcases, then look for Daddy. And if a hoe or pimp or child-lovin sick pervert come anywhere near me, cuss 'em out and keep on walkin. "They hicks. They'll leave you alone then," she said.

The man who was givin people their luggage from out of this door on the side of the bus was the first normal person I saw in Jacksonville. He was smilin and friendly with everybody and sayin junk like, 'You the man' and 'It's yo world, bro,' and played-out stuff like that. When I got up to him and handed him my suitcase ticket, I don't know, but I sensed that maybe he knew my daddy or somethin. I don't know why I thought it, but I did. So I asked him. He didn't hear me at first cause he was too busy talkin to somebody else, so I pulled on his uniform and asked him again. He still didn't hear me. He just kept on grinnin and talkin. I jerked harder on his uniform, causin his body to tilt sideways like he was losin his balance. When he finally looked down at me the grinnin and jive talkin stopped. He looked at me like I was somethin scary to look at, and he frowned big time. "What the fuck you want?" he asked me.

I moved back from him, or jumped back, until I was clean across the sidewalk and against the brick wall. I must of looked like a fool to him. I knew he just knew I was crazy as a bedbug, as Mama used to say. But I didn't care. Cause he looked crazy as a bedbug to me too.

My bus arrived in Jacksonville at seven thirty that Friday morning. Daddy showed up around ten. I didn't see him at first because I had stopped lookin for him. I didn't call his office neither, like Mama told me to do if he wasn't on time. I didn't care if I sat in that station all night. I wasn't stuttin him neither. I wasn't gonna call him up and beg him to come and pick up his own son, he had another thought comin if he thought I was gonna do that. I started hatin Mama too. She had no right, no right forcin me on some stranger man who barely knew my name. He didn't want me. He told her he didn't want me, that I was her problem, not his, but Mama sent me on down anyway. And forever. She said I had to stay down here with Daddy forever, whether I liked it or not. It wasn't up to me. Nothin about my life was up to me. I was just a nobody thirteen-year-old with nothin to say about it. I hated Mama then. I sat down in that old smelly bus station and hated the shit out of my own mama.

When Daddy finally came, I didn't even know it was him.

Ain't that somethin? I didn't know what my own daddy looked like. I saw somebody tall and very well dressed come into the station, but it didn't dawn on me that he could be my daddy. Not *my* daddy anyway. He was somethin like six feet tall, with real smooth-lookin light brown skin, a thick mustache, and a short, kind of curly-lookin afro. He had on a dark blue suit that wasn't buttoned up, causin him to show his kind of big stomach. And although he wasn't what you would call fat or anything, he was like big, like when he was a young man he was a football star. I saw him come into the station, but I didn't get any feeling that he was any kin to me at all. I just knew he looked out of place. A man who looked like him, I figured, don't be ridin no buses nowhere.

He knew it was me though, right off, probably because I was the only black boy in the whole station and I was starin at him so hard. Or maybe he knew how I looked. Maybe he knew more about me than I thought. I hoped so, anyway.

He started walkin slowly toward me without takin his eyes off me. His shoes were so black and shiny they sparkled when he walked. He moved like a fat man, like he was climbin up a mountain and had to kind of hunch his shoulders cause he was gettin worn out. You would of thought he was the biggest drug dealer this side of livin the way he carried himself, even bigger than Blade Montgomery, but only Daddy wasn't flashy like Blade and he didn't have one single gold chain around his neck. And Daddy looked legit, like a businessman or somethin. And I'm not talkin bout no businessman like Mr. Peterson or Hank Slappey or Mr. Priest or none of them. He looked like those businessmen you see in Manhattan, who carried briefcases and went into banks and law offices. No strut, no lean, no foot glide to his steppin at all. Even the white people gave him second looks. And that was my daddy? I couldn't believe it. I expected him to be some loudmouth, wise-crackin, hip-walkin hotshot who thought he was down because he owned a little property. I expected him to come chargin into the station, tell me to grab my bag, and then kick my ass on out the door just to let me know who was in charge of things. But the man who came in that station that day wasn't nothin at all like I thought. That man, my daddy, looked like he didn't even know what an asskickin was.

I stared at him and stared at him until he was right in front of me. Usually I'm too shy and self-conscious to check out somebody that long, but I forgot all about me when I realized that man could be my daddy. Let me tell you what it felt like. It felt like I was dreamin, that this big man standin in front of me hell no ain't true. All those years I prayed to just see him on a picture or from a window, anything, just let me see him. And to see him, finally, after all those years. It was too much, man. I can't swear to it, but I think I kind of froze up. I couldn't move. I couldn't for one second take my eyes off that man.

He was checkin me out too, starin bout as hard as I was starin at him, like havin to meet me wasn't no roll in the hay for him either. Then he opened his mouth to speak to me. When he spoke, I remembered his voice from the telephone. I blinked. I knew it wasn't no dream.

"Are you Ralph Dawson?" he asked me like he wasn't at all sure who I was. When I didn't say nothin, he even looked away from me and started checkin out other people in the station, like maybe there was another black boy around there somewhere. Up close, I could see why he had his doubts. I don't mean to sound like I'm braggin, but my daddy looked good, man. I couldn't believe how good. He had gray, hazel-like eyes, long, long eyelashes, and a face that looked so perfect you would of thought it was a girl's face. He was tall. He was rich. He was built like a mack daddy. The only bad thing about him was that he was kind of on the old side. Like fifty or somethin. And he had some gray hair in his mustache and sideburns. But the point is, I could understand how a guy who looked like him would be surprised to have a son who looked like me. I mean, if I was my daddy and I saw some weird-lookin, red-haired joker like me sittin up there, I'd look around too. Ain't no way he's kin to pretty me, I'd say, like I'm sure my daddy said. But we belonged to each other. Mama said ain't no doubts about that. But I sure couldn't see the resemblance.

He asked me again if I was Ralph Dawson. When I didn't say nothin again, but just kept on starin at him like a fool, he lowered his head down to where his chin was touchin his chest and looked at me real hard. Then he put his big cold hand on my chin and lifted my face back a little to where we were almost eyeball to eyeball.

"What's your name, boy?" he asked.

But I couldn't say a word. Swear to God. It was like I was too mad to talk. I guess it all kind of got to me, you know? It was like I wanted that dude to suffer. I wanted him to realize, like I was realizin, how terrible it was that he couldn't recognize his own thirteen-year-old son. Here he was, this great-lookin, great-dressin, high-livin big shot, and he couldn't recognize his own son. It was my turn to sit and be quiet. It wasn't no on purpose silence by me, because I really just couldn't say nothin to him, but the more uncomfortable he acted, the better I felt. It was like

I wanted him to hurt. I wanted him to know he was a big fat zero. Any man who would forget his own children, never call them, never see about them, no matter how powerful he was, how much money he had, how many backwater swamp-land pieces of property he owned, wasn't shit.

After a while he let my chin go. I guess he could sense how much I hated him, I don't know, but he put his hands in his pants pockets and started actin all nervous like. He even apologized for bein late. "A messy eviction," he said. "I got held up." Then he sat down beside me. I could smell a strong, pretty odor as he sat down. It was almost as sweet as ladies smelled when they went on dates, but only it was stronger and louder. He didn't seem to care, though, that he smelled sweeter than a lady, because he crossed his leg too, actin like one.

He started askin me a lot of questions about when did my bus get in and how did I like Jacksonville and dumb stuff like that. I still didn't say a word. Damn. Didn't he get it? I wanted to cry, not talk. I wanted to kick his ass, not listen to his stupid questions. But just as I was gettin bold about it, he did somethin that scared me: he inhaled, then exhaled real loud. Mama told me a lot of things to check out about Daddy, about how he was a "sir" freak and all that, and she told me to watch myself when he exhaled loud. That meant he was runnin out of patience and was gettin upset. That meant trouble, Mama said.

And I remembered somethin else about Daddy. I remembered what Mama said to Miss Cency one night when they was sittin up in the front room with their beer cans in their hands talkin bout all those no-good men they've had in their lives. "Yeah, Tom Bach used to kick my ass sometimes," Mama said. "But he didn't break my bones or nothin."

I remembered how crazy that sounded to me. It was like Mama was justifyin an ass-whippin. It was like she was sayin Daddy could beat her, kick her, tie her up and knock her down, but because she didn't die or get paralyzed and junk, then it was no big deal. I remember Joe Nathan tellin me no, that ain't what Mama meant. She meant Daddy was so fucked up, so down and dirty mean, that if he kick your ass a little you had better shut your mouth and be glad that was all he did to you.

That was the way he seemed that day in the bus station when he exhaled loud. He was gettin tired of me. He didn't have to take my shit, who was I kiddin? So for my own good, if I didn't want to end up sayin things like Mama was sayin, I figured I'd better knock off the silent treatment and quit fuckin with him.

And I was about to do it, I could even feel my lips formin to say somethin, but Daddy looked at me quick like and rattled me so that I froze up again.

"Now look here, boy," he said real blunt like and low, like he didn't want other people to know he was gettin mad. "I'm not going to sit up here and keep repeating myself. I know you're upset and don't feel I deserve to hear you speak. But I'll put you on a bus back to Harlem before I put up with this nonsense any longer. Now let's be like Finnegan and begin again, shall we? My name is Tom Bach. Are you Ralph Dawson?"

AM I RALPH DAWSON? I wanted to yell from the top of my lungs. *Who the hell else am I supposed to be? You see any other little black boys sittin in this stank place? You see any other human being sittin around here lookin for his long-lost daddy like a fool? What's wrong with you? Don't you understand how bad that makes me feel? AM I RALPH DAWSON? You dumb ass. Couldn't you at least have pretended you knew?*

"Everybody calls me Bay," I said.

Daddy looked at me and smiled. But his smile lasted only a half second. It wasn't like he thought what I had said was funny or anything, it was more like he just did that all the time when people said somethin to him, he just smiled for half a second and then looked serious again.

He put his smooth-lookin hand on the knee of the leg he had crossed. "I know you don't really know me, Ralph, and I don't know what-all your mother has told you, and don't want to know, frankly, but I do want you to understand one thing."

Uh-oh, I said to myself. Here it comes. Here comes that *I'm the boss* speech; that *I'm in charge of this scene and if you don't like it you can sail your ass right back where it came from* speech. I knew his smart mouth was gonna come out, I knew it.

He leaned over by me. His eyes were a soft gray, almost like glass. Mama used to tell Miss Cency that Daddy had eyes like Smokey Robinson. Mama was right.

"I know I haven't been anything remotely resembling a father to you," he looked me dead in the eye and said, "and I know it's too late for me to try to be. But I want you to know that I'm sorry I've been a bastard, and I'm glad you decided to come."

He apologized. He actually apologized! Not that the apology wiped away the pain, nothin was gonna do that. I mean, you can't kill somebody and then apologize to him. But it meant somethin still. It meant that he knew. He knew how much he hurt me. He knew how he denied me and Joe Nathan the one thing that only he could give to us. And it was hurtin him.

His long eyelashes covered his eyes. It seemed like he was asleep, but I knew he was just lookin down. I guess he was kind of sad about not bein a real father and all, and he couldn't face me anymore. And all the things Mama said about Daddy seemed like they could be true. Maybe he was a good man who really did care about us. Maybe he didn't pay Mama off, like Joe Nathan said, or run us out of town, like Miss Cency said. Maybe he was providin for us in one lump sum. He was still a nothin for a father; I mean, he kicked our ass when it came down to him doin the right thing and bein a real father to us. But he apologized for it. That made a difference. That made the difference from him just kickin my ass and breakin my bones too.

You ever seen a really ugly guy walkin with a Miss America–lookin woman? And you figure he's got to be rich for her to even be seen in public with him? That's how I felt walkin out of that station with my daddy. We didn't match, I guess is the best way to put it. Men as well as women were starin at Daddy. There was somethin distinguished about him. It was like they were sayin, "Hey, who is this guy?" as if they had spotted a movie star or somethin. And there I was, walkin beside him, lookin like a little roach I'm sure.

I grew to hate the stares. Not because I didn't want people lookin at and admirin my daddy. Hell, it was a compliment to me, in a way. But I hated the stares because they always started starin at me too. Only when their eyeballs got down to me you didn't see the approving nods and smiles. A look of terror would cross their faces. It was like they was surprised somebody like my daddy was walkin with somebody that looked like me. It made me feel real bad, you know. Made me feel like I had no right to claim a daddy like that. Not that I didn't understand how those people felt, because I did. It just didn't seem right to them that he could be any kin to me. I mean, I didn't look nothin like him. I was too short for one thing. And I had this really pale, high-yellar kind of skin and reddish-brown cropped-off soft hair, yet my eyes were black as coal. Joe Nathan used to say I looked funny. Not sissy funny, I guess, but stupid funny. I was too short and too yellar and too redheaded, he said, that when you put it all together it just didn't look right.

    Girls thought I looked funny too. All through school they couldn't believe me and Joe Nathan were brothers. They would call me Shorty or Red or Yellar Boy. It didn't bother me too much, because the girls weren't mean or nothin, and some even liked me. But then came Sheneka Johnson. I'll never forget Sheneka Johnson. She was new to our school and was kind of pretty. Naturally I tried to impress her. I would see her comin down the hall and would jump out in front of her doin cartwheels and flips. Or I would write her love notes about how pretty she was and how mature she acted. Then, and also naturally, I asked her to be my girlfriend.

    She put her hand on her hip, I'll never forget it. "Like are you crazy?" she said. "*Me* be *your* girlfriend? Is you on dope? There ain't no way on the face of this earth that some short, high-yellar, redheaded, black-eyed fool like you is gonna be anything to me but a short, high-yellar, redheaded, black-eyed fool!"

    She said it in front of everybody too. Even Joe Nathan said the guys told him how Sheneka Johnson read me that day. It was like she said what I always thought was true. I really was ugly. Or, if not puredy ugly, so funny-lookin I might as well of been ugly. She sized me up good that day. There ain't no ands, ifs, or buts about it.

    And there I was, years later, with my short, high-yellar, redheaded, black-eyed self, standin outside that Greyhound bus station, with my tall, rich, great-lookin daddy, wishin that Sheneka Johnson had seen *him*, that Sheneka Johnson had known that I had a daddy who looked so good. That would of changed everything. I just know that would of changed everything.

Daddy's car was parked down the street from the station on the side of the road. It had stopped rainin but we had to do a lot of sideseppin to avoid all the puddles. Daddy looked funny, sidesteppin that way, like he was dancin, and a couple of times I even giggled. He looked back and asked me what was so funny, but I was still too terrified to just hold a conversation with him like that.

Out on the street against the curb was a beautiful Jaguar, and we were walkin straight to it. My daddy drove a Jaguar. That's right. A Jaguar. It looked just like the one The Equalizer used to drive on that TV show. Only Daddy's wasn't black but a kind of light gray. That car was kickin, man. Prettiest car I think I had ever seen. A Jaguar! I could just see myself back at school tellin Sheneka Johnson and all of those other loudmouth girls how my daddy don't drive no jive Cadillac, not my daddy. He's above that Cadillac crap. He drives a Jaguar, jack. A 200-mile-an-hour, can't touch this, super cool, gangsta 'chine, man. Don't tell me they wouldn't be impressed!

Not that they would know much about cars. I mean, none of us do. Our ideal of a fancy car is what we see those drug dealers flyin around in, or the pimps. Before my daddy, Big Ike was the only person I ever knew personally with a fancy car, and it was an old beat-up-lookin Cadillac that looked like it had been in two, three major wrecks somewhere. I remember when Big Ike first got his car. He took me, Mama, and Joe Nathan for a ride.

We were so poor and so used to walkin everywhere we went, we thought ridin around in this Cadillac was like a great thing. Very big deal. We wasn't two miles from our block when that hunk of junk broke down. We had to push it back home. I'll never forget Mama, who was kind of proud, noddin her head and cussin as she pushed with us. "Ain't this some shit?" she kept sayin. "I can just beat your ole bony ass, Big Ike!"

Daddy lifted the trunk to the Jag and started puttin my suitcases in it. He would grunt every time he bent to pick up one like they were too heavy for a big man like him. He even asked me what I had in them, like those old clothes and two pork chop sandwiches were just weighin him down. I couldn't believe it, a big man like him. It made me wonder though. It made me wonder if my pretty daddy didn't have some sugar in his tank.

When we were about to go get in the car—and I was tryin like hell to act like I was unimpressed by his car—somebody started yellin Daddy's name so loud we both turned around nervous. We looked across the street and saw this dark-skinned lady with big hips comin toward us. She wore a really short, tight-fittin black dress with shoes so high she looked like she was walkin on stilts. Even from across the street I could tell she was nothin but a hoe. And there the bitch was, yellin my daddy's name like she knew him and shit.

Daddy smiled a little when she got up to us, but you could tell he didn't mean it; you could tell she wasn't somebody he wanted to be seen in public talkin to.

"Hey, Mr. Bach," she said almost out of breath, like that walk across the street wore her out.

"Hello, kid. How you doing?"

"I'm doin good, Mr. Bach. Got me a job."

"Yeah?"

"Yes sir."

"Where?"

"At this temporary agency. They send me to different job sites. It only pays five dollars an hour, but it's an honest livin."

"Damn straight."

"About time I did somethin," the hoe said with a big smile on her face. She wasn't nothin pretty to look at, that's for sure. I couldn't understand why Daddy was even foolin with her. And he even smiled back at her.

"You're still young," he said. "You're entitled to a few false starts."

"A few? Been more like a steady stream, Mr. Bach. But I'm straight now."

"Good for you."

They smiled at each other for a while, like there was more goin on than just small talk between them. Then the hoe took a look at me. Daddy was right, she was young, maybe as young as twenty or somethin like that, but she was still loaded down with makeup like a hoe, and dressed like a hoe, I don't care how young she was.

"Who is this?" she asked, smilin that stupid smile of hers.

But I was glad she asked. I wanted Daddy to tell her I was his son, like he was proud of it. I mean, what difference would it make tellin a nobody like her? Who's she gonna tell? It's not like she would know Daddy's wife or anything (if he even had a wife).

"This here is Ralph," he said to her. "Ralph Dawson."

I prayed she would get nosy and ask if I was his nephew or somethin, but I guess she wasn't comfortable with Daddy to be askin him all those personal questions. She didn't even mention me again.

"Well, I guess I better make it on home before the rain start up again," she said.

"Where are you living now?"

"I got me a room on Julia Street. It ain't fancy, but it's what I can afford."

Daddy had his hand in his pants pocket jigglin around some change. He was lookin at her funny, like she was lyin to him or somethin.

"Taking care of yourself, Trish?" he asked.

"Oh, yes sir. Like I said, I'm workin now."

"Off the junk yet?"

"Oh, Mr. Bach, I been off that."

Daddy kept lookin at her funny. She started frownin, like she knew she was lyin but she was gonna make him believe her anyway.

"May God strike me down, Mr. Bach, I been bein straight for months. I don't even know what that shit taste like no more. I got a job now. And I ain't messin up for nothin! I'm gonna get my kids back one day."

"I hope so, babe," Daddy said and she smiled. He called her *babe*.

"You know me. When I make up my mind about somethin, I do it."

Daddy gave one of his half-second smiles and kept lookin down at her body, like he was undressin her with his eyes.

"Seen that husband of yours lately?" he asked her.

"Yeah. Sometimes. I see him around."

"How's life been treating him?"

"Bout the same, from what I be seein."

"He's still at it, huh?"

"Big time. You oughta see him, Mr. Bach. Sometimes I think he's crazy the way he act like he don't care."

"You ever try to talk to him?"

"Hell yeah. But you can't tell that brother nothin. He's sick, Mr. Bach, I'm tellin you. Crazy. Guess what he did last week?"

"What?"

The hoe was about to tell it, but she looked down and saw me. Then Daddy looked at me.

"Get on in the car, Ralph," he said to me. "I won't be long."

Rememberin that Daddy was a sir freak, I said "yes sir" and hurried in the car. As soon as I opened the door, I could smell Daddy's perfume everywhere. The whole car smelled like him. If that car had of been a girl, I'd be in love with her just for smellin so good. The seats were so shiny red leather, and so thick and cushiony, that I found myself rubbin my hands all over them. And it had a radio in it and a cassette deck (not an old 8-track player like in Big Ike's car). It had buttons for the air conditioning and heater and even a sliding button for the windshield wipers! Everything looked and felt and smelled so good, I almost cried. Ain't that somethin? I almost cried over a car. I guess I never seen nothin so beautiful. And it was my daddy's car. My daddy's! Who wouldn't cry over somethin like that?

I can't swear to it, but I think I saw Daddy give the hoe some money before she walked off. Then he sat down in his car and just stared at her as she walked on down the street and around the corner. It was like he wanted her the way he was starin. I couldn't figure it out. What in the world would he want with that? He's like Mr. Universe and she's like somethin the cat drug in. Why was he even givin her the time of day? What was Daddy thinkin about? I tried with all I had to imagine my daddy foolin around with somebody that looked like her. But don't even think about it. She was a hoe, that's all. He didn't want her. I was certain of that.

Then Daddy said, "Ah, forget it!" when the hoe had disappeared around a big old deserted-lookin building, and then he cranked the Jaguar up. Crankin up was so easy I couldn't believe it. Daddy didn't have to keep pattin the gas pedal and turnin the key over and over. He just turned the key one time and that baby was hummin like a bird. You couldn't even tell it was cranked. And when we started movin, it drove so smooth I thought we was floatin. I mean, I don't mean to go on and on about no car and I know goin on like this makes me sound like I was poor as mud and not used to nothin, but damn. You should of seen that car, man. And you should of seen my daddy in it. He was so cool-lookin, so big and all, I had to pinch myself a few times to be certain he was mine.

"You all right, champ?" he looked over at me and asked as he turned that corner like the steering wheel was a feather.

"Yes sir," I said. Then I said, almost before I realized what I was sayin, "That tape player work, Daddy?"

I almost covered my mouth from shame after I said *Daddy* to him. I was embarrassed big time. I looked at him, expectin him to tell me to never call him that name again as long as I lived.

"Sure it works," he said, like me callin him that name wasn't nothin. "You like music?"

"Yes sir."

"What kind?"

I had to think about that. Mama was into all that old sixties Motown crap so it wasn't like we had a lot of hip records around the house to brag about. "I like R. Kelly and Boyz II Men and Snoop Doggy Dogg and Tupac and... Michael Jackson too."

By this time Daddy was smilin. He pressed a button and a small drawer slid out. Daddy pulled a tiny round record from the drawer and slipped it into the tape player. It was a CD. He had a CD player, man. I had heard about them things but it was the first time in my life I had seen one in person before. All Daddy had to do then was press another button and the music started. It was some white-soundin guy singin some slow song about some woman treatin him bad and givin him the blues in the night. I looked at Daddy. This had to be a joke.

Daddy smiled. "I like Frank Sinatra," he said. Then he laughed out loud and turned another corner like a feather.

Three

The name BACH'S RENTAL PROPERTIES was printed on the glass window of the office near downtown. Daddy's car stopped at the curb. I was relieved. I was kind of scared that he was gonna take me straight to Grandmama Dawson's house from the bus station and just leave me there. Not that I didn't like Grandmama Dawson or didn't want to see her. I did. The little I remembered of her wasn't bad, and she would call us up there in New York every now and then and check on us. But I kept rememberin how Mama said she was poor and how Miss Cency said that house Daddy gave her was a shack. I was tired of poverty and shacks. I wanted to wear clothes like Daddy wore and drive cars like he drove. I wanted to have thick stacks of money I could throw to a hooker. I was tired of lima beans and black-eyed peas and waitin on the welfare check mailman. Seein Daddy made me tired of it. Seein Daddy made me know there was a lot more to life than I could of ever imagined. I loved Grandmama Dawson and all that. But she could forget it if she thought I was goin her way.

Daddy must of spoke to six or seven people before we even made it across the sidewalk to his office good. There were poor-lookin people, rich-lookin people, everybody knew my daddy. And he knew how to talk to people too. When there was a rich-lookin guy talkin he'd say stuff about politics or how's business or somethin like that. With poor-lookin people he was really cool. I mean my daddy was old and all, but he was kinda hip. He said to one guy: "It's your world, blood. I'm just visitin."

I know he probably heard that line on TV or somethin, but it worked for him. It wasn't like he was some old rich guy tryin to act hip. Man, I hate when I see that! With Daddy it was more like bein hip was natural. He knew how to work that thang.

Daddy's office was kind of small, with wood-paneled walls, a radiator, and a tiny TV sittin on top of a file cabinet. There was a little desk with stacks of papers on it and an oversized-like desk over by the window. That was Daddy's desk. He looked through a few papers on the little desk and then went over to his own desk. There was a pile of mail on it, and he stood there readin every piece. I sat on the radiator. I was tired and kind of hungry but Daddy was forgettin me again, the way he did when the hoe came up to him, the way he probably always will do when somebody else hits the scene.

But I didn't care. I was in my daddy's office. I was sittin on the radiator in my own daddy's office in downtown Jacksonville, Florida, and I didn't care for a minute if I was forgotten. I kind of was lookin forward to all of the changes. This was what I wanted. This was where I wanted to be.

Then the front door opened and a short, dumpy, gayish-actin man came flyin into the office. He scared the shit out of me, the way he just flew in, but Daddy didn't even look his way. He stood in the middle of the floor with one hand on his hip and looked at Daddy. "Well," he said, kind of shakin his big head, "if it isn't D.B. Cooper. I thought you'd never come out of those woods, Mr. C."

Daddy looked up at him for a second, and then looked back down at his mail. "Oh," he said. "Hey Peete."

Peete dropped his shoulders and kept his mouth open like he couldn't believe it. It was like he wanted to say, "Is this nigga for real, or what?"

"*Oh hey Peete?*" he said, really overacting. "Is that what you said? Oh hey Peete? We're in the middle of one of the most important days this business has ever seen, dear heart, and all you can say is 'hey Peete'?"

Daddy kind of smiled, but he still hardly looked at the man. "What you want me to say, sport? I don't know what you're talking about."

"Of course you don't, dreamboat. You're too busy. You can't be bothered with the pettiness of running a business, oh no. Not you."

Daddy sat down, or rather he dropped down in the chair behind his desk and leaned back. Man, did he look good behind that desk. I had never met anybody like him before. He had like class, you know? He looked like he was *somebody*. Like if you did him dirty, he could get you back.

He put his hands behind his head and for the first time started payin attention to that Peete man.

"What's going on, Peete?" he asked.

"For openers," Peete said, shakin his hip a little bit. What a zero. "Where were you all morning?"

"You know I had to go to the bus station."

"All morning, Thomas?"

"Not all morning, no."

"Then where were you? You certainly weren't home. I called there. Six times."

Daddy didn't say anything. He was rubbin the back of his head and starin at Peete like his mind was a million miles away. But that Peete, he had balls. He didn't act scared of Daddy at all. If it was me, and Daddy got quiet like that, I wouldn't keep on talkin like a fool. But Peete kept on talkin. And shakin and wigglin too.

"So where were you, Thomas? This is getting to be a problem."

"How about that."

"I mean it. Your absentees are becoming problematic."

"Just chill out, Peete, all right?" Daddy said that like he didn't mean nothin by it, and Peete took it light too.

Peete waited, then did what I figured was a curtsy. "All right. I'll be happy to chill out. And I suppose that means you don't want to know what happened while you were cavorting around the bus station all morning."

I looked at Daddy. I wanted to know what happened even though that guy Peete made me sick. Daddy looked out of the window first, like he was tryin to decide if he really wanted to know at all, then he looked at Peete.

"What happened?"

"Are you sure you want to know, Thomas?"

"Come on, Peete, I'm not in the mood."

"After all, you did tell me to—what was it?—'chill out'?"

"Peete!"

"All right," Peete said, with a wiggle. He then walked behind his desk and sat down. He put his hand on his chest and smiled.

"Varnadore agreed to terms."

Daddy hesitated, and then he smiled too. "Get outta here!"

"He said he tried everywhere, but nobody was coming close to what we offered him."

"Get outta here!"

"We seal the deal Tuesday. No revisions."

"That's great. That's great, Peete," Daddy said like a kid in a candy store, his gray eyes all wide open. "Do you realize what this means? We can build it up to our first middle-class community—for working people. No HUD allowed! Jesus, this is great! Do you realize how great this is, man?"

For nearly an hour Daddy and Peete talked on and on about Varnadore and him sellin some property to them. I just sat up on the radiator and listened until it was so boring that even they were gettin tired of it. Then everything just died down. Peete started goin through those papers on his desk, readin some and throwin some in the wastebasket, and Daddy called somebody on the telephone. Naturally he was braggin about the new deal. I guess he forgot to introduce me to Peete (not that I wanted to be introduced to that fruit, but still). I also guess he forgot I had nothin to eat all day. I told him in the car, that I had nothin to eat all day, and he said we was gonna stop by Burger King, but he didn't stop and never mentioned it again. I don't know, but my daddy didn't seem to pay much attention to things. He was always actin like he had somethin else to do or somethin else on his mind, even if he's lookin you dead in the eye. And he never seemed to remember anything either. Like I told him over and over, everybody called me Bay, yet every time he said my name he called me Ralph. I hated that name. It was a fat, old man name. Ralph. What kind of name is that for a little boy? But Daddy wouldn't call me anything else. That's just how he was, I guess.

When he got off of the telephone, he turned on the TV and stared at some reporter talkin about O.J. Simpson. Then he started rushin toward some door in the back of the office. I thought it was the back door and I got scared. All I could think about was Daddy goin away and leavin me with that crazy faggot Peete.

I jumped off the radiator and hurried up behind him. He turned around fast and stopped me in my tracks. I almost backed up, I was so scared.

"Where you goin?" I asked in a low, nervous voice. He didn't say nothin. He just stared at me for what seemed like a long time, like he was wonderin how a boy as funny-lookin as me could ever be any kin to him. I tell you I wanted to run out of that place right then and there.

Then he said; "I'm going to the bathroom, Ralph. Is that all right?" He said it kind of low and smart, like he thought I was crazy for even askin him somethin like that. I started noddin and lookin around as if it was no big deal to me anyway. I felt like a natural fool just standin there like that. But he didn't seem to care what I felt like. He went on to the bathroom.

For a while I tried to act like I was just wanderin around the office lookin at stuff. But it didn't work. I felt more foolish than before. I managed to wander back over to my radiator and sit my ass back down real fast, that's how bad I felt.

Peete, by now, had stopped his paper-shufflin and was watchin the television. "CNN Live," it said on the screen. Some funny-lookin old cop was tellin a room full of reporters that the Los Angeles police department couldn't find O.J. Simpson, who the cop said they wanted to arrest for murdering his ex-wife and some other man. Peete jumped up laughin.

"That's right, O.J.," he said to the TV. "I would've got the hell out too!"

Peete was a trip. He was shakin his head and flippin his wrist like somethin was wrong with him. Mama always said guys like that were fun to be with because they were so crazy. "But don't cross them," Mama said. "They'll cut you in a heartbeat."

Then Peete looked at me. There was somethin, I don't know, childish and sad about him. "Isn't this exciting?" he said with a big smile. "O.J. got away. And they got it live on CNN. That's modern technology for you. I mean it's like Rodney King and those riots all over again. I was simply glued to my television set."

What was he talkin about? What the shit Rodney King got to do with O.J. Simpson? He went from O.J. Simpson offin his ex-wife to Rodney damn King. What was he gettin at? I knew more about Rodney King than anybody in America because I saw the whole thing on TV. The day those white jury people said those cops were innocent, man, I could of told you they were gonna riot. Even my Mama got mad that day. "Them crackers somethin else," she said when she heard about the verdict. "How the hell you gonna beat the shit out of somebody on national TV and be innocent? Let that of been a black cop beatin on a cracker. They wouldn't of had to take that brother to no trial, no ma'am. He would of been dead within the hour!"

Mama wasn't politically active or any kind of civil rights person, so she said her two cents and forgot about it. Until Miss Cency came bustin in our door.

"They mad as hell out in L.A., Nita, can you believe it?"

"Mad about what?" Mama said.

"Hell, them police! Who else? They said they innocent, Nita, can you believe that? They said those no-good, racist police ain't touched Rodney King. Ain't that some shit? But them niggas gettin even, girlfriend, and it's all on TV and I got a ringside seat!"

Miss Cency ran back out the door and back to her apartment, and me and Mama ran behind her. We was havin some tough luck up around that time because our phone was disconnected and our TV was in the pawnshop.

"It's in the shop," Mama always told Miss Cency when she asked where our TV was.

"It was broke?" Miss Cency would ask.

"No," Mama would say. "But I was."

By the time me and Mama got to Miss Cency's apartment it was so crowded with people we had to sit on top of the kitchen table just to halfway see. Miss Cency was one of the few people in our building with cable, and we watched it all on CNN. And man did we watch. Almost all night we watched. It was like the whole city of Los Angeles was burnin down, the way they had it on television. Blacks and a lot of Spanish people were talkin bout if they don't have no justice, the cops ain't gon have no peace. They threw a garbage can through a store window and stole everything they could get their hands on. Some Puerto Ricans even had sofas and chairs, pilin them on top of cars and junk. I mean these dudes were stealin big time and it was all on

TV. They were beatin people too. Some dudes pulled a white guy from this big truck and just beat him like he was a dog. One dude, in some big shorts, threw a brick or somethin at the man's head and you could just see the blood gush out. That made Miss Cency happy. She jumped up then.

"Beat that cracker's ass!" she screamed at the TV. "Kick that cracker's lily-white ass!"

Others joined in, sayin they should beat the white folks just like those cops beat Rodney King. Big Ike even ran to the window and yelled in the alley. "They beatin white folks! They beatin the mess out of white folks!"

More people came and jammed Miss Cency's apartment. We were glued to the TV. Everybody kept wonderin where the police was, how in the world could all that be happenin and ain't no police around. I was scared. I was scared because it didn't seem like nothin mattered no more. They were robbin stores and beatin people like they had a right to do it. But nobody in the room seemed to be scared but me. Everybody else was enjoyin it. Even my mama said she wished she could get her hands on that couch those Puerto Ricans were haulin out the door.

That was what Rodney King was about. That was the day America went crazy. And Peete was tryin to compare that to some O.J. Simpson crap? I mean, if Juice did what they say he did then he should swing, man, and I mean from a tree! Ain't nobody gonna riot over no O.J. Simpson, especially if he did it.

But that Peete kept talkin like O.J. and Rodney King was the same thing. He even said he hoped O.J. made it to another country.

"We're talking about frying in the electric chair, honey

bun," he said to me, I guess. "You don't be too excited about putting your life in the hands of white folks when it comes to electric chairs. My God, they said the police didn't beat Rodney King when clearly they had. What on earth would they do to poor O.J.?"

Miss Cency was an O.J. fan too. She said there was no way one man could possibly kill two people, go home, wash off the blood, hop in a limousine, then catch an airplane out of town all in less than an hour. And everybody who saw him said he looked normal and relaxed. Miss Cency said people don't kill two people every day, especially with a knife, especially since it's probably impossible for one person to cut up two people. You can't kill two people and then act normal, she said. O.J., she was sure, was framed.

Mama didn't buy that line at all. O.J. killed those two people one at a time, she said. She also said she never did like O.J. Simpson. Mostly because he married a white woman, she said, but also because there was somethin dumb about him. And she could easily see somebody dumb as O.J. committing murder and then believin he could get away with it. I was with Mama on that one. Old Peete had another thought comin if he thought I was gonna cheerlead for O.J. Simpson.

But Peete kept talkin about it with a happiness that seemed too happy. He reminded me of those guys you see actin so happy all the time and then the next thing you hear they've blown their brains out. I sat up on that radiator and let him talk and be as happy as he wanted to be. He was high-yellar, not as high as me, but almost, and had a small afro. His eyes were light brown in color and real big, like they were almost popeyes. He was a loudmouth girlish-actin joker who was always shakin one of his legs like he had a nervous condition. He had gray in his hair like my daddy did and, like my daddy, lines came around his mouth when he smiled. He was just a jumpy little odd-lookin man that I just couldn't figure out. He was dangerous. Joe Nathan used to say a cat you can't get the lowdown on was dangerous. That was why I kept my eyes on that man Daddy called Peete.

Not long after he had left, Daddy came back from the bathroom just as Peete was gettin really excited. He was tellin me everything he knew about O.J. Simpson and Rodney King and President Clinton for that matter. He was gettin on my last nerve.

Daddy looked at Peete and shook his head. "What in the world are you going on about?" he asked.

"O.J. got away," Peete said, grinnin.

Daddy looked at the television set. Then he looked at Peete. "What do you mean he got away? There's a million reporters right outside his house—what are you talking about?"

"I'm talking about what I said, dear. O.J. is doing what he does best: he is running. The police went to arrest him for those murders and dreamboat was gone!"

Peete snapped his finger and rocked his body when he said "gone." After that it was more and more O.J. talk until Daddy finally got tired of it. He started searchin for somethin on his desk.

"Did I give you that Henderson file?"

"You certainly did not."

"I did give it to you, Peete. You remember. Number 12. She was coming by today."

"Oh! Her? Yes, I took care of that."

"Did she have it all?"

"A month and a half."

"Like hell! She was supposed to have all of it or she's out." Peete smiled and shook his head. He was really very crazy.

"That's not what she told me. I reckon I was duped big time, lover."

Daddy kind of looked over at me. You could tell he was embarrassed that some jumped-up mammy boy like Peete called him lover. But old Peete didn't think nothin of it. Old Peete just kept right on talkin.

"She was so convincing, too. 'Tommy told me to pay a month and a half today and the rest in two weeks.' She even told me I could ask you myself. I did not see any reason to disbelieve her, dear. She appeared so sweet and innocent."

Daddy smiled. "Sweet and innocent? That bitch?"

It seemed like a man who looked like my Daddy wouldn't call a girl a bitch. It seemed too streety. But I didn't know the man at all, and every minute he was full of surprises. Like havin Peete workin for him. Or givin money to some ugly hoe. Or ignorin me like I was invisible.

"I don't know our tenants up close and personal the way you do," Peete said. "I base all my impressions on half-minute conversations. Besides, if you were so insistent upon all of it at one time, you should have noted it in the record. Or even better, you should have been here when she came."

"Pamela's slick, Peete. If I would've been here, she wouldn't have come."

Peete nodded. "I get your point."

Daddy pulled out a pack of cigarettes. After he removed one and was about to put the pack back inside his suit-coat pocket, he looked at me. "You smoke?" he asked.

I didn't know if he was bullin or what. "No sir," I said.

Daddy stuffed the pack of cigarettes in his pocket. "Just asking," he said, wavin his hand in a way he probably picked up from Peete. "You never know these days. You never know what a big-town northern boy like you could be capable of."

It sounded like a putdown, the way he said it and looked at Peete, and I felt kind of bad that he said it, but I knew I had to let it slide. But that got Peete goin, Daddy lookin at him after puttin me down, that gave Peete the excuse he needed to jump into my business.

"Well," he said, lookin at me, "this must be young Ralph."

"Everybody calls him Bay," Daddy said and smiled.

Peete smiled too. "Hello, Bay," he said.

I hated Daddy for tellin that clown my nickname. He had no right doin that. I didn't want no F-boy like him callin me Bay. He might of let it go to his head. He might of changed it all around, like faggots do, and started callin me baby or babe or even lover like he called Daddy. I was damn mad. It was very uncool for Daddy to do that to me. That was why I played crazy and acted like I didn't hear Peete talkin to me. I wanted Daddy to know I didn't like it.

But Peete, bein who he was, read me wrong. "It must be quite a cultural shock for you, being transplanted from a city the size of New York and plopped down here. In the land that time forgot."

"Oh, I don't know, Peete," Daddy said, leanin back and rockin in his rockin-like desk chair. "It's not so shocking, is it, Ralph?"

Daddy knew I was iggin Peete, I guess, so he decided to try me too. Of course I couldn't ig him. He was my ticket out, like Mama said.

"No," I said.

I guess Daddy didn't like my one-word answer. "No what?" he asked.

"No, it ain't shockin," I said.

Daddy and Peete kind of looked at each other and smiled.

That was when I knew I had gave the wrong answer. That was when I knew Daddy meant for me to call him Sir.

"In any event," Peete said as he stood up and began sashayin toward me, "I'm Luther Peete. That's P-E-E-T-E. I manage your father's properties."

He stuck out his hand for me to shake. At first I stared at it, but I knew Daddy was lookin so I shook it.

"Jacksonville is no New York, let me be the first to tell you. But it has its few perks here and there that make it unique."

After he shook my hand he started starin at me. That made me real nervous. If I looked to the right, his big old gigantic eyes followed my head. If I looked down, he looked down at me. It was so stupid! That cat was somethin else. He was really the most craziest person I had ever met. I mean, it was bad enough he was jumpin all around like Peter Pan and Mary Poppins and shit, but to have a cat like that starin at you and watchin your every move was just too much.

But Daddy didn't seem to mind one bit. He just sat there and watched Peete watchin me. He had to know I hated the stares, but he didn't do a damn thing about it. I learned a serious lesson about Daddy that day. I learned that he was kind of insensitive like. That he wasn't the kind of man you could depend on.

"You know what?" Peete said mostly to Daddy, although he was still starin at me. "He bears a remarkable resemblance to you, Thomas."

I could of died. That was all I needed. That old crazy Peete couldn't do anything right in my sight that day. There he was tellin a beautiful man like Daddy that some ugly old high-yellar boy looked like him. I wanted to kick his blind ass. How in the hell could I look like Daddy? Where was the resemblance? I looked like some redheaded, black-eyed albino, and Daddy looked like Mr. America. That was really the straw for me. Peete had done it then.

Yet Daddy played it off. It was like he didn't really care either way. "How about that," he said to Peete. And that was all he said about it.

Daddy was like that. Cool, I guess you'd call it. He never would let things get to him for too long. He would get mad a lot, I mean, he was really impatient with people, but he would get mad and then forget about it. It was like he'd forget that people weren't as superior and perfect as he was, and he'd get mad at them for not bein that way. But then he'd realize that people were just stupid, crazy, ignorant people, and he wouldn't be mad anymore.

I knew I could be tight with a man like Daddy. We was gonna get along just fine, I knew it.

Peete, however, was another story. The longer I hung around him, the more I didn't like him. He finally stopped his starin though, and carried his fat, twistin ass back to his desk. But I still didn't dig him. He was just too weird. He was just too ready, willin, and able to let the whole world know how girlish and generally fucked up he really was.

That bothered me. For nearly an hour I sat up on that radiator worryin about that. How could Daddy have a cat like Peete around? I mean, he didn't even try to hide bein a sissy, it was like he was proud of it or somethin. He could cause Daddy to lose a lot of business, I thought. People would come to the office lookin to rent an apartment or whatever, and they'd see Tinkerbell flyin all over the place. They'd probably run out of Daddy's office real fast. And they'd tell other people not to do business there. "Don't go in there," they'd say. "Sissies in there!"

How could Daddy not worry about that happenin? I knew he was cool and all, but it ain't that much cool in this world, not when it came down to money. Mama said Daddy was stingy and shit, so I just couldn't figure out how he would let Peete run with him. And I know it wasn't like Jacksonville was so progressive and junk. Jacksonville was just a little southern outhouse compared to New York. And they really hated sissies in New York. I remember how one of my teachers, Mr. Saulsbury, got fired because he was one. And you couldn't even tell he was.

After about an hour of sittin up on that radiator thinkin about Daddy and Peete, I got tired. Daddy was writin a lot of stuff in some files he got out of the back room, and Peete was still watchin that O.J. crap on TV. For a whole hour they did this.

I missed Mama. It took a lot for her to send me away, because she really loved me, and I missed everything about her. But I didn't want to go home. I wanted to stay with Daddy. I wasn't about to go back to Harlem, after bein with Daddy.

I thought about Grandmama Dawson too. Mama told me to call her as soon as I got in town. I felt I needed to call her and get that over with. I also felt I needed to go to the bathroom real bad.

So I said to Daddy, "Excuse me." He didn't hear me. I stood up. "Sir?" I said, louder.

Daddy looked up. His soft eyes looked so beautiful, it looked like I was starin into glass. "Yes?" he said.

"I need to call my grandmama and use the bathroom."

Daddy smiled that half-second smile of his and looked at Peete. I don't know why he was always lookin at Peete when I said somethin to him. "You don't need to call Bessie," he said. "I'm going to take you over there in a few."

I got scared. I had to know. "To stay?" I asked.

"For a day or so. That's all."

"Why?" I asked. That was when Peete got into the act.

"My my," he said, and me and Daddy looked at him. "It talks."

I looked at Daddy. What the fuck he's talkin bout, I wanted to say, but Daddy was smilin at him. They had a bond.

After a little while Daddy looked at me and, naturally, stopped smilin. I always felt when he looked at me that I reminded him of somethin bad. "You'll spend the night with Bessie, your grandmother," he said. "That will give me a chance to discuss some things with my wife."

He said "my wife" like it was the most natural thing in the world to say. He said it like he knew I knew about her. I felt doomed. I felt like my dream had just told me that it wasn't gonna come true so I might as well quit thinkin about it. Daddy had a wife. And the way he was talkin, he had a wife who didn't know I existed. I felt doomed. No woman was gonna accept some other woman's child. Daddy should of told her about me. And Mama should of told me about her, cause the way I saw it,

I didn't have a chance. Women don't go for stuff like men do. And what with the kind of people Daddy liked to hang with, people like Peete and that hoe, I just knew that wife of his had to be a trip too.

"As for the bathroom," Daddy said, ignorin the startled look that had to be on my face, "you should know where that is by now."

Daddy gave one of his half-second smiles again and went back to writin what he was writin. I looked at Peete and he was watchin the TV again. I felt stupid. I felt the same way I felt when Sheneka Johnson read me that day. I felt alone. I felt like I was all by myself in this whole wide world.

I stayed in the bathroom kind of long. I couldn't do anything on the john so I just looked at myself in the mirror. I kept wishin I was better-lookin. That if I looked better people would like me. I guess I was feelin sorry for myself. My daddy had a wife and nobody told me about it. I cried in that bathroom of Daddy's. I cried because I had that reddish-brown hair, yellar skin, and coal-black eyes. And if that wasn't bad enough, I had the nerve to be short and scary and stupid-actin.

I was really more down on myself that day than I usually was. I guess I was havin what they called a pity party in that there bathroom of Daddy's.

When I came out, dry eyes and all, a skinny boy was sittin on the edge of Daddy's desk talkin to him. He was the exact same skin color as Daddy and he looked like him across the forehead. But he wasn't great-lookin or anything. He was average. He just looked like an average old skinny black boy to me.

I heard Daddy say, "I don't care" to the boy, and the boy

said somethin back to Daddy. Then Daddy looked up and said, "Does it look like I care, Coleman?"

That was when Coleman looked up at me. I knew he was Daddy's son.

He smiled. "Hi."

I kind of shook my head. I didn't know if Daddy didn't want him to see me or what.

But Coleman kept smilin. "You must be Ralph Dawson," he said.

Daddy told him that I existed, at least. But that still didn't mean he knew I was Daddy's son.

Peete said to Coleman, "Everybody calls him Bay."

Peete and Daddy looked at each other and smiled. My name was becomin a runnin joke between the two of them.

"They call you Bay?" Coleman asked.

"Yeah," I said in a nervous voice.

Coleman grinned. "Why?"

Daddy and Peete looked at me. I wanted to run. Nobody never asked me why before. It was just a name. Damn!

"I got a uncle name Bay," I lied and said. It worked. Coleman said, "Oh," and everybody kind of stopped lookin at me.

Coleman started walkin over to where I was. I was sort of standin behind Daddy, near the bathroom. The boy was about a foot taller than I was and he didn't stop smilin. He had small gray eyes and hardly no hair. But you could tell he was Daddy's son. Lookin at him from the forehead down, he looked almost just like Daddy.

"I'm Cole," he said, reachin out his hand. "Cole Bach."

I shook his hand, as if I knew all along Daddy had a son.

"You live in Harlem, don't you?"

I nodded. I was too scared to really talk.

"I heard people get shot in Harlem every night and drug dealers run the community. Is this accurate?"

He wasn't as young as he looked because he talked like a schoolteacher or somethin. I started wonderin if Joe Nathan was right, that Daddy left Mama because of this whole other family, and Coleman was just one of a slew of sons.

"It's kind of bad there," I said. I could just hear my voice echoing around the quiet room.

"Jacksonville isn't bad," Cole said. "I mean, it has its bad places, but it's hardly New York."

I smiled. I didn't know what to say.

"I went to New York once. When I was about ten. My mom had to speak at this convention and she took me along. It's a big place, boy. But Mom wouldn't go near Harlem. She's like that."

He said "she's like that" like he was apologizin to me. I didn't know what to say, so I smiled again. He went on to tell me he was sixteen years old, went to Ed White High School, played the trombone in the school band, wore size 8 shoes, didn't like any kind of sports, looked at movies all the time, and was a jack-leg preacher. He didn't say jack-leg, but that was what he had to be. I never heard of a sixteen-year-old preacher before in my life. He didn't even act like no preacher. He didn't tote around a Bible or tell me I was goin to hell. He didn't even mention Jesus name once. He just said he was a preacher like it was no big deal, like sixteen-year-old preachers were just fallin off of trees in Jacksonville. It was really hard to take. Here was this grinnin boy standin in my face tellin me he was a preacher. And Daddy didn't even flinch when he said it. It was really somethin to hear.

Southern life was nothin like Harlem life. In the south you got your sissies runnin round loose like it was nothin; sixteen-year-old boys preachin the gospel; and Daddy lettin it all go on, just sittin behind that desk of his and lettin the whole thing get out of control.

By four thirty we were in the Jaguar goin to Grandmama Dawson's house. It was located in a part of town Cole called *out east*. Cole sat up front with Daddy, and I sat in the middle of the back seat alone. The car was so clean, you couldn't find a piece of trash nowhere. It was so clean, I kept my hands on my lap. I couldn't be comfortable in a car like that. But Daddy was. It fit him like a glove. His whole body just relaxed in that car. Cole was relaxed too. His beany head kept bobbin as he kept askin Daddy if he could go to some Sunday school convention or somethin in Miami. I was amazed at how easily he could talk to Daddy. He even argued with him. At one point, he even called Daddy mean.

"I don't care how mean I am," Daddy said, "you're still not going."

"I'll be the only one who couldn't go. And I'm a minister! How's that going to look?"

"I don't care how it looks."

"It's just for a weekend, Dad, goodness. We'll be back Sunday night."

"Coleman?"

Cole waited, like he knew what was comin. "Sir?"

"What part of my 'no' didn't you understand?"

"Daddy, please! Everybody's going."

Daddy turned the corner and started drivin fast.

"Apparently not," he said.

Cole kept beggin, givin all kinds of reasons he should go, but Daddy had nothin else to say. He just let the conversation die. I think Cole was cryin, but I couldn't tell for sure. I felt like Daddy was wrong. He had a good son who wasn't on dope and wasn't a rogue. All he wanted to do was go to church things. He didn't seem all crazy about it either. He just wanted to go to church. My mama would give a million dollars to have a boy like Cole.

Out east was the stankest part of Jacksonville. It smelled like a big old chemical plant. Grandmama lived on Franklin Street. She lived in a tiny little wooden house on the corner. It looked like it had never been painted in its life. It looked like it would just drop to the ground if you touched it wrong.

Daddy got out of the car and started takin my suitcases out of the trunk. There was somethin like fifteen people sittin out on the porch. There was two men, three women, and a whole lot of nappy-headed little barefeet children. The men didn't have on shirts and were drinkin cans of beer. They looked like escaped convicts or somethin. The girls looked rough too, with hair standin all on top of their heads, and I could just see them stabbin me while I was asleep and stealin my fifty dollars. I didn't want to get out of the car. I decided to be bold like Cole, and not get out of the car. I was goin home with Daddy if that was the last thing I did. I wasn't about to spend the night in that old run-down shack with all those crazy-lookin niggas.

Daddy carried my suitcases up to the porch and was runnin his mouth with one of the men. The girls up there were just starin at him like he was somethin good to eat. I looked at Cole. Him bein a preacher and all, I felt like I could trust him.

"I don't wanna stay here," I said. Cole turned around. Like Daddy, he had those dreamy eyes. But only his weren't glassy, but gray and blurry-lookin.

"This is where your grandma lives, isn't it?" he asked.

"Yeah. But I still don't wanna stay here."

"Then tell Dad."

"Yeah, right. Tell him and watch him kick my ass."

Cole looked at me kind of hard, like he couldn't believe I said ass. Just that fast I had forgot he was a preacher. Just that fast I had forgot all those manners Mama begged me to use when I met up with these new people in Jacksonville.

Cole smiled. "I wouldn't worry about that. Dad won't hit you."

"He won't?"

"No! Of course not. Unless you make him really mad. Then he'll beat the living snot outta ya!"

Cole started his gigglin and grinnin and I looked at Daddy. He was walkin back to the car. I decided to try it, to glue myself in the seat and just try it.

Daddy opened the car door. "Okay, let's go," he said, leanin in.

I folded my arms and looked straight ahead. Cole started his grinnin again, but I was dead serious. Daddy didn't get it.

"I want you to behave yourself and do what your grandma says. I'll probably get you sometime tomorrow. Now let's go."

I didn't budge. I couldn't believe I was tryin Daddy like that, but I felt like I had to. I felt like if Cole could stand up to him without gettin beat up, then I could too. I was his son just like Cole was. And he owed me a whole lot more than he owed Cole.

"Do you hear me, Ralph?" he asked like he wasn't used to sayin my name.

"Yes sir, I hear you," I said.

"Then come on, I don't have all day."

"I don't wanna stay over here," I said and looked at Daddy.

He exhaled. "Now didn't I tell you at my office you had to stay with your grandma for a day or two? Didn't I tell you that, Ralph?"

"Yes sir. But I don't want to."

"Whether you want to or not hasn't anything to do with it. You're getting out of this car and going into that house and staying until I come for you. These are your relatives; all of them on that porch are some kin to you, boy. They aren't going to hurt you. Now stop acting like some overgrown baby, and let's go!"

Daddy moved aside for me to get out. He really didn't want to be bothered with my mess that day. Cole stopped lookin at us and turned around. I slowly slid across the beautiful red leather seat and got out of the car. Daddy held me by the wrist and closed the car door. Then he put my hand in his and we walked toward that raggedy porch. Daddy smelled so good and fresh that I walked as close up to him as I possibly could. I knew I was too old for my daddy to be holdin my hand like that, and I knew all the people on the porch were just watchin us like we were crazy, but I didn't care. I wanted to be with Daddy. I was tired of shacks and poverty. I wanted to go home to Daddy's clean, pretty house like Cole was goin home to. I wanted to sleep in a big soft bed that I didn't have to knock the rats and roaches off of before I could lay down. That was what Mama kept tellin me. Daddy don't have roaches, she said. "And ain't no furry-tailed critters in his house."

But who was I kiddin? Daddy and Cole, they didn't want me in their house. To them I was just some ignorant poor ghetto boy who was an embarrassing part of Daddy's past. He didn't have to talk nothin over with his wife. That didn't even sound right anyway. He planned it like this all along. He planned to pick me up from that bus station (two and a half hours late!), show me his office, and then bring me out here in these boondocks to rot, for all he cared. I wasn't about to live with him. He had his own family, his own life, his own son! I didn't belong in a world like his. I belonged in Grandmama Dawson's world. I belonged in a world of shacks and rats and roaches and nappy-headed children runnin all over the place. I would of been better off in Harlem. It would of been better if I never seen my father that day, if I just got right back on that bus like I started to, and went right back where I belonged. I guess Daddy figured he was givin me what I was used to by takin me to Grandma's house. And I guess he figured a poor joker like me had better be glad to get that much from somebody like him.

Grandmama Dawson was in the back room of the narrow, creaking house. Daddy said she was sick and that's why she was layin in bed in the middle of the day. But I knew better than that. Grandmama Dawson was drunk as a skunk. I could just smell the liquor when Daddy opened up her room door. She looked like a big old, fat, curly-headed, drunk bear layin up there in that bed. I couldn't believe she looked like that. I couldn't believe my mama had a mama that looked like that.

But I might as well believed it cause Daddy wasn't playin. He got in a hurry like. As soon as he saw Grandmama and told her who I was, his ass was gone. He barely said goodbye to me. It was like he couldn't get out of that house fast enough.

Soon as he left, Grandmama raised her big arms and started

in with that *gimme some sugar, baby* shit. I hugged her neck and like to died from her stank liquor breath. It was a trip situation, man. I felt more trapped in her arms than I ever did in Harlem.

She looked at me. She had an oversized brown face with a big mole on her cheek. But her eyes danced like Mama's. That was how I knew for sure she was the grandmama I hadn't seen since Joe Nathan's funeral, when her eyes started dancin.

"I'm glad you came, baby," she said, holdin me against her big chest. "We gon do a whole lotta things together too. We gon fish, you like to fish, Baby Boy? We gon be partners in everything, you and me. Oh, it's gon be wonderful. It's gon be like when you and Joe Nathan was little and y'all use to follow me toe to toe. Ha! You remember that, Baby Boy? You remember when you lived in this very house right chere and wouldn't let yo ole grandmammy piss by herself? You remember that, baby? You remember that?"

I really didn't remember it, none of it, but I smiled as if I did. She was this big, poor, old somebody, and drunk as a motherfuck, but I smiled and held onto her. She wasn't much, she sho wasn't much, but I just knew she was all I had.

Four

Sittin on the porch was like a way of life for Mama's people. It was like a job to them, the men as well as the women. They just sat on that porch of Grandmama's and watched the cars go by. All day. They didn't even take baths in the morning. They just got up out of those beds and went on the porch. You could just hear them in the morning, gettin on their shoes and gettin on the porch. At first, I thought it was a fire or somethin, the way they jumped up all at once. It made me jump up too. But this little boy name Peanut, who was supposed to be my cousin and slept in the same bed with me, told me to lay back down.

"Ain't no fire," he said. "Dey goin on da porch."

I couldn't wait to get up, to find out what was out there, but I learned right away not to rush things in Jacksonville. Especially if you was in Grandmama Dawson's house in Jacksonville. Everybody took their time. Everybody acted like they had all the time in the world to do what they had to do. Gettin on the porch was about the only thing those people did with any life in them, and early on, I couldn't understand why. It wasn't until Peanut explained it to me, when we were in the back yard catchin bumblebees.

"Dey want da big chair," he said. "Jason want it, and Waterman do too, but Chinesa she always beat everybody to it, dough."

Chinesa was Grandmama's daughter, my mama's sister, and she looked just like Grandmama. Every morning she sat her big self in that chair on the porch like it was her job to keep the chair down. Jason, Grandmama's youngest boy, and Waterman, her oldest, sat in the less comfortable torn-up kitchen chairs Grandmama had on the porch. They took their meals out there (three times a day Grandmama cooked, three times a day they ate), they joked around with neighbors out there, and they talked a whole bunch of trash about what they was gonna do when their ships came in out there. It was really funny seein them talk this way, about ships and shit, and me and Peanut would just sit in the yard and listen to them. Then Peanut would grab a mason jar and we would go huntin bumblebees.

"How old Waterman is?" I asked Peanut one time.

"Forty-two," he said.

"His ship ain't in yet?"

Peanut looked up for a moment, his beady eyes kind of closin cause of the sun. He was twelve years old but he always acted kind of funny, like he was retarded or slow or somethin. "I don't think Waterman got no ship," he said.

But that was what they talked about, ships and shit, all day long. And they were all really ugly, just some of the ugliest people I ever seen in my life. I couldn't believe they was related to my pretty mama in any way, shape, or form.

And they were also alcoholics. From Grandmama on down. They usually started around ten in the morning, when Waterman would go buy some beer: Colt 45 for Grandmama and Chinesa, Miller High Life for himself, and whatever he could get his hands on for Jason. Jason was probably the worst one in terms of drinkin. He didn't drink no beer all day, he was always tryin to get whiskey and gin and hard stuff like that to drink. Accordin to Peanut, Jason had a girlfriend name Myesha who got a crazy check every month from the government and that was how he got his drinkin money, but I think it took more than one girl's money to pay for all that liquor Jason drank. And he sho didn't work. None of them worked nowhere. Chinesa got a welfare check and food stamps for Peanut and her other four kids, and Grandmama got social security. That was it. Waterman said he was laid off and waitin for his boss man to call (Peanut said that was a lie, that Waterman ain't had no job in all Peanut's life), and Jason kept talkin about catchin the lottery and some job he had years ago.

Funny thing is, I liked Jason most of all. There was somethin sad about Jason to me. He had a big nappy afro and liked to wear bell bottom pants and sandals, like he didn't know it wasn't the seventies no more, but he was the only somebody that never gave me no funny looks. He took me with him when he was goin on the corner to hang with his homies, and right away he told them I was his nephew. And he called me Bay, not Baby Boy like all those other Dawsons called me, or Ralph.

"This Bay, y'all," he would tell his friends like he was proud of me. "He from New York City. The Big Apple. The Great

White Way. The city that never sleeps. The capital of the world!"

The homeboys would nod in my direction, not really knowin what the hell Jason was talkin bout, mostly because Jason was a college graduate and knew a lot more than the average homie, but also because the boys were all drunk and ain't cared what Jason was sayin.

"What yo nephew wanna come to jive-ass Jacksonville for if he from New York City?" the man Jase called Dollar Bill asked.

"What wind blew him this way, is that what you mean?" Jason asked, and Dollar Bill would look at the man Jase called Airvoid. They would both nod.

"Yeah," Dollar Bill said. "That's what I mean."

"The wind of his misfortune, as García Márquez would say," Jason said. "Or fortune, dependin on how you look at it. We never look at it the same way. I might look at a horse and think nothin of it; whereas Freud's Little Hans might look at that same horse and declare it the end of life as he knows it. We never look at it the same way. Misfortune or fortune, it depends on how you look at it."

Dollar Bill looked at me. "Why you come to J-ville, boy?"

For some reason I wasn't scared to talk around Jason and his friends. They reminded me of home, I guess.

"My mama want me to start livin with my daddy."

"Yo daddy? Who yo daddy?"

I took an unnecessary deep breath and said, real proud like, "Tommy Bach," but Dollar Bill and Airvoid bust out laughin.

"Tom Bach?" Dollar Bill asked like he was shocked sho nuff. "You gots to be jivin! That uptown brother ain't gon be foolin with you. Not Tom Bach! Not that mean motherfucker

Tom Bach! Shit! You gots to be jivin! You can be just two days late with his rent and he'll kick yo ass in the street!"

"Ah, nigga, shut up," Jason said. "What you know about rent? You ain't never paid nobody no rent in yo life! Don't listen to him, Bay. Tom Bach all right. He's just a businessman."

"Businessman my ass!" Dollar Bill said. "I know Tom Bach. I seen what that nigga will do to you. He'll fuck yo ass up! Remember Hop Scotch, man? Remember him? Remember how he was late payin rent and told Tom Bach he ain't had no money, and Tom Bach got so mad he threw Hop ass out the goddamn window? And Hop was a cripple, man."

"Hop Scotch ain't got nothin to do with this. Every time we say Tom Bach name you always bringin Hop Scotch up. You have a serious problem with that, Dollar Bill, you know that, man? Always mixin apples with oranges. Always takin one isolated incident and blowin it out of proportion. A man spend his entire life doin good and he makes one stupid mistake. People like you will concentrate on his mistake only and bump the rest of his life. Hop Scotch is irrelevant to this conversation."

"He ain't mimerivant to me, or whatever the fuck you said. I seen Hop come flyin out that window, man. I seen it wit my own two eyes. I said, 'Damn. Ain't that Hop Scotch flyin out that window?' And old Tom Bach come walkin out tellin them police Hop must of lost his balance. And them damn police believed him!"

"He might of lost his balance, hell, you weren't there!"

"I seen him comin out that window, I was there for that!"

"Y'all borin, man," Airvoid jumped in and said. "Bump all that Tom Bach shit. Do the dance, Jason, do the dance, man. Let's put some life on this corner. Do the dance!"

The dance was Jason's imitation of James Brown. He had the slide down good and he knew how to shake his leg and jerk his head back and forward. He couldn't sing much like James but it was fun to see. We all would laugh and laugh at Jason doin that dance. Later, when they all got a few more drinks in them, they would sit under a tree in a vacant lot and Jason would talk about the time he was a schoolteacher. It was like paradise, let Jason tell it. I never knew school could be that much fun. But he would never tell why he wasn't teachin anymore. I figured he was fired on account of he was an alcoholic. But I could never tell him that.

If I didn't know anything for sure, though, I knew one thing: I missed Mama. That was the worst thing about bein in Jacksonville, not havin my mama with me. It broke my heart to tell her that Daddy didn't come back the next day, like he promised, that he didn't even call. She cried on the phone. She didn't get angry or anything, because I guess she realized me and her both were kind of wishin for too much, but she couldn't stop cryin. She wanted to know everything: how did he look at me, what did he say to me, what did he say about her, did he hug me, did he tell everybody who I was? I guess she had a dream about how it was gonna be too. He was supposed to hug me and cry and tell the world I was his son. He was supposed to say great things about Mama too, like she was the only woman he had ever loved, and he would then rush to New York to be with her again. We was supposed to be like a family.

"Don't worry," I told Mama on the phone. "I like it with Grandmama. I'm havin a lot of fun down here."

Mama probably knew I was lyin, but she went along with

the game. It was like we had to pretend because the truth was too scary. We had to act like everything was all right or it would just change us forever. Daddy lied to her and me, but that was all right. We couldn't look at it that way. I was out of Harlem. I was safe. I was with a grandmama who at least cared about me. That was what we talked about.

The first week was the hardest. Every morning I got up expectin Daddy to be outside leanin against his Jaguar and waitin on me. I missed seein his pretty eyes and bad clothes and straight-back walk. But mostly I missed the way he smelled. Sometimes in the middle of the night, when Peanut was sleepin and the whole house was quiet, I thought I could smell his perfume. Usually I just smelled beer, but sometimes I smelled Daddy. It was really weird. I would wake up in the middle of the night smellin Daddy. It would give me a good feeling at first, because no matter how bad he treated me, how out of sight and mind he wanted me to be, he was still my daddy, but then I would get kind of down on myself. I was no kid. I was thirteen years old. I seen hookers get so beat up they couldn't walk no more. I seen old ladies get cut all up in the hallway and little babies get drop-kicked down flights of stairs because they was cryin too loud. I seen the only friend I ever had in this whole world get blown away by his own daddy, and I was standin right there, and it could of been me. I was no goddamn kid. But I was actin like one. I was wakin up in the middle of the night smellin some old man who didn't give a shit about me. That was kid stuff. Dreamin about daddies and wakin up smellin daddies was strictly for kids.

After seven straight days of not seein or hearin from him, I got the picture. He didn't come back the next day because he didn't want to come back. It wasn't because his wife said no or Cole didn't want me around. *He* didn't want me around. It was painful to admit, but it kind of made me get on with my life. And I'd be fine for a day or two. I'd even almost forget about Daddy. But then somebody would say somethin, when I sort of least expected it, and I'd start feelin bad again.

Like Chinesa. I really didn't like Chinesa because she was always sayin the wrong thing. She was always callin me and Peanut punks or sayin all we needed was a good fuck. And when I was feelin almost happy there in Jacksonville, she would start talkin about my daddy.

"You heard from yo daddy, Baby Boy?" she said to me one night when me and Peanut was comin up on the porch.

"Uh-uh," I said.

"That's a shame," Waterman said and shook his nappy, drunk head.

"He ain't even called you since you been here?" Chinesa asked.

"Uh-uh," I said again and tried to go on in the house.

"Not even one half-minute hello goodbye since you been here?"

It was how she got her kicks, I guess, downin my daddy, so I decided to remind her of what kind of man he was. Why I wanna do that?

"My daddy a real busy man," I said. "He ain't got no time to be callin me."

Chinesa leaned her big body back in her chair and looked at me funny. "Negro please, who you jivin?" she said. "Yo daddy ain't shit."

Then her and Waterman would start laughin real hard and drinkin more beer.

I grew to hate Chinesa and Waterman and everything about them. I hated beer and cigarettes and laziness and that goddamn porch. I hated the way they walked and talked and called me Baby Boy. But I took it. For nearly two weeks I took the name-callin and jokes about my daddy and the drinkin and the stank and everything they did. I took it for nearly two whole weeks. Until a Saturday afternoon, when Chinesa started talkin about how my daddy wasn't shit, and I kicked her ass.

I don't know why I did it, because it wasn't like she was lyin or nothin, but I couldn't control myself anymore. She was sittin her fat ass up on that old raggedy porch, drunk as a skunk, downin my daddy. "He ain't shit," she was tellin Waterman and Jason and their drinkin buddies. "Picked Baby Boy up from that bus station, sat his butt down in Mama's house, and hog-tailed it away from here. Won't even call Baby Boy, that's what kind of zero Tom Bach is. A big zero, a nothin! I remember how he used to come around here lookin for pussy. That ole horny motherfucker would of banged a damn dog if the dog would let him. And Nita let him. I sat right here and told her she was the biggest fool in J-ville lettin the likes of Tom Bach lay with her. But she wouldn't listen to me. 'Chinesa, you just jealous,' she said. 'Tommy so pretty, and he likes me.' I said, 'Nita, you's the fool if you think Tom "Hard On" Bach want you. He want what he can get out of you and nothin else.' But sister girl wouldn't listen to me. And let that joker knock her up twice. Twice! And both times he left her ass! He's a stone cold somebody, that Tom Bach is. Tom Bach. Tom Bach ain't shit!"

She kept on and on downin my daddy, sayin he ain't shit so many times that it seemed like she just wanted me to jump her ass. So I did. I jumped on her and started swingin. She was a big somebody but I was fast. It was like she was sayin I wasn't shit when she said my daddy wasn't, and I just couldn't deal with that no more. I started knockin her all in the face. I guess I wanted to kill her. I guess I wanted to see blood in her face. I wanted her to wish she never met me when I finished with her.

Waterman and Jason was able to pull me off her. But not before Chinesa had fallen out of her chair and was rollin on the porch. She looked like a pig rollin down there on that porch, and there was blood all over her face. I was thirteen and short and redheaded and poor, and had a daddy that wasn't shit, but I sho kicked her ass that day.

It worried Grandmama real bad. She said I was nothin but a juvenile delinquent. She said Chinesa could of called the police and had me thrown in jail. She said I disappointed her. She said I scared her and she didn't see how I could live with her anymore.

That was when she called Daddy. And that was when I found out the arrangement she had with Daddy. It seemed he was payin her a hundred dollars a week to take care of me. But she told him that wasn't nearly enough money to raise a child like me. I was becomin just like Joe Nathan, she told him. I was trouble, she said. Either Daddy was comin and get me, or she was sendin me back to Harlem.

I knew right away what that meant. It was crazy for Grandmama to even tell Daddy that. I mean, it wasn't like he knew I was alive. It wasn't like he called me or came by to see me or even asked about me every once in a while. He would of been glad for me to go back to Harlem, what was Grandmama talkin about? And why was she bringin up Joe Nathan? He didn't even go to Joe Nathan's funeral or call Mama back or nothin. Me endin up like Joe Nathan wasn't gonna mean shit to a man like that.

I wanted to take that phone from Grandmama and tell him to kiss my ass. I wouldn't live with him if he was the last man on earth, I wanted to say. Me and Mama waited for him. We waited for him to call and tell us he was comin to the funeral even after the funeral was over. He hurt us so much. He treated us like dogs so many times. And I still defended him. I hated myself for jumpin Chinesa when it was *his* ass I should of jumped. I defended a man like that. And now my whole future was in his hands.

Mama said I would probably get killed if I stayed in Harlem. Grandmama said I was probably gonna die if I went back to Harlem. And Daddy wasn't sayin nothin. It was like it wasn't fair. I wanted to take that phone from Grandmama and tell Daddy it wasn't fair. He should be beggin me. He should be runnin me down. He should be apologizin to me for every minute I wasted my time thinkin about him. And Grandmama was on that phone tellin him how I was out of control and she couldn't take it no more, like he was supposed to care or somethin. I wanted to take that phone from her and tell him hell, I didn't care either. Bump him! I rather be dead than fool up with a fool like him!

But I didn't tell him nothin. I didn't have a chance to. While I was gearin up for the showdown, actin it all out in my head,

Daddy had already hung up in Grandmama's face. It seemed like all the life had just seeped right out of her. She looked up at my pitiful-lookin face and then down at her big, tired old hands.

"Yo daddy the devil," she said like she was finally admittin it. "Yo daddy the puredy devil straight from hell."

Two hours later, when the sun was goin down in the woods across the street and the evening wind was shakin the mailbox at the end of the yard, that old devil was standin on our front porch.

Five

I was in the utility room lookin for mason jars with Peanut. We were gonna trap bumblebees again and then let them go. I really hated doin it, because it didn't make no sense, but Peanut loved it more than anything in this world. He was gonna be a bumblebee catcher when he grew up, he said. That was when Waterman came in the utility room and told me my daddy was on the porch. I almost believed him at first. I almost dropped that one jar we did find to the floor and run like hell out of there. But Waterman was always jokin around about stuff. It would be just like him to mess with me like that.

"Is he, now?" I said and smiled. Peanut giggled.

"Ain't nobody lyin about a thing like this, ole crazy boy," Waterman said. "He on the front porch waitin on you."

"Sure he is, Waterman. And I'm Michael Jackson." I then put one hand on my hip and started poppin my fingers and goin around in a circle tryin to sing and act like Michael Jackson. Peanut was laughin so hard he started coughin. Then we gave each other high fives right in Waterman's face.

Waterman got so mad he couldn't do nothin but shake his head. "Go look for yourself, crazy boy. He out there just like I said."

"Yeah, right."

"I ain't lyin, fool."

"Look, Waterman, I'll tell you what. You kiss my ass. All right?"

I liked cussin out Waterman because he always would get real mad about it, and start preachin and shit, but he would never hit me.

"You better learn how to respect yo elders, Baby Boy. You ain't nothin but thirteen years old and you cuss like a sailor. One day I'm gonna kiss it, you just keep askin me to, one day I'm gonna do it."

My back was to Waterman so I stuck my butt out at him. I was wrong, but I was havin too much fun. Me and Peanut was laughin like crazy. "Go head on, man. You bad. There it is. Kiss it. Puckle yo fat, juicy lips up and kiss the mess out of it!"

Peanut was bent over laughin. It was like he was havin spasms he was laughin so hard. He was really gettin to be my best friend. He was retarded or slow or whatever, and when the summer was over and school started back up he was goin to a special school for people like him, but I still liked him. I even beat up a boy for him, and I had never done that for nobody before. But this cat needed beatin. He just kept messin with Peanut and callin him Problem Head and shit. He needed somebody to bust him up a little.

While I was still bent over beggin Waterman to kiss my ass, and while me and Peanut was still laughin, I felt a cold shoe rest against my butt. Then I felt a hard push. The next thing I knew, I had flipped over the foot tub and had crashed into the wall. Before I even looked up at Waterman I got up ready to beat his ass. I knew I was gonna break Grandmama's heart again, and Mama's too probably, but I wasn't about to let some joker like Waterman jump me from behind like that.

When I got up and turned around, I saw Daddy. He was standin in front of Waterman, lookin all wide and big like, and I knew right away he was the one who kicked me.

"Sure you want me to kiss it?" he said.

I remembered what Cole said, that if you made Daddy mad, he would knock the fire out you. So I kind of moved back and got quiet. I didn't know what Daddy was capable of doin to me and I wasn't gonna try him. I tried him once and that didn't work. I was through tryin a man like that.

Then Daddy looked at me funny. "You're just a regular street punk, aren't you?"

It hurt me when he said that, and I didn't know what to say. He was the one who never showed any interest in me in my whole life, he was the one who didn't go to his own son's funeral, he was the one who left me with Grandmama Dawson and lied about comin back the next day. But *I was the street punk*? I thought about tellin him off right then and there. But I couldn't. I *couldn't*. Truth is, I was sorry he saw me actin bad. And I was too glad to see him to even think about readin him. It was like I was tellin myself yes, he was a bastard and the devil straight from hell and all that, but he came. That was all that mattered. I guess I was just like my mama. "Tommy kicked my ass sometimes," she once said, "but he didn't break my bones or nothin."

Seein Daddy was what changed it for me. Just seein his face again with those sad-lookin glassy eyes made me almost forget what I was so mad about in the first place. When I saw him, I just couldn't believe he could hate me. I couldn't believe he could let me die young and poor in some cold gutter somewhere in Harlem. It was like a man with eyes like Daddy's had to be decent, he just had to care what happened to his own son.

But Daddy had a way of starin those eyes at me until it made my skin crawl he stared so hard. What the hell was he lookin at, was what I wanted to know. I mean, I knew I was funny-lookin and all that, but damn! And I had to just stand there and take it, just stand in the middle of that wet-clothes-smellin utility room of Grandmama's and take the stares. And, of course, Waterman and Peanut were starin too. It seemed like whenever Daddy was around, everybody did what he did. So they all just stared at me, waitin for Daddy, I guess, to say somethin, and he wasn't about to speak. It was really too much for me. I mean, it was bad enough that Daddy was starin at me like I was some alien or somethin, but Peanut and Waterman was doin it too. I wanted to run. I wanted to run right out of that utility room and never stop humpin.

Then Daddy folded his arms and kind of leaned against the wall. "Come here," he said, lookin straight at me.

I looked around though, as if he might of meant somebody else, and then moved slowly toward him. When I got up close I could just smell that same perfume all over him. It was like there was a beautiful sweet scent underneath his skin and no soap and water in this world could wash it off.

"You make it a habit talking to your uncle like that?" he asked in that kind of smart-alecky voice he used on me before.

"No sir," I said. I was tryin my best to look as innocent as possible.

"Yes he do!" Waterman jumped in and said, talkin all loud and ignorant and embarrassin the hell out of me. "He talk to me like a dog, Mr. Bach!"

I knew right away I had to deny everything, or I could just kiss any chance I had with Daddy goodbye. "I don't be talkin to you like no—" I started sayin, talkin as loud as Waterman. But Daddy stopped leanin against the wall and stood up straight. I nearly jumped out of my skin. I knew he was gonna knock me upside my head for interruptin Waterman, I just knew he was gonna kick my ass good for havin the nerve to open my stupid mouth. But he didn't even touch me. He looked at me hard, like he was real tired of me, but then he looked back at Waterman. And Waterman was ready to talk. Waterman was ready to read me good that day.

"He cuss me out all the time, Mr. Bach. He won't do what I tell him to do, he won't listen to Mama no mo at all. You should of seen the way he beat up Chinesa. I declare he would of kilt that girl ifn't I hadn't of knocked him off her. Calls me all kinds of nasty names I don't wanna repeat myself. Be beatin on the chirren round here like he was they daddy or boss man. He beat a boy so bad the other day the boy's mama wanted to call the police on his butt. He talk back to Mama like she was another chile he be talkin to. He called her a drunk, Mr. Bach. 'You don't tell me what to do,' he told her. 'You can just go on from round here, wit yo ole drunk self.' And he cuss worse than a sailor, Mr. Bach. You should hear the thangs he say to people.

Just cuss folk out like it was nothin. He just a little ole mean, hateful somethin. And he know he lyin when he say he don't sass me. He sass me and everybody else. Don't he, Peanut?"

I looked at Peanut. He had to talk up for me. He just had to tell my daddy it wasn't true, that I wasn't mean and hateful and treated people wrong. He had to tell Daddy I beat up that boy for him, and that was the only fight I had in the whole two weeks I've been in this stupid town. Peanut more than anybody knew how bad I wanted to be with my daddy. He had to speak up for me. He had to make Waterman look like a fool for talkin about me like that. Peanut couldn't mess it up for me. He couldn't let my daddy believe Waterman and not want me more than he already didn't.

But Peanut wasn't seein it that way. He said, "He bad wit everybody," like he'd been wantin to say it out loud for a long time but was scared of me. I couldn't believe it. I fought for that boy and there he was downin me. I wanted to knock his dumb ass through the wall. I wanted to take his peanut head and shove it through that beat-up old foot tub.

Daddy had started lookin at me all the while Waterman was talkin. He didn't seem surprised by what was bein said and he didn't change his look when Peanut agreed with all that talk. That bothered me. I wasn't considered bad back home. Everybody kind of thought of me as a good, mama's boy who wasn't never comin out of the house. I didn't steal like Joe Nathan and I never once got in no trouble with the police. I got in a lot of fights but I usually got beat up, and when I wanted to join the jivest gang in Harlem, the Vitals, they wouldn't let me. I never went to school too much, but that was because Mama didn't push me or make me go, and I only cussed a lot because Mama,

Joe Nathan, Big Ike, Miss Cency, Monroe Oliver, and everybody I ever knew did too.

But Daddy was lookin at me like I was a troublemaker from way back. His glassy eyes were just fixed on me. I wanted to tell him I was a good boy, honest, that I didn't know why I was actin so crazy around Grandmama 'n'em, but it wouldn't of done any good. I looked bad. There was somethin about the way I looked, I guess, that made people hate me. I could tell Daddy how good I was till I was blue in the face. But it wouldn't of mattered. My ass was goin back to Harlem.

"Get your things," Daddy said after he was tired of starin at me. "I'll be in the car."

And then he turned around and walked out of the utility room. He wasn't walkin straight-back like I remembered but kind of hunch-shouldered, like a worried old man. He even looked much older than I remembered him, with what looked like more spots of gray all over his hair and mustache. He wasn't the same person that met me at the bus station two weeks ago. He had gained weight and was kind of spacy-lookin. Even his clothes looked wrinkled as he walked up out of that utility room. Somethin happened to him since I last saw him. And all he needed was to deal with me right now—and my foolishness.

I punched Peanut in the chest with my elbow and then hurried to do just as Daddy told me to. If I was goin back to Harlem, so be it. I wasn't gonna throw no fits or beg nobody gettin there either.

My brother Joe Nathan used to have this thing about gettin in trouble every Saturday night. I don't know what it was about Saturday nights, but one didn't pass without the police, or a neighbor, or some stranger man comin and tellin Mama about the trouble Joe Nathan had gone and got into. I remember one Saturday night in particular, a few months before Joe Nathan was killed, when Mama, Miss Cency, and two of their men friends were listenin to records. I was in the back room in bed, but because my bedroom wall was next to the living room, I always would lay awake listenin to everything that was goin on.

They were all drinkin that night, especially Miss Cency, who Mama said couldn't hold her liquor. Mama was arguin with the rest of them because she wanted to listen to Smokey Robinson records and they wanted to hear some jazz. It was a joke at first, with Mama puttin on her record and Miss Cency takin it off. It started as a joke. But then Miss Cency said somethin to Mama that everybody who knew Mama knew was true, but she still shouldn't of said it. She told Mama that Mama wanted to listen to Smokey Robinson records because Daddy had eyes like Smokey Robinson, and listenin to Smokey made her think of Daddy. I sat up in bed. Daddy was Mama's secret in New York. She didn't talk about him in front of just anybody, and Miss Cency knew she didn't. Night after night sometimes, Mama would just sit around listenin to Smokey Robinson sing those sad songs of his, and sometimes, if she missed Daddy bad enough, she would call Daddy on the telephone. She wouldn't even tell Miss Cency about those phone calls, or that she was still in love with Daddy, because she was probably too embarrassed to admit it, but Miss Cency still knew better than to mention Daddy in front of those men.

Mama headed for the kitchen. She was gonna get that butcher knife and cut Miss Cency if it was the last thing she did. I jumped out of bed. The two men were pretty drunk and were staggerin around laughin and shit. Miss Cency was laughin too. "Ain't it some mess?" she was tellin the men. "Just cause he got them damn weirdo eyes like Smokey damn Robinson. Ain't that some shit?"

They all thought it was funny, that Mama was gettin upset about records, and they thought she went into the kitchen to get more drinks. But I knew my mama. I knew what she was capable of when she got enough of that liquor in her. I ran into the kitchen just as she slung the spoon drawer onto the floor, with spoons and forks flyin everywhere, and she grabbed that big old butcher knife.

"What's wrong, Mama?" I asked, scared as hell.

But it was like Mama didn't hear me. "Who she think she is?" she was sayin. "I'll cut her ass, that's what I'm gonna do. Gon cut her black ass!"

Mama had the knife in one hand and a glass of liquor in the other and she started headin for the living room. I knew she meant it because her eyes weren't dancin anymore. I knew she was gonna kill Miss Cency, cause her eyes stopped dancin.

But Miss Cency was too drunk to see the danger. She and those drunk men were still laughin it up in the living room. That's what liquor do for you: you don't see the danger. I tried to hold Mama back, I even tried to grab the knife, but I was so little, and when Mama got mad she was strong as a horse. So I ran in the front room ahead of Mama. "She's got a knife!" I yelled. "Run, Miss Cency! Mama got a knife!"

But Miss Cency only laughed at me and told those men how cute I was. "Cute my ass!" I said to her. "Mama gon kill you!"

But she didn't see the danger. Even when Mama pushed me aside and was in the front room with the knife, Miss Cency was still laughin. It wasn't until Mama actually lunged at her that she saw the danger. She rolled off that couch and jumped to her feet real fast.

"What the hell is wrong wit you?" she screamed.

"I'm gon cut yo ass, that's what wrong wit me!" Mama screamed back and chased Miss Cency to the door. Just as Miss Cency opened the door, Mama slashed her shirt. That made Miss Cency scream even louder, and one of the men, who suddenly realized it ain't funny no more, went to grab Mama, but Mama turned on him.

"You want some, motherfucker?" she said, wavin that knife. The man backed off and held up his hands, like Mama was the police.

Miss Cency made it out the door and started screamin and runnin down the stairs. But Mama kept chasin her. She probably didn't even know anymore why she was doin it, but she was gonna cut Miss Cency, that's all she knew.

Then Joe Nathan showed up. He was comin in the building just as Miss Cency was about to run out of it.

"Yo mama crazy!" she yelled to him.

"You crazy too, bitch!" he yelled back at her, without even botherin to find out why she thought Mama was nuts. Joe Nathan was like that. He didn't care nothin about respectin his elders and shit like that.

But then he saw Mama runnin down the stairs with that butcher knife.

"Where you goin, Mama?" he asked her and bear-hugged her as she was about to run past him.

"Let me go, boy!" she yelled at him.

"I ain't lettin you go nothin. What you doin with that knife?"

She tried with all she had to get away, but Joe Nathan wouldn't let her.

"Miss Cency gone now, Mama," I ran down the stairs and said. "See. She gone." I opened the building door. People were beginnin to come out of their apartments and I wanted Mama to hurry up and calm down, before trouble really did get goin.

Mama did calm down and Joe Nathan helped her back upstairs. One of the men, Mama's date I guess, was still in our apartment. Joe Nathan, thinkin he had somethin to do with it, turned Mama aloose and hurried toward the man. "What the fuck you doin in here?" he said.

The man jumped up scared to death and I was screamin for Joe Nathan not to mess with him. "I ain't done nothin," he said like he was about to cry. "Tell him, Juanita!"

But Mama wasn't stuttin him. She dropped the knife on the couch and started headin for the back room. "I'm goin to bed," she said without turning around. She was worn out.

The man couldn't believe it. "Juanita? Juanita? Tell this boy I ain't had nothin to do wit it. Nita?"

But Mama was gone. Joe Nathan, who could tell the man wasn't even worth the energy to talk to, moved away from him. "Get yo punk ass outta here," he said and the man, shakin all over, sat down the glass of liquor he was holdin and ran.

After the man was gone Joe Nathan looked at me. "What happened around here? Why was Mama chasin Miss Cency like that?"

I had to catch my breath first. Joe Nathan hit me upside my head. "What happened, boy?"

"She said somethin bout Daddy," I said.

"Man," Joe Nathan said, shakin his head. "What she said?"

"She said Mama wanted to play Smokey Robinson records cause Smokey Robinson got eyes like Daddy."

Joe Nathan shook his head. "I don't believe it," he said. "I don't believe this shit!"

Then he went runnin in the back room, to Mama's room, and I just knew he was gonna try to hurt her. I ran behind him, peein in my clothes.

Mama was layin across her bed, hung over big time. Joe Nathan reached and turned her over, grabbin her by her blouse.

"What's the matter with you?" she said to him. "What kind of Sadday night shit you done got into now?"

"You was gonna cut Miss Cency cause of Daddy? You was gonna hurt somebody over that piece of shit? I don't believe it! Are you outta yo fuckin mind? That motherfucker ain't stuttin you! Don't you get it? He don't give a shit about you! Bury his ass, Mama. Stop takin us through this shit and bury his goddamn ass!"

Joe Nathan was cryin. He was grabbin on our mama and cryin like a baby. But Mama didn't say a word. She just pushed him off her and turned over. He stood up straight. He knew it was no use.

Like all the other times, Joe Nathan got in trouble that Saturday night too. He and Iceberg got in a brawl with some other boys from Bed-Sty and ended up in the hospital. Big Ike took me and Mama to see him. His jaw was wired for weeks. He got in trouble that Saturday night too. But only it was Daddy's fault that night.

Daddy threw my suitcases in the back seat of his Jaguar and opened the door for me. I brushed past him as I got in the car and I could feel him cringe when we touched. It was like he was scared of me. It was like he didn't know if he could trust me at night in his car and shit. It's a terrible feeling when people don't think you're good enough. It makes you mad as hell when they act like they're better than you. But that feeling is twice as bad when it's your own daddy actin that way. I mean, he didn't try to hide it either. The way he looked at me and handled me was a trip, man. But I still didn't lash out at him. No matter how bad I felt sittin in that car that night, I didn't show no sign of pain.

He didn't take me to the bus station that night. He took me home with him. It was a long drive from Grandmama's house, and the longer we drove the better I felt about where we were goin. I was gettin excited. Waterman told him all those bad things about me, and he was still takin me home with him? Maybe it was just for that night and tomorrow he was gonna ship me off to Harlem. Maybe he had other things in mind. I didn't know. I was too excited, though, to worry about it.

He was quiet all the way. He kept his glassy eyes glued to that road out there. I tried to get up the nerve to say somethin, to let him know I was glad he came to get me, even if he was two weeks late, but I was too scared. I didn't know him. I didn't know how to talk to a man like him. He was mean. I knew he was mean, the way he kicked my ass proved that. But he came and got me. He came as soon as Grandmama told him how bad I was gettin. Maybe he was worried about me. Maybe he didn't want me to end up like Joe Nathan. I didn't know. I couldn't figure him out that easily. Grandmama said he was the devil out of hell. Joe Nathan said so too. But Mama loved Daddy. She couldn't see the bad about him. She couldn't see that he didn't come and get me until Grandmama almost begged him to come. He came. That was all she would see. And I was like my mama.

Daddy's Jaguar turned a corner and ended up on a long,

curving street. All the houses on this street were big and beautiful. They looked like somethin out of a movie star magazine. Some of the houses were made of brick, some stone, and some with wooden fences so high you couldn't tell how they were made. In one driveway was a gang of fancy cars like it was a car lot. Another house was so long it almost took up half the street. It was so different. I just couldn't believe that a black man could live like this, let alone a black man who was kin to me. I always figured Daddy would have a nice house and shit, but damn! I wouldn't be surprised if Bill Cosby had a house in this hood.

Daddy drove around another curve and started drivin straight toward a house at the end of the street. It was a big two-story house made of all brick. It had a double front door and big windows with fancy-lookin curtains in every window. The driveway was arched up and the whole house looked like it was sittin on a hill. It was the most beautiful house in the world to me. I knew it had to be Daddy's.

"That your house?" I asked him as we kept drivin slowly toward it.

Daddy smiled his half smile. "How did you know?"

I didn't know how I knew, just that I knew, so I didn't say anything else. We drove up the arch in the driveway and stopped beside a red sports car. Daddy seemed surprised to see the car and just sat behind his steering wheel starin at it and lookin over at his house.

Then he exhaled. "Here goes," he said and hurried out the car. My heart sunk to my knees. That had to be his wife's car, I thought, and he probably didn't expect her to be home when he came with me. He probably figured he could get me off to bed or somethin before his wife got back home and he could explain me in the morning. But now she was already there, and I was there, and a showdown was comin up.

I followed close behind Daddy as he walked across the grass and up the steps to the front door. The house was lit up like a Christmas tree, both downstairs and up, so it was clear right off the people inside weren't asleep or anything. Daddy went to turn the knob. Before he opened the door, though, he looked down at me. His gray eyes were tired and scared-lookin but they stared at me hard, like somethin was really wrong with me.

"Put your shirttail in," he ordered, and I quickly obeyed. I guess he was thinkin how it was bad enough that I was funny-lookin and short. I could at least be neat. I could at least have somethin goin for me when he presented me to his wife.

He opened the door and we stepped into the big house. The first thing I noticed was the soft, thick rug that was all over the floor. It was real light-blue-lookin and didn't have no spots nowhere. It even went up the beautiful stairs that led to the second floor. It even covered all of the front room to our right and another room that kind of sunk down from the front room and had a sliding glass door in it. It even covered another room to our left that had a beautiful big table and high-back chairs in it. It was a big, long room with a huge light and a lot of small lights hangin down to the center of the table. I had never before that night seen a dining room, so I thought it could be a real big kitchen, but no stove or refrigerator or nothin was in it. And the rug covered that whole room too.

Just as Daddy closed the door, a short, kind of chubby young man came walkin from out of the dining room. He had these really droopy-lookin, sleepy eyes and walked like he was hunchback. But he was real good-lookin, like Daddy, but only he didn't look nothin like him. He didn't even look at me. It was like his eyes were just glued on Daddy.

"Hey there," Daddy said to him with a put-on-lookin big smile. The man must of known he didn't mean it cause he sho didn't smile back.

"Hey," he said and stopped walkin when he got up close to us.

"Whose car?" Daddy asked.

"I'm driving it," the man said.

"I know you're driving it, Dave," Daddy said like he was tryin to keep from losin his cool. "But that's not what I asked you. I asked you who owns it."

"A friend, Dad, okay?" the man said real mean like, and I kind of almost moved back. Dad? Did he say Dad? Cole and me ain't it? I couldn't believe it. I hadn't even thought about there bein more children to meet. And he wasn't no child neither. He was a full-grown man! Not for a minute did I think there would be more.

I guess I didn't hide my shock too well, because before I knew it that man was lookin his droopy eyes at me. "This must be your son," he said, with a hard sound to the word *son*. Then he looked up at Daddy.

"Yeah, this is him," Daddy said.

The man just stared at Daddy, and for a long time seem like. He then walked over to the door. "Tell Mom I'll be in the car," he said.

"She's here?" Daddy asked. "Where?"

"Upstairs," the man said, openin the front door.

"I thought she was—" Daddy said, but before he could

finish talkin, his son had slammed the door behind him. What a bastard, I thought.

Daddy looked real embarrassed by it all and avoided lookin me in the eye. He started to head toward the living room but before he got movin, Cole and some woman started comin down the stairs. Cole started walkin slower when he saw me, like he was shocked I was in his house, but the woman kept hurryin down, almost marchin down, and she kept her eyes on me.

She was an uptight-lookin woman with brown skin, brown cat eyes, and round, full lips. Her hair was jet black and fluffy and curled all under like a mushroom. She was small around the waist and she wore a nice green dress that bounced with every step she made. She looked a little younger than Daddy, and from the way she carried herself you could tell she just knew she was pretty. But she wasn't. My mama looked way better than her.

When she reached the last step she looked at me and just kept starin. My heart must of sank through my shoes. I thought, why she had to be mean too? Why she had to give me that same funny look Daddy gave me, Cole gave me, the droopy-eyed boy gave me, and even my own mama probably gave me when she first laid eyes on me? That look that became so much a part of my life early on, that I started callin it *that look*, where I stopped knowin how to explain it because no matter what it meant it didn't mean nothin good for me.

The woman hit the last step and came marchin up to me and Daddy like she caught us doin somethin wrong. Daddy spoke to her and put his hand around her waist. She liked his touch, I could tell. He then moved her up close to him and they kissed on the lips. She asked where was he all day and he started givin some lame excuse she didn't buy for a minute. And she didn't take her eyes off me. She was one of them uppity yams, you know? The kind that think they're white and shit. The kind that I could just tell wouldn't be caught dead around poor people. That's what I had to deal with, man. I wasn't gettin no breaks. None.

Seein her, though, made it clearer to me how Daddy could of fooled around with somebody like my mama. She and Daddy didn't match. There was somethin odd couple about them. Daddy looked serious but with a strong fun-lovin side to him. His wife looked like she wouldn't know what a joke was. Foolin around with other women was probably the only way Daddy could survive havin a wife like that.

Soon as Daddy finished his drawn-out story about what he had been up to all day, his wife, provin she had other things on her mind at that moment, said, "Is this him?"

Daddy ran his hand across his hair. "I was going to explain it to you…"

"Explain what?" his wife said, like she was gettin upset. "We're certainly beyond explanations now."

"What I mean is, I was going to explain to you why I had to bring him here, to the house, but you weren't home at the time. Bessie called and said he couldn't stay with her any longer."

"Why couldn't he?"

Daddy took his hand from around her waist and slipped both hands in his pockets. "Apparently he and Chinesa got into a fight of some kind."

Daddy's wife leaned her body back, as if she couldn't believe what Daddy had said. "Chinesa? Wait a minute. He fought Chinesa? She's a full-grown woman! What do you mean he fought her?"

"Exactly what I said, Ellie. They fought."

"They fought? Chinesa and this boy here were *fighting*?"

"That's right."

"And you brought him here? Why, Tommy? So he can fight me?"

Daddy looked at his wife hard, but he didn't say anything. You could tell he wasn't in the mood for her mess. You could tell he was goin to pop her if she kept on. But she kept on.

"You know how I feel about bad children, Tommy. If Bessie can't handle him, what makes you think I can?"

"He's not so bad, Mom," Cole said, tryin to defend me. But you just can't argue with somebody like Daddy's wife. She wouldn't let you get away with it

"Was I speaking to you, Coleman?" she asked. Cole stayed quiet. "Was I?"

"No ma'am," he said and glanced at Daddy. Daddy pulled out a cigarette.

The wife looked at me again. "What's your name?" she asked me.

My lips kind of stuck together and it took all I had to pry them loose. "Ralph," I said.

"Ralph?" she said. "Why your mama named you Ralph?"

She was gonna try and dis me if it was the last thing she did, like I was her competition or somethin. Daddy must of hurt her big time gettin my mama pregnant like that, and she was determined to let the whole world know it hurt.

"My granddaddy was name Ralph," I said.

"What granddaddy?" she said. "Bessie Dawson never had a husband."

But my mama had a daddy, bitch, I said to myself. But I couldn't say nothin to somethin like her. I never could talk up to people like her.

"I don't know, Tom," she said, still givin me the look-over, still tryin to get even. "You sure it's yours?"

The half-smile Daddy kind of had on his face turned to a hard frown, like he couldn't believe she said that. But I wasn't surprised. I had wondered the same thing myself.

"He's mine," Daddy said real confident like.

"I don't know," his wife said. "You might have been duped."

"He acts like Dad," Cole said, tryin to help me out again. But his mama didn't even look at him.

"Red hair. Yellow as I don't know what. He don't even look like his mama."

She kept lookin at me, like I was just the most amazing-lookin thing she ever seen.

"I used to hear about you for years," she said to me. "'He got red hair,' they said. 'He almost albino-looking.' 'He short.' 'He tall.' Then the talking died out. So naturally I thought you *and* your brother were simply a rumor, like all the rumors I had to endure since I hooked up with our Mr. Bach. Ha! Some rumor."

Cole looked down and then kind of away from his mama. I guess he felt sorry for her. I guess I did too. She looked all emotional, like she was gonna cry and shit. But Daddy wasn't touched at all. It was like he was tired and just wanted to go to bed or somethin.

"I expected you to be already gone to that banquet," he said.

"I see you did," she said and looked at him. That lady was bitter as hell. "And it's not a banquet. It's a fund-raising dinner. I was hoping you'd change your mind and go with me tonight."

Daddy started shakin his head, like ain't no way he was goin. "Not tonight, Ellie. Not tonight."

"Why not, Tommy?" she asked, still emotional. "You can go this one time. It'll mean so much to David."

"I'm not going anywhere tonight, Ellie, I told you that."

She kind of took her big eyes and looked up in the air and then rolled them. When she did that, water came drainin out.

"I'm tired of being unescorted, Tommy."

Daddy looked at her. God, he was beautiful. Everybody seemed to freeze in place when he looked at her.

"Every night you've been going to something or other with that law partner of David's by your side. I wouldn't call that being unescorted."

That did somethin to Daddy's wife. Water was still in her eyes, but it was gettin hard fast. "You got a lot of nerve," she said with her teeth all together and shit. Her head started bobbin back and forward and she put a hand on her hip, like my mama did when she got hot. "You come waltzin in this door, *in my house*, with some child you had by some other woman while you was married to me, and you're trying to question what *I* do every night?"

"Come on, Mama," Cole said, touchin her arm. "Let's just go. David's waiting."

"Bump David!" she said, snatchin her arm from Cole. Man, was she like my mama! "I'm getting sick and tired of this nonsense I've been taking from your father day in and day out. And you don't get it. Do you, Tommy? You don't realize that any other woman would have left you a long time ago. Do you, Tommy? Do you?"

Daddy kind of eased his hand out of his pocket. I thought he was gonna slap her for sure. But he just puffed on his cigarette and cringed a little, like he couldn't stand the smell of his own smoke anymore.

"Why don't you go on to your dinner," he said real cool like, and that must of blew her mind. There she was, veins and all, lookin like some wild woman, and he was Mr. Cool. It was a great strategy, I thought. It was the only way to handle a high-flyin, big-talkin, get-on-your-last-damn-nerve bitch like her, I thought.

She stared at Daddy for a long time after that. Daddy stared back, and there was a sadness between the two of them. Cole put his hand around his mama's arm. He was sad too.

"Come on, Mom," he said to her. I guess she was too hurt to say anything else because she let Cole lead her on out the door. Daddy hesitated for a moment, like he didn't know what to do, then he walked over by the window on the side of the front door and looked out. The way he acted made me figure he loved his wife. Only he was always doin stupid stuff, like bringin me home with him—or havin me in the first place—so even if he said he loved her a million times, she wouldn't believe him.

He pulled his shirttail completely out of his pants and looked at me. He smiled. But it looked too painful when he did it, it was too phony-lookin. And it came and went so fast, I didn't have a chance to smile back. But when Daddy smiled, lines came around his mouth and on the sides of his eyes. He was too old for this shit, and he knew it.

"Go on in the Florida room and watch some TV," he said to me and then went on upstairs. He didn't even look back, to see if I was doin what he said, to see if I even knew how. It was like he didn't care anymore. Nobody would believe he cared anyway, he probably figured, so why keep tryin? Man, was my timing bad. Of all my thirteen years on this earth Mama could of picked to send me to live with my daddy, I came to stay at the same time he was givin up. I'm unlucky. I swear to God I am.

It didn't hit me until Daddy was clean out of sight that I was standin alone at the front door of a stranger's house. Everybody had gone on with their business and left me so alone I could almost cry. I couldn't believe they would do this to me. I was only thirteen years old—how could they leave a thirteen-year-old alone like that? Daddy said for me to go in the Florida room and watch some TV. What the hell was a Florida room? I didn't know if it was the room with the velvet chairs and the lights, or the sunk-down room beyond the living room. Or maybe the living room was the Florida room, and Daddy called it the Florida room on account of he lived in Florida. Or maybe it was some kind of outhouse. I was all turned around there for a while. I felt confused and anxious and more alone than I could remember ever being. How could Daddy leave me like this? It wasn't my fault he knocked up Mama. How could he just go on upstairs and leave me alone like this?

But what was I expectin? Daddy was supposed to bring his bastard son home and they were supposed to welcome me with open arms? I should of been glad his wife even let me in the door, what the hell was I bullin about? And Daddy, well, he was Daddy. He was gonna help you just so much, I had already figured that out. So I figured I might as well find the Florida room and sit my scared ass down, like he told me to.

It turned out to be that sunk-down room with the slidin glass door. It was easy to find because of all the rooms I saw, it was the only one with a TV. It was a big, wide room with wood-paneled walls and a couch that went from one wall around to another one. The TV was big too, so big that it didn't even have to sit on a table. But I couldn't turn it on. I tried to. For nearly an hour I tried to. But I just couldn't figure the damn thing out.

I fell asleep after hours of starin at nothin, and woke up to the sound of a loud noise. I looked out and saw Daddy and his wife standin in the room with the fancy lights yellin at each other. I couldn't hear what they were sayin, because they were too far away from me, but I knew it was bad. Then Daddy, who didn't even have a shirt on, grabbed his wife by her arm and slung her with him as he went up the stairs. I got scared, cause Daddy looked out of control. I started wonderin if I should make a run for it, before the shooting started. But then I saw Coleman. He was comin in the front door. I stood up, to make sure he saw me. But that didn't work. He went runnin up the stairs and didn't even look my way. I waited for hours for somebody to come back down and tell me what to do. But nobody came. They all went on up those stairs the way they probably did each and every night, and not a one of them came back down to just say hey you, dog, here's a sheet, a blanket, or even a worn-out old bedspread, for the cold.

Six

One day in the middle of summer, two years before Joe Nathan got killed, it rained all day long. Mama kept walkin around smokin cigarettes and talkin bout how the dog days were the worst time of year for her. Mostly she didn't feel that way because of the rain, but because Joe Nathan had been gone for two whole days. The round-face nice policeman who came to our house after the first day said most all the kids in Harlem run off like Joe Nathan every once in a while but they always come back. "All a part of growin up," I remember him sayin to me and Mama, but that did nothin to stop us from worryin. Joe Nathan wasn't all the other kids in Harlem, he was my brother, and Mama's favorite child. He had never stayed out all night in his life before, let alone disappearin for two whole days.

It was hard to deal with. Joe Nathan was like the glue of our family, the only person me and Mama both could depend on to be strong and protect us when trouble came around. I really didn't know how to deal with him bein gone like that. It was probably almost as hard to deal with as dealin with his death two years later. At least then we could picture in our minds what happened to him and how it happened and where it happened. But this was different. I couldn't eat, I couldn't sleep, I couldn't think about anything but my big brother Joe Nathan.

It was hard. Especially that second night. Especially after we walked every step in Harlem lookin for him, checkin out all his runnin partners and hangouts, annoyin the shit out of the police. Especially after all that and he still didn't show. I remember layin on my big old bed in a ball, holdin my stomach, cause I couldn't stand the waitin. Mama told Miss Cency that Joe Nathan could be in a gutter somewhere, bleedin to death, crawlin around callin for her and ain't nothin she could do about it. For two whole days our eyes hardly blinked. For two whole days I kept seein my brother, crawlin through the rain and the mud callin for me, and I just stood there like I couldn't figure out what to do about it.

But then he came home. He wouldn't even tell us where he had been. He even looked at us like we had no right askin where he had been. And after a while, Mama stopped askin him too. I couldn't believe it.

"You gonna let him get away with worryin you like that?" I asked her.

"Ain't got no choice," she said. "He growin up."

I felt the same way tryin to live in Daddy's world. I felt like I was growin up too. It was like I was gone off like Joe Nathan went, with no mama, no friends, no nobody to look out for me. Every day it was somethin different. Every minute, seemed like, I had somethin new to deal with. It was like my life had been taken away from me and all the things I knew about didn't make sense no more.

And Daddy was terrible. He didn't give a shit about me. He just dumped me in his world and forgot about me. He didn't tell me nothin. I used to think all I had seen in Harlem, all the stabbings and killings and poverty, made me an automatic man at thirteen. But I was wrong. Harlem wasn't nothin compared to Daddy's world. In Harlem, I had Mama and Miss Cency and Big Ike to care for me. In Daddy's world, I was on my own.

I couldn't of realized it more when he woke me up the next morning, mad at me for not sleepin in a bed. It was like he was expectin me to do somethin I didn't know how to do. He was standin over me like a giant, tellin me how any fool would of known to get into a bed, especially when there were so many in his house. Did he have to tell me everything?

I listened to him go on and on, screamin at me and downin me before I could even open my eyes good. He had on a fancy suit and a tie and was wavin around the newspaper in his hand. He looked like a weirdo to me. He looked like one of those weirdos on any street corner in Harlem, preachin from the top of their lungs about nothin. I remember sittin up on that couch listenin to Daddy and wonderin if it was gonna end, if I was gonna ever know what it was like to be a part of a normal family again. Daddy was too crazy, I couldn't never peg him. He was meaner to me that morning than I ever thought he could be. I didn't know how to deal with a moody man like him. All I did was sleep in the Florida room because nobody told me nothin different, and he was actin like I just killed somebody or somethin. He was wavin his hands in the air and talkin real loud and frownin at me like it hurt his eyes to even look in my direction.

Even his wife saw how he was overreactin and came down in that Florida room in her housecoat and junk. But Daddy wasn't stuttin her. He told her to mind her own damn business, that I was his son, not hers, that she didn't have nothin to do with it. She looked at me like she felt sorry for me or somethin and just walked back out the room. It was like she was tellin me, okay, hotshot, this is what you wanted, you wanted to be with this fool, now you with him, you happy?

Happy? How the hell could I be happy? It couldn't of got any worse for me. Daddy couldn't of acted any meaner. "This isn't Harlem," he said as if that said everything. But why he had to say that? It was true, but truth always made me mad. I couldn't handle truth, not when it came from him, not when the only person I had in this world able to help me didn't think I was worth a shit.

"You can kiss my Harlem ass!" I said back to him in a high-pitched, cracking voice, but I looked him dead in the eye after I said it, as if I was darin him to not like it.

That was when he grabbed me, with both hands, and slung me off the couch. I thought he was gonna throw me through the wall the way he looked. For a minute I wanted to scream. It was like it wasn't happenin. It was like my whole life was somethin dirty and shameful and doomed to end in tragedy and there was nothin I could do about it. Cause no matter how many big houses they put me in, how many fancy clothes they put on me, I knew I'd never be able to escape who I was, how I grew up in

Harlem, how I grew up poor, how I grew up funny-lookin. That's why I cried. That's why I was danglin by the catch of my daddy's hands, cryin like a baby.

I don't know what Daddy made of my cryin, but it did somethin to him. His angry look was still there, but he seemed more mad at himself than at me. I could just see the pain come all over his face, and that hard grip he had on my arms started easin up. Then he let me go. I stood up beside him, wipin the tears from my eyes. I stood close to him, almost touchin him.

He just stood there starin at me with his hands on his hips. "What am I gonna do with you?" he said like he was thinkin out loud. It was a great question, but I didn't near bout know the answer. I knew what I wanted him to do with me. I wanted him to love me and be proud of me and treat me like I was somethin special to him. But I was dreamin and I knew it, so I didn't say a word.

He put the newspaper under his armpit and just kept starin at me. His eyes were soft as ever, but they was still sad-lookin and wide open, like he was in a trance. It was like he wanted to say he was sorry, but his eyes were sayin it for him. It was like he wanted me to know he didn't mean it like that, he didn't mean to hurt me like that, but he just couldn't help himself. That was how I felt when I looked in his Smokey Robinson eyes. Cause what I did when I cussed him, I couldn't help myself either.

And before I knew it, I threw my arms around his waist and fell against him. But he didn't hug me back. He patted me on the top of my head with his newspaper, said somethin about how late he was, and slowly started walkin away from me and up and out of that Florida room.

He barely said two words to me for a week after that. He would go to work early and not come home till after dark. I would look out for him, secretly, and when his Jaguar would lift up into that arched driveway, I made it a point to be passin by the front door just as he would be comin in it. But he would only say "hey" or somethin like "how you doing" and go on upstairs. I didn't know what to make of it. I knew him bringin me to his house was gonna be hard, not just for me, but for his wife and children too. But I never dreamed he'd bring me here and forget about me. It was like he'd decided to let me be a part of his world just so much, and he wasn't goin no further.

And it was hard for me hangin round that house all day. I followed Cole around every time he went someplace, but Cole ain't hardly go nowhere. Most days he'd get up, do a little work around the house (whatever Daddy's wife Eleanor made him do before she went off), then he'd go back in his bedroom, get on his bed, put his headphones on, and read books. I used to lay across the edge of his bed and act like I was interested in all those weird books he read, but I got tired of that put-on with the quickness. I mean, every one of his books was about dyin and goin to hell and stuff like that. I was too scared to read them books cause every time I read or heard somebody talkin bout dyin, I thought about Joe Nathan. And every time I thought about Joe Nathan, I started feelin real bad. Reverend Ruby said he was gon burn up in hell. I couldn't deal with that, you know?

One day, after Daddy's wife made me and Cole vacuum the whole house and sweep off the patio, Cole started askin me a lot of questions about if I was saved or not. We was sittin out on the patio drinkin cans of Mountain Dew and eatin some tuna salad

Eleanor fixed us for lunch. It was hot. We was both wearin shorts and sandals, and I was hittin mosquitoes and fannin flies every two minutes seemed like.

"You saved, Bay?" he asked me and drank his Mountain Dew. I was waitin for him to ask me that question since I arrived in Jacksonville. I was shocked it took him almost a week after I moved in with them to ask me.

I leaned back in my chair and answered the way I heard my mama tell Reverend Ruby one time. "It depends on what you call saved," I said.

Cole looked at me and smiled. He had one of those hard-to-figure smiles like Daddy, but only his lasted longer than half a second. "Good answer," he said. And that was all he said about it.

When Mama gave that answer to Reverend Ruby, you could hear Reverend Ruby's mouth a mile away. She went off on one of her preachin fits that lasted all day. She called Mama everything but a child of God. Accordin to Reverend Ruby, everybody that ain't saved ain't nothin but filthy rags that was gonna bust hell wide open if we didn't ask God to forgive us and clean us up from unrighteousness.

But Cole didn't say nothin else. He was cool with me, you know? I guess he figured I wasn't ready to be saved or whatever, so he didn't waste his breath talkin bout it.

I felt like I could talk to Cole, but I never said much to him. From the time I first met him in Daddy's office, I wanted to get a second opinion on whether or not Joe Nathan was in hell. But I couldn't push myself to come out and ask him. The closest I came was later that same day, after we got too hot out on that patio and went back into Cole's room and laid across his bed. He was just about to put his headphones on when I asked him if a person that don't go to church can go to heaven.

He put his headphones on the bed and looked me dead in the eyes. "Not if they aren't saved," he said.

I nodded like it was no big deal and grabbed one of his books to read. He wanted to know why I asked, but I told him I didn't have no reason. Thinkin about Joe Nathan burnin up in hell's fire made me wanna forget I ever brought up the subject in the first place. I couldn't hear no more.

I got up off Cole's bed and went into my room, which was next to Cole's. I turned on the TV and turned it up loud. *The Young and the Restless* was the only program I could get a clear look at cause Daddy ain't had no cable hooked up upstairs. But I didn't care that all I could see was the stories. I even watched that, cause anything, anything was better than even thinkin about hell's fire.

My best days was when Cole decided to go out the house and hang with some of his homeboys. It was all good then. We'd go over to Rodney Cramer's house and get in his parents' big swimmin pool or sit on his patio and listen to rap. I loved those times. Cole was nothin like he was at home. He'd laugh and joke around and try to act cool like Rodney. He wouldn't never even mention Jesus. In fact, I don't think Rodney or any of his friends knew he was a jack-leg preacher. I started to tell Rodney a few times, but Cole told me to stop tellin his business.

But I loved those days at Rodney's house. We would horse around so much that I had to pee from laughin so hard. I remember one time when Cole got so carried away that he took off his trunks and jumped in the pool naked—and right in front of the big fat lady that lived next door too. Man, did her face turn red!

"I *will* be tellin your parents about this when they get home, Rodney!" she yelled across the fence.

Rodney tried to act all innocent. "What'd I do?" he yelled. "That's Cole actin crazy." But the big fat lady wasn't stuttin him. She went on back in her house. "Fat bitch," Rodney added when she was gone.

Other times we might hang over to this other dude name Drummer's house. Drummer was a trip cause he was always talkin bout stuff ain't nobody never heard of, like how fast light travels through time and junk like that.

Cole liked Drummer and could sit down for hours and listen to him go on and on about his scientific theories. But me, I wasn't wit that program at all. He bored the shit out of me. But I acted like it was real excitin to hear him talk, cause it sure as hell beat layin around in Cole's room.

But even hangin out in Cole's room wasn't as bad as the days when Daddy's wife didn't go nowhere. Damn. Them days were rough, you hear me? She made me and Cole work from sunup to sundown. We had to vacuum and sweep and mop floors and clean out toilets and polish furniture. Man. I wanted to tell her a time or two that I wasn't her damn slave, but I ain't said nothin. I just worked harder than Cole and hoped she'd tell Daddy what a good worker I was, but I was wastin my time hopin that. I ain't never heard her tell Daddy nothin good about me.

Besides, Daddy was in his own world. After that day in the Florida room when I told him to kiss my Harlem ass, he didn't hardly say two words to me. At first I worried about it. Maybe he was thinkin bout sendin me back home or somethin. But I didn't feel too bad about it, cause he wasn't sayin too much to Cole or his own wife either.

He got mad a lot, when the trash wasn't out or the yard wasn't cut right, and once he hit Cole upside his head just cause Cole forgot to water the hedges like he was supposed to. But mostly he just worked all day long and came home, always at night, looked at TV a little, and went to bed. His job had to be his life, cause he sho didn't have one at home. But Cole said it wasn't like it seemed, that Daddy had a lot of girlfriends and did all kinds of bad things to people. He said Daddy always came home and went off to bed because he was too tired from humpin women to do anything else. He said his mama was a saint for stayin with Daddy like she did and for even lettin me stay in her house. "You just don't know," Cole liked to say to me. "Daddy somethin else."

They all saw Daddy that way, from his wife to Cole to that droopy-eyed boy David, who they called "Wine" for some reason. Only they didn't badmouth Daddy to his face, they never hardly argued with Daddy to his face. But they talked up a storm when he was out of sight.

Like his wife. Every time me and Cole would go in the kitchen to get some water or a banana or somethin, she'd stop shellin peas or tossin salad to say somethin negative. It would be like she was makin a point of it, like she was the head of the committee to trash her own husband.

"What time is it, Cole?" she'd usually start it off by askin.

Cole would look at the clock that would be right in front of her. "Eight fifteen," he'd say, or whatever.

"Uh-huh. And your daddy ain't home yet. But see if I wait

for him this time. As soon as I finish this salad, we're eating. He has no interest in considering our feelings, so why should we consider his? Uh-huh. He must think I'm crazy."

"Why don't you call his office?" Cole would ask.

"I did."

"Is he there?"

"No."

"And watch how he'll claim he was at the office."

"One day I'm gonna follow his butt. See if he wiggle his way out of it then."

And she'd go on and on like that. She was always throwin hints about Daddy, and Cole was always backin her up. Everything I came to know about my daddy was negative. Everything. He couldn't do nothin right in the eyes of his family. When he came home late, they'd say he'd been with a woman. When he came home early, they'd say he'd been with a woman. When he came home on time it was on account of the woman he was supposed to of been with. It was like a broken record. And Daddy never even heard the tune.

Then there was all them girlfriends of Daddy's wife, all them preacher wives or undertaker wives or Dr. So-and-So's wives, who'd come over to our house every week and throw down on Daddy. It was like they were a club, the way they went at it, with one after another tossin the dirt.

"I wouldn't put up with his mess another day."

"You got too much going for you, Eleanor, to let Tom Bach treat you like this."

"Divorce him. And take everything!"

"That's exactly why I don't fool with no pretty man. They ain't nothin but trouble."

"Women look at your husband like he somethin good to eat, girl. They don't care nothin about him being married, and apparently he don't care either."

"Tell him you ain't nobody's fool, girlfriend. Tell him about his butt. Don't take that from him. Let him know you're just as independent as he is."

"Have an affair, girl."

"Leave his ass. He'll get the message then."

But he didn't get the message because she wasn't about to leave him. No matter how bad she talked about Daddy and let her friends do the same, I never once saw her packin no bags. I guess she felt like I felt about it, that somebody that looked like her and me should be glad to be associated with somebody that looked like Daddy. When her friends weren't around, you could tell she was glad to have him too. She was always sittin up under him and kissin on him. They were in the Florida room one time when I saw her put his thing in her mouth.

But one night everything changed. Daddy acted just like her friends thought he would, and for the first time since I moved in with Daddy, his wife not only left him, but took Cole and me with her.

It was a bad day all around. The summer of 1994 was over and it was the first day of school. I was so nervous about goin to school in Jacksonville I couldn't sleep at all the night before.

The day before school started, Daddy told me I had to be dressed and downstairs by seven that next morning so he could register me on time, but I was dressed and downstairs before six. I sat on the couch in the living room and couldn't stop shakin my leg. The whole house was dark and quiet. I kept prayin

Daddy didn't oversleep, but I was too scared to go back upstairs and make sure. I tried to wake Cole up when I got up, but he pushed me and told me to get out of his room. So I went downstairs.

Eleanor came down around seven and was shocked to see me sittin in her living room.

"You know better than that," she said and told me to take my "narrow behind" in the Florida room and wait. She was still in her housecoat and slippers and her hair was standin on top of her head.

Mama used to always treat the first day of school like a big deal. She would get up early and fix me and Joe Nathan a real big breakfast. Then she'd go on and on about how proud she was that we passed and was goin to a brand-new grade.

I guess I expected Daddy and his wife to treat my first day of school the same way. But I must of been out of my mind. Nothin about Jacksonville was like New York. The parents in Jacksonville didn't fix a big breakfast and congratulate their children for passin to the next grade. They expected them to pass. That's why Eleanor didn't treat me no different on the first day of school than she did every day. Goin to school was like breathin to her. And she wasn't about to get all excited about that.

Daddy and Cole came hurryin downstairs around eight thirty. Daddy was walkin fast and tyin his tie and Cole was complainin that his pants were too short.

"Too bad," Eleanor said. "You should have gotten up on time. It's too late to change now."

"But *Dad*!" Cole said, rushin up to Daddy. "These are high waters."

"Too bad," Daddy said and told me and Cole to come on.

Daddy backed that Jaguar down that arched driveway so fast his tailpipe scraped the street. It was crazy, man. Daddy drove faster than I had ever seen him drive, and me and Cole kept beggin him to slow down before he killed us. But it didn't seem like he was stuttin us. He was gonna get us to school on time, and if he killed us in the process, well, that was our problem.

The car clock said eight thirty-nine when we drove up to Jeb Stuart. It was a long brick building that looked more like a hospital than a school. Plenty of yellow school buses were in the parking lot, and all the students seemed in a hurry to beat the bell. And man did they all look good. I mean, they knew how to dress. They had on clothes I dreamed of wearin, like them big jeans that hung off your butt and those bad Nike tennis shoes that pumped up.

I looked down at my clothes and I knew I was doomed. I could see the girls laughin now. Eleanor picked out all my school clothes, and I didn't have the nerve to tell her that she didn't know what she was doin. I was just too happy to be gettin new clothes. But damn. Everything she bought me looked like somethin a four-year-old would wear, from my Barney book bag to my Oshkosh B'gosh shorts and shirt. She said I had the body of a little kid, so she shopped for me in the little kid section. I tried to tell her that I wasn't too small for big boy clothes, but she told me to be quiet or she wasn't gonna get me nothin.

When I stepped out of Daddy's Jaguar at Jeb Stuart that morning, I wished to God she had got me nothin. Cole stayed in the car while me and Daddy got out, and even Cole started pickin on me, tellin me to sing the Barney song before I left.

I wanted to tell him to kiss my Barney song ass, but I didn't. Daddy was still around and I wasn't about to cuss in front of him. I just told Cole to have fun at Ed White, which was the school he went to, and me and Daddy got out of the car. I felt like I was the center of attention right away, though nobody seemed to be lookin at me no harder than they looked at Daddy. But there was nothin wrong with Daddy. He wasn't dressed like a fool the way I was. And Cole had the nerve to complain cause his pants were high. Please. I'd trade my Oshkosh B'gosh any day for high water pants!

Daddy told Cole to be sure and stay in the car till he got back, and me and him walked into the school and headed for the main office. The school was so clean I couldn't believe my eyes. There wasn't no drawings on the walls or no gang symbols or no nothin. Nobody had no boom boxes, and the only music you heard was some mall music somebody was playin over the loudspeaker.

Because I was new to Stuart, me and Daddy had to wait in the guidance office for my class assignment. We sat over by the window, and Daddy crossed his leg and flipped through some magazine. Student after student who came into that office would speak to Daddy and giggle at me. At first, I just knew it was because of my clothes. But the students didn't laugh until some girl that worked in the office would point at me and whisper somethin to them. By the time I went to my first class, which was English, word had spread throughout the school that the man some of their parents rented houses from had a funny-lookin little son that didn't have the same last name he had. And that son was a student there!

Kids would come up to me askin me if I was really Tommy

Bach's boy, and when I said yeah they would fall out laughin. That's when I realized my clothes ain't had nothin to do with the laughin. It was all about how I looked versus how Daddy looked. That was why them stupid students was doin all of that laughin.

I remembered runnin in the bathroom at the end of fifth period and cryin like a baby. I never thought I was much to look at, but damn. Those students acted like I was the weirdest-lookin boy in the whole wide world. I had high hopes for my school days in Jacksonville, but by the time that first day was over I would of been glad just to get through another day without being laughed at.

After school, me and Cole sat on the patio drinkin lemonade. He asked me how did my day go, but I didn't tell him the truth. "Okay," I said. "What about yours?"

Cole said his day went okay too, and that was all we said about school.

We went over to Rodney's house later that day to shoot some hoops. Rodney and Cole talked about school like it was the best time they ever had. I kept my mouth shut. Sayin school was okay was one thing. But goin on and on about it like it was the best fun I ever had was somethin else.

It was almost dark when me and Cole got back home. Daddy was pullin up in the driveway just as we was crossin the street. We ran up to Daddy's Jag. There was somethin like five cars parked all around our house. Daddy got out of his car lookin mad, like he sho didn't feel like bein bothered with no whole lot of people.

"What's all this?" he asked Cole as we walked up to his car. He was wearin a kind of wrinkled-up-lookin suit and he smelled funny, like his perfume and somebody else's perfume was all mixed up together on him.

"I think it's Mom's social club people's cars," Cole said.

"What social club?"

"I don't know, Dad. Those goofy ladies she's always having over."

Daddy exhaled hard and shook his head. Then he looked at me. "Hey," he said without even a smile.

"Hey," I said back, and that was the only word we spoke to each other that whole day and night.

Me, him, and Cole decided to go in through the back door in case a party was goin on or somethin. That was a mistake. The kitchen was full of people, from those women who were always comin around to a big black man with jheri curls. I knew he had to be Taylor King, a man Daddy's wife was helpin to win some election. It wasn't like it was a party, though, cause everybody was all quiet and Daddy's wife looked like she'd been cryin.

As soon as we closed the door good, every eye in that kitchen fell on us. There was the short, skinny lady with long hair sittin at the table next to Daddy's wife, while a taller lady with a ponytail was sittin on her other side. A woman with a short, neat afro was standin against the refrigerator holdin a glass of water, and two other ladies were standin by the sink. Taylor King, the only man in the group, was leanin against the drainboard with his big arms folded and his legs stretched out. He was standin directly behind Daddy's wife's chair. For some reason, Daddy didn't like Taylor King. Whenever his wife would even mention him, Daddy would start callin him all kinds of names, like Mr. King was a crook or somethin.

Yet it was Taylor King who was the first to look up at us

when we came in the back door. And for all the negative things Daddy had said about him, he looked like a nice, decent man to me. He didn't smile or nothin when he saw me, but he didn't frown either, and I appreciated that.

Then Daddy's wife looked up. Her eyes were bloodshot red and her hair, that great mushroom style she was always bouncin around in, looked straggly like a wig. There was nothin pretty about her. In fact, she was kind of ugly. She looked so ugly to me that night that I started wonderin for the first time why in the world Daddy would of married somebody who looked like that.

"Good evening," Daddy smiled and said to the group, but didn't none of them really answer him back, except maybe Taylor King, who grunted. "Ellie, what's going on?"

Daddy was always smilin and tryin to act easygoin around other people, even though he was kind of mean and always yellin at us. But his wife didn't go for his put-on that night. She was too mad-lookin.

"Where have you been, Tommy?" she asked.

Daddy smiled. "What?"

"Where have you been?"

"I've been to work. What is this?"

"You have not been to work, don't tell me that lie."

The word "lie" did somethin to Daddy, cause he dropped that unnatural-lookin smile of his like a hot potato.

His wife kept talkin: "You can't get out of it this time, because I saw you."

"You saw me? What are you talking about?"

Daddy was frownin now and lookin at his wife like she was crazy.

"I saw you in Cleveland Arms."

For the first time Daddy lost eye contact with his wife and kind of glanced at the other people. That eye movement made him look like he was embarrassed, or guilty. I couldn't tell which. "So what if I was in Cleveland Arms? Just what are you insinuating?"

The short lady sittin next to Eleanor moved in her chair. "Huh! As if you don't know!"

"Stay out of it, Gwen," Taylor King told her.

"I ain't stayin out of nothin. Standin his sorry ass up here actin like nothin's going on. She caught your ass, Tom Bach! With Mary Wright! That's what she's insinuatin!"

Daddy just stood there for a long time. He looked like he was too mad to even talk. He stared at that lady Gwen because she said what she had to say and kept shakin her head, as if she had just proved somethin. Watchin her made Daddy speak up.

"You don't know what the hell you're talking about, Gwen."

"Oh child, please," Gwen said. "Nobody's falling for your line anymore. I don't know why Ellie put up with your ass this long! All that working late. Yeah, you was working late all right. On top of somebody!"

Daddy charged toward the table and everybody seemed to jump. "Get the hell out of my house!" he said to Gwen, and she stood up fast and Taylor King kind of moved in front of her. "You get out before I throw you out!"

"Now let's not lose our cool, Mr. Bach," Mr. King said.

"You kiss my ass!" Daddy said. He looked like he wanted to cry he was so mad. "You get out too!"

"Nobody's going anywhere," Eleanor said and stood up just as he got near her. There was somethin sad about what was goin on, when they faced each other like that. "These are my friends. They came over here to support me, and they're staying."

Her voice was cracking, like she wanted to cry some more, and it seemed like it was hard for her to stare Daddy in the eye.

Then Daddy said, out of the blue like, "So, you want a divorce?"

That seemed to throw everybody in the room. It was like Daddy wasn't interested in workin it out anymore and he was gonna have the last laugh. His wife had overreacted, and the way she looked I could tell she never expected Daddy to mention no divorce. Cole didn't expect it either. And although he tried to hide it, I could see him turn and wipe the tears from his eyes.

"You promised me, Tommy," Daddy's wife said. "You promised you had stopped seeing her."

"I did."

"I saw you over there today, Tommy. I saw your car at her apartment for hours today, Tommy."

"I don't care what you saw. And where the hell do you get off following me? I don't care if I stayed over there for ten days, that's my damn business! You understand that, Ellie? And if you don't like it, if your friends don't like it, then all y'all can get the hell out of my house!"

Daddy was tremblin he was so mad. But Eleanor was mad too.

"It's your fault!" she yelled back at him. "You're always trying to make me feel guilty when you do something wrong! And you don't have the decency to admit you did it."

"Then divorce me, Ellie, all right? If I'm so damn bad, divorce me. Because you don't know what you're talking about, you're listening to the wrong damn people, and you're jumping to conclusions when you don't know what's going on!"

"Don't even try that, Tommy," Ellie said. "You stayed there for hours. Hours!"

"Did you see what went on inside that apartment, Ellie?"

"I didn't have to see! All I needed to know was that it was Mary Wright. And I know you don't hold Bible studies when you're with Mary Wright. You was humpin that bitch just like you used to do!"

Why she wanted to say that? Daddy, without thinkin about it, took his fist and hit his wife so hard in the face she fell into the dish rack, causin forks and spoons to fly everywhere. Her friends let out a quick scream of horror. Cole yelled, "Daddy, no!" real loud, and Taylor King grabbed Daddy and stopped him from goin after Eleanor again. Then Daddy snatched away from Mr. King.

"Get out of my house now," he said nearly out of breath, pointing at his wife, "before I hurt you. I don't mean an hour from now, I don't mean a day from now, I mean right now." Then he looked back at me and Cole for some reason and walked on out of the kitchen. His wife got her balance back, although she was bleedin at the nose, and told her friends she needed to get a few clothes from upstairs.

"Wine can come back for your clothes," Gwen said. "Let's just leave before that fool comes back."

She agreed to leave, and she even told me to come with her and Cole. I felt funny doin it, since I knew she didn't like me and I reminded her of what that Mary Wright lady must of reminded her of, but I didn't like what I saw in my daddy that night. He seemed so mean. He seemed like he didn't care who he hurt anymore, cause he was gonna do whatever he wanted to do. I don't know, but I felt like if I stayed with Daddy that night, he might of hurt me or somethin. So I went with his wife. I swallowed my fear and all those bad feelings I had, and latched on to whatever part of her I could.

Taylor King and Gwen dropped us off at a really nice apartment out in a part of town they called Arlington. It was David's apartment. I later found out that he wasn't just some droopy-eyed boy who didn't much like his own daddy, but he was a lawyer, the only lawyer I ever knew in my life, and he was nice.

That first night we all sat up in his quiet living room and tried to figure out what we was gonna do. Eleanor had stopped bleeding but was holdin a bag of ice on the side of her nose, where she had a bad bruise.

"I can't go back to him, Wine," she said to David.

"You should have seen how he talked to Mom," Cole said. "Then he hit her."

"Are you sure it was Mary Wright's apartment he went into?" David asked his mama.

"Of course I'm sure. I saw him."

"Jesus, he's a trip!" David said. "After all that crap, he's right back up to his old tricks again."

"He promised me it was over. He promised me, Wine, and I believed him. Now I don't think it ever ended."

"It ended," David said. "He's simply starting it up again. He's tripping again."

"But why? Tell me that. He knows how that heifer almost destroyed our marriage. Why would he go back to that? And I do everything for that man. Everything, David! I want somebody to tell me why."

She ran her fingers through her hair and leaned her head back. The tears were comin in her eyes again. "I couldn't believe it when I saw his car parked at Cleveland Arms. I actually did a double take. I just couldn't believe it."

"How did you end up in Cleveland Arms anyway, Mom? Is that one of your projects now?"

"Don't be ridiculous. Taylor had to meet with the manager out there about a rally we're having this weekend. But when I saw your father's Jaguar my heart raced. After all we went through. Unbelievable."

"Damn," David said. "No telling how long he's been seeing her again."

Eleanor looked at David real fast like. She was pitiful. "You really think there've been other times, Wine?"

"Please. Of course there have! You just happened to catch him this time. Come on, Mom, think about it. That'd be a helluva coincidence if the one day your job takes you into Cleveland Arms apartments is the same day Dad decides to start it up again with Mary Wright. Please."

"But why, David? I know I'm involved in Taylor's campaign and I'm not home as much as I used to be, but…"

"But nothing, Mom. Stop trying to justify it. Even if you weren't involved in Taylor's campaign, he still would have done it. That's how Dad is. He doesn't care who he hurts."

"He told Mom she should divorce him," Cole said.

"When?" David asked.

"Tonight!"

"He's got some nerve."

"You think he meant it, Wine?"

"I have no idea what that joker meant."

"And you and Tommy used to be so close," Eleanor said. "Sometimes I used to believe you knew exactly what he was thinking."

"Yeah, well, that was a long time ago," David said and drank with one upturn almost a whole can of Pepsi.

Eleanor stood up and started walkin around. She would fold and unfold her arms like she was so nervous she couldn't control herself. I should of felt out of place there with my Daddy's family talkin bad about him the way they were, but I didn't. I felt like I was supposed to be with them, that God was givin them a chance to like me.

"What am I going to do?" Eleanor said as she walked all around David's living room like she couldn't be still for nothin.

"Go to the house tomorrow when he's at work and get some clothes," David said. "Don't call him, don't drop by his office, don't do anything to make him think you're coming back."

"But I want to go back home already, Wine. To him." Tears started to stream down her face.

"I know you do, Mom," David said, "but you can't. You ran back to him the last time and the time before that. And nothing changed. You've got to let him run to you this time. You've got to know if he wants you back."

"But what if he doesn't come, Wine? You know how he is."

"Then you'll know he doesn't want you and you'll divorce him, take everything you can get, and get on with your life."

Nobody said nothin else after that. A scary kind of quiet

came over everybody in the room. It was like we all felt the same way, that we couldn't bear leavin Daddy. I guess we all loved him so much in our own way that it was too personal to talk about. So we kept quiet, lookin at everything but each other, knowin the only thing we had in common was a man who, I really believe, none of us really knew.

Later that night Cole told me all about that Mary Wright woman that caused all the trouble. Seems she used to be Daddy's girlfriend and Daddy almost divorced his wife over her. Cole told me about how he and his mama and Wine used to go over to her apartment and tell Daddy to come home. Once Cole even grabbed Daddy by the leg and started cryin and beggin him and junk, but none of it did any good. Daddy would accuse them of followin him and he'd yell at them like it was all their fault. Daddy and his wife separated for almost a month one time, Cole said, and his mama like to died it hurt her so bad. Sometimes in the middle of the night she'd get so desperate to know where Daddy was spendin his nights that she'd call Mary Wright's apartment and and then hang up the phone. Cole said he kind of hated Daddy during those times because of the way he treated his mama. I told him I knew exactly how he felt.

But Mary Wright wasn't all, Cole said, cause Daddy had other women too, including a girl David was thinkin about marryin. They would call the house sometimes and ask for Daddy like there was nothin to it. Cole said he got so mad one time that he lost his religion and cussed one of them out. When Daddy found out what Cole had done, though, he took off his belt and beat him so hard, Cole said, that he couldn't sit down for a week. Daddy said those women were his tenants and Cole had better treat them with respect. But Cole said he wasn't stuttin them. They was tenants all right.

    I should of known Daddy would be that kind of man. Joe Nathan said he was, and Miss Cency said he was, but I guess I was hopin my mama was right. But reality wasn't on Mama's side, and whenever I got down to it, there wasn't much to praise about my daddy. He left my mama when I was first born and again when I was four, and when we moved to New York, not one time did he come to see me or even call to check on me. Mama had to beg him to let me come live with him, and then when I got in town he shipped me right to the ghetto and out of his sight. Maybe he had good reasons to do it, what with his history of runnin around on his wife, but good reasons ain't mean nothin to me. And how could he fool around with David's woman? That's sick. That's like a snake in the ground ain't low as that. I couldn't sleep that night. I kept seein Daddy ballin up his fist and runnin up to his wife. If he would do that to her, after all the shit he's put her through, what the hell would he do to me? My days in his world were numbered. I could feel it in my bones.

Seven

A week later me and Cole skipped school and took the city bus to Daddy's office. It was more a dare than really meanin to do it, but when we got off that bus a block away we knew we wasn't turnin back. We didn't talk. Cole kept his hands in his pockets and walked like he wasn't in a rush. I walked slow too, kickin rocks along my way. We had planned to sneak off and see Daddy almost the very next day after we moved in with Wine, but we could never get up the nerve to do it. We were both scared of Daddy. We knew how mean he could be when he was in one of his moods. But we missed him, both of us, and after a week of not even gettin a phone call from him, we knew we had to do somethin. I was more scared than Cole, though, and all during our bus ride I kept tryin to back out.

"Why don't we call him first?" I said.

"No," Cole said. "He doesn't like to talk on the phone and he might get mad if we call him."

"He might get mad if we show up at his office door."

"He'll get mad but he'll still have to see us."

"He might peep through the peepholes and don't even open the door," I said.

"He won't do that."

"How do you know?"

"Because I know."

"That ain't no answer."

"It is an answer."

"I asked you how you know. You didn't tell me how."

"No duh!"

"How you know then?"

"How do I know what, Bay?"

"That Daddy gonna let us in his office."

"Because I know, all right? Goodness!"

Cole had a temper just like Daddy. He never cursed or nothin like that, but he sho got mad a lot.

"I don't know why we're even doin this," I said. "Daddy don't care nothin bout us."

"He does care."

"I ain't seen it."

"I have."

"Since when? I thought you hated him."

"I don't hate him," Cole said. "What an asinine thing to say."

"A what?"

"Stupid."

"It ain't stupid. You act like you hate him."

"I'm saved, Bay. I love everybody. I could never hate my own daddy and still think I'm going to heaven."

I turned around and looked at Cole. "Heaven? You figure you goin to heaven?" I had never known nobody who thought they was goin to heaven.

"Of course I'm going to heaven. Why do you think I go to church and believe in God and tell people about Jesus? For my health?"

"Damn, man," I said. "It was just a question. I didn't mean nothin by it."

In a lot of ways, Cole was just like Daddy. They had the same kind of way of gettin annoyed at people, and you're always scared to ask them a question cause you might not ask it right and junk. He was always talkin bad about Daddy, always sayin how Daddy somethin else, but of everybody in the family, he seemed to miss Daddy the most. He would bring up Daddy's name when nobody was even thinkin bout him, and when some black man would be on TV who looked and acted nothin like Daddy, he would talk about how that man reminded him of Daddy.

I think Cole was scared. He told me the day after we moved in with Wine that his mama was always leavin Daddy, and Daddy never, not one time, asked her to come back to him. It was always Cole's mama who made the move. But this time was different. Wine, Cole said, used to always push their mama up to call Daddy or to go see him, but this time Wine was makin her stay away. And after a whole week, Daddy hadn't even called. That kind of made Cole nervous, I think, and so without lettin his mama know, and tellin me about it only after I promised not to let her know, Cole and me skipped school and rode the bus to Daddy's office.

"But what about the victims?" some old white man was sayin to Mr. Peete when me and Cole walked in the office. Mr. Peete was standin over a card table pourin coffee, and the white man was sittin on the edge of Daddy's desk restin his hands on a cane. Daddy's car wasn't out front, so we already knew he wasn't there.

"I understand that, Lou," Peete said. "But we're talking about O.J."

"I'm tired of talking about O.J. That's all I hear about: O.J. this, O.J. that. But what about the victims? That was a brutal, heinous crime. And so young they were!"

"And so white. Right, Lou?"

Peete waved for me and Cole to come on in, but his attention was totally on the white man.

"What does race have to do with this?" the white man asked. "I never mentioned anything about race."

"But that is exactly what this case is now about and will always be about."

"Race? What are you talking about? This is a murder case. Race has nothing to do with who murdered those two innocent people."

Cole, who was good at relaxin, moved quick over to Daddy's desk and sat in the chair behind it. I fumbled around, causin Peete and his friend to stop talkin and stare at me until I sat down on the radiator.

"Say Lou," Peete said. "You know Tom's children, don't you?"

"Tom's children? I didn't know Tom had children."

"He has three, actually. That's Coleman behind you. And this right here is Ralph. But, of course, everybody calls him Bay. Right?"

I tried to smile but was too nervous. "Yes sir," I said.

"Hello, Bay. And hello, Coleman. I'm Lou Borowitz. I do business with your father."

"It may be a longer wait than I expected, Lou," Peete said. "Sure he couldn't call you when he gets in?"

"No, because he never calls me! For twenty years I'm selling property to Tom Bach and not one time has he returned my telephone calls. Not one time! Not even when the deal depended on it. He would rather lose out than to pick up a telephone."

Peete smiled like he knew it too and sat behind his desk. He wasn't actin all jumpy and girlish the way he was when I first met him. He wasn't limpin his wrist or jerkin his body or talkin a whole lot of trash. I wondered if I had read him wrong, if maybe he wasn't an F-boy after all.

"I agree, Lou, that this is a murder case. Two people were murdered, that's true. But race plays a part of everything in America, Lou, let's not pretend that it doesn't. O.J., I guarantee you, will be crucified because he is black and those two victims are white. Pure and simple."

"Nonsense," Lou said and stomped his cane on the floor. He was an old guy with hanging jaws who talked like he was from another country. "It is not pure and simple. It is complicated, as most murders are, and it is more than likely that this

O.J. you seem to idolize actually killed two people. And if he gets the death penalty it will not be because he is black, okay? I get sick and tired of that excuse."

"You weren't sick and tired of those excuses white people made for treating blacks like second-class citizens. Where was your outrage then?"

"Second-class citizens? I don't know what you mean. I do not treat any man like a second-class citizen. I can't speak for what others do, but for me, no. Never."

"Good for you, Lou."

"Besides," Lou said. "I'm a card-carrying member of the NAACP."

Peete let out a loud, high-pitched laugh. "Child, hush," he said and wiggled his body. I was right all along. He might of tried to hide his sissiness from that Lou man, but it was too deep in him not to come out sooner or later. I looked over at Cole. He raised his eyebrows and smiled.

They kept on talkin. All day, seemed like. They went from O.J. Simpson to Bill Clinton to somethin called Whitewater. Peete didn't even ask us why we was there or why we weren't in school or nothin. He just kept on talkin and grinnin and wigglin. I fell asleep. I must of slept long and hard because when I woke up, Lou was gone, Peete was gone, and Cole was shakin me to let me know that Daddy was comin in the office.

Every time I saw Daddy he looked different to me. When we left him a week ago, he looked mean and fat, like a crazy old man with wrinkled-up clothes on. Now he looked great again, all tall and strong and dressed to kill. His glassy gray eyes were clear again, and although they still had that blank stare about them, it was more a happy stare than a sad one. Of course, that might not of been a good sign for Cole and me, since Daddy seemed happier with us out of his life, but I didn't look at it like that. When I saw him for the first time in my life at that bus station, I wanted him to have a hard time, I wanted him to suffer. I wanted him to know he should of came to Joe Nathan's funeral and he should of called me sometimes and he should of treated my mama better. But when Cole woke me up and I saw him comin in that office, I felt differently about it. I felt like he had suffered enough, and I was glad he was happy.

We caught him off guard. When he first opened the door he wasn't exactly smilin, but there was somethin peaceful about him. Seein me and Cole seemed to shake that peace, and he almost gave the look of wantin to turn and run back out. Everything just froze when he saw us. Even Cole, who I expected to be overcome with emotion when he saw Daddy, didn't hardly move. He just stood there starin. Like always, I wanted to hug Daddy and tell him I didn't mind him bein happy, but I didn't have nearly the nerve to do it. I was still scared of him. He was still like a stranger to me.

"Well," Daddy finally said, with a slow-comin weak smile. "No school today?"

"We wanted to see you," Cole said all pitiful like, as if he wanted Daddy to feel sorry for us. He even put on that mad look he liked to put on whenever Daddy came around.

"I understand that, Cole," he said, "but you know better than skipping school. Does Ellie know you're here?"

"You act like you don't want to see us," Cole said.

"Of course I want to see you," Daddy said with his put-on smile. "I just don't think skipping school would have been the way to do it."

"Look," Cole said like Daddy just called him a bad name, "we can leave."

I looked at Cole like he was crazy. Leave? He was the one dyin to get here. Now he was talkin bout leavin?

Daddy ignored Cole's sly remark and closed the door. Then he started walkin toward us. Cole and me both couldn't stop starin at him. There was somethin special about our daddy. He walked special. He didn't talk like no daddies I ever knew. And when he walked up to us, and I could see his clear eyes up close, I knew what Cole's mama's friends meant about how Daddy looked like somethin good to eat.

"How long have you guys been waiting?" he asked.

"All morning," Cole said.

"All morning? I'm sorry about that. I got tied up. Where's Peete?"

"Gone to lunch," Cole said. "Him and some white dude. What was his name, Bay?"

Cole and Daddy both looked at me and I got so scared my heart started beatin fast. I hunched my shoulders like I didn't know, although I did.

"He had a Jewish kind of accent," Cole said.

Daddy shook his head. "Borowitz," he said. "I was supposed to get back with him on some old piece of property he's trying to get rid of. Oh well."

For what seemed like a real long time nothin happened. Me and Cole were waitin for Daddy to do somethin, and Daddy was actin like he was waitin for us to do somethin.

Finally he gave up. "You boys had lunch yet?"

"We ain't even had breakfast," I said before I knew it. Daddy looked at me. Naturally, he frowned.

"'Ain't' is not a word," he said. I almost died. I guess he thought I was the dumbest, stupidest boy on the face of this earth, the way I never did anything right around him. But he always made me so nervous. It was like seein my best friend Monroe get shot and killed was easy compared to just talkin around my own daddy.

He acted like he was waitin for me to say somethin about him tellin me that "ain't" ain't no word, but I wasn't about to open my stupid mouth again.

"Well," he said, "I had planned to get some paperwork done, but let's go get some lunch. Then we'll see what's next."

That was fine with me because I was starvin for real. I jumped off the radiator right away. Cole tried to act like it didn't matter either way to him.

Daddy put a *Gone to Lunch* sign outside his office door, and we walked across the sidewalk and got in his car. For some crazy reason, Cole got in the back seat with me. He'd never done that before. It was like he was tryin to hurt Daddy's feelings or somethin. Daddy got in and kind of kept lookin at Cole through his mirror. But he didn't say nothin about it.

We went to McDonald's because Cole said they had Big Macs on sale for 99 cents. Daddy ordered me and Cole Big Macs, french fries, and shakes. He ordered himself a Coke. I went to the bathroom. When I came out, Cole and Daddy were sittin at a table by the window talkin all intense, like they was talkin about personal stuff, and Daddy was smokin a cigarette. I was scared to interrupt them. But I knew I couldn't just stand by the bathroom like a fool, I had to move on. So I went on up to the table. Naturally, when they saw me, they stopped talkin.

"Got the lead out?" Daddy asked and kind of smiled. I froze

like I always did when Daddy asked me somethin. And naturally, my mind shut down.

"What?" I asked.

Cole smiled and pulled me by the sleeve. "Sit down, Bay," he said. "You'll understand it better by and by."

Daddy smiled at Cole. He was proud of him, I could tell. I sat next to Cole and tried to keep my eyes lookin down. Daddy and Cole, I later learned, had been talkin bout why he hadn't called us since his wife left him. Cole said Daddy gave some lame excuse about givin us time to sort things out, but that he was gonna call us eventually. I didn't buy that. Our Daddy wasn't the kind of man who would make the first move. Cole believed if we hadn't skipped school that day and went to see Daddy, we might never of seen him again. That was the kind of daddy we was dealin with. That was the kind of low-down, dirty, insensitive so-called daddy we was dealin with.

Cole went and got the food Daddy had ordered. While he was gone, Daddy kept starin at me. I kept lookin out the window, pretendin to be all interested in the cars drivin by. I felt real sad about it. I felt like nothin could be sadder than a boy not bein able to look his daddy in the eye, and a daddy not bein able to say two words to his own son. I felt like nothin was gonna change, that maybe deep down he hated havin me, the bastard boy, around, but he just didn't know how to tell me to get lost. I was still dreamin about him most every night, and every time I woke up and realized he didn't hug me like my dream said, or he didn't take me to no ball game, or he didn't give me a good reason why he didn't come to the funeral, I felt worse than before. It was like I couldn't feel good for feelin bad.

And even though when he first came in the office and I was glad he was happy, I changed my mind at McDonald's. The way he stared at me and didn't even know how to talk to me made me mad. Why should he be happy? He didn't deserve happiness, not with the way he was treatin me. I never asked him for nothin, I never even asked him to let me live with him. But he acted like it was all my fault! I didn't tell him to sleep with my mama. I didn't tell them to have me. But he treated me like I plotted the whole damn thing and was forcin him to be in the same room with me. Boy, did I feel like cryin that day. I could just feel that rush of water try to come to my eyes as I looked out that window that day. But I was tough. I wasn't about to cry.

Cole came back with the food and started eatin like he was starvin. I was starvin too, but I ate slow, bitin my Big Mac like I didn't hardly want it. I was so conscious of Daddy starin at me that right then and there, though I was starvin to death, I lost my appetite. I couldn't eat it. And Cole, the meanest preacher I ever heard of, had the nerve to say somethin about it.

"Don't be scared to eat," Cole said and smiled and looked at Daddy. I couldn't believe it. I wanted to cuss his ass out but I couldn't even think about havin the nerve to do that.

"I think he's starving for attention, Dad," Cole kept talkin. "Why don't you tell him to eat, then I think he'll do it."

But Daddy didn't even pretend to act like he cared what I did. He blew a cloud of smoke in the air and drank his Coke. He looked like he was too pretty and too important to be bothered about whether some ugly boy like me ate his lunch. His eyes were clear as glass, and they danced like he had other things on his mind. I excused myself and went to the bathroom. And cried and cried. I felt so embarrassed. I felt like Daddy could read my mind, and he knew I was dreamin about him, and he was mad that I did.

We spent the afternoon collectin rents with him. He took us to four or five different houses and every one of them had a pretty lady to answer the door. Daddy acted like every one of them was his girlfriend, callin them sweetie and babe and honey and junk. They would all giggle and act like Daddy was doin them a favor to take their money.

"Hello, Tommy," one lady said.

"Hey, sweetie, how are you?"

"Fine now."

Daddy would smile and drive on to the next house.

"You sho lookin good today, Tommy."

"Thank you, babe. You're looking mighty good yourself."

Then every last one of them would ask him that famous "You wanna come in?" question. But he said no to all of them. Until we got to the last house. He told us to wait in the car this time. Cole, of course, wanted to know why, but Daddy just said he'd be right back and he grabbed his receipt book. When a real pretty, dark-skinned girl with long hair answered the door, it didn't take no genius to know why he didn't want us with him. It wasn't because she was that much prettier than the other ladies, but she was dressed real skimpy in a pair of skintight jeans and a halter top. And she had the figure to fit it all too.

Daddy went into that house. He didn't stay real long, but it was longer than it took to collect money. When Daddy came out, Cole stared at him like he just walked off Mars. You could see the hate in his eyes. I guess Cole couldn't believe it. After all

Daddy put us through, even to where we had to leave him, he was still doin everything in his power to keep us from regainin faith in him.

But Cole didn't say a word to him, and after stoppin for gas, Daddy drove us straight to Wine's apartment. I got out fast, without sayin nothin, but Cole moved real slow. He even asked Daddy if he wanted to come up.

"No," Daddy said, "I don't think so, Cole."

"Why not?"

"You know why not."

"But I wanna go home, Daddy. I'm tired of living here."

"That's all up to your mother, Coleman. I don't have any control over that. She left me."

"But she'll come back if you just ask her."

"I told you I'm not going to get into that right now."

"But she told me she'll come back if you ask her to."

"Coleman—"

"All you got to do is just ask her."

"Coleman, you let me and your mother handle this, all right?"

"But you aren't handling it. I wanna come home, Daddy."

Cole was beggin him. He was leanin against Daddy's car and beggin with all he knew how. I was no help. I was too scared to even beg.

Daddy reached his hand out of his car window and touched Cole on the back. "I know you want to come home, Cole," he said. "And you will. But your mother is going to have to be the one to make that decision."

"Wine says you don't want us back."

"Oh really?"

"He says you like being free, and we'll never go back home waiting on you to come get us."

"Yeah, well, as usual David doesn't know what the hell he's talking about."

"Then why don't you take us home?"

Daddy exhaled real loud and looked up at Wine's apartment. For the first time it looked like Cole's sad routine might be gettin to him and he just might take us back. But then he removed his arm from around Cole and cranked up his car.

"You and Bay go on up. Tell your mother I'll call her."

He backed out that parking lot like he was a cop on a call.

And then he was gone. Cole stared at him until he was clean out of sight, and then me and him went on up to Wine's apartment. Words couldn't say how sad it all was.

We waited every day for Daddy to make that phone call. Every time the phone would ring, everybody would kind of freeze until they found out it wasn't Daddy callin. For nearly two weeks we waited. Until one night, when it seemed like all of us, especially me, had pretty much given up on Daddy, he showed up at Wine's front door.

We were hangin out in the living room listenin to a bunch of old white guys on TV talkin bout O.J. and his trial comin up. They talked like they knew the brother was guilty, with one of them sayin that O.J. ought to confess now and throw himself on the mercy of the court. That got Eleanor goin big time. She said white people think black people some crazy fools who ain't got enough sense to know that you ain't got to say nothin until you have your trial. O.J. got framed by them white police, she said, and Johnnie Cochran gonna prove it. David tried to explain to her what those white folks really meant, bein that he was a lawyer and all, but Eleanor was a lot like my mama when she got goin. You couldn't tell that lady nothin!

The doorbell rang just as Wine and his mama was gettin all hot and actin like their life depended on whether O.J. should fess up or not. They was yellin and carryin on so loud that we almost didn't hear the bell. Cole, in fact, was the only one who did hear it and ran for the door. You ever seen those cowboy pictures on TV when a gunslinger walks in the saloon and all the talkin and the piano-playin stop all of a sudden? That's what happened when Daddy came in the house. I mean, he was in the house, man, hear what I'm sayin? You could of heard a pin drop. And when Eleanor saw Daddy, she flew in his arms so fast it made me dizzy just watchin her fly. We wasn't stuttin that O.J. shit by then. O.J. and No J. could rot in prison for all we cared by then. Wine tried to act funny, like he always did when Daddy came around, but he was wastin his time. Daddy was our knight in shinin armor that day. Bump Wine, O.J., and everybody else. We were goin home!

Eight

"Telephone," Cole said to me as I came in the kitchen from the back door. I threw my schoolbooks on the table and grabbed the phone. It was my mama—I knew it. She was the only somebody who ever called me.

"Mama, this you?" I asked as I grabbed the phone.

"Hey there, Bay! How you?"

"I'm fine, Mama. You all right?"

"Oh yes, honey, I'm fine."

"Why didn't you call me, Mama?"

"Call you? Call you when?"

"When I was stayin at Wine's house."

"For yo information, I did try to call you. But that bitch yo daddy married wouldn't let me talk to you."

"Really?"

"Yes, really! What, you think I'm lyin to you?"

"No—"

"She wouldn't let me talk to you. But I betcha I cussed her ass out! And then I called yo daddy back and cussed his ass out too! I told him I didn't let you go all the way to Florida to live with his bitch."

"You said it just like that, Mama?"

"Hell yeah, I said it just like that."

"What'd he say?"

"What he always says: 'I'm busy, Juanita. Is it somethin you want from me, Juanita?' I tell you, Bay, I was tempted to fly down there and bring you back to Harlem, that's how mad I was."

"You only called the one time, Mama? To talk to me, I mean?"

"What you mean 'one time'? I told you the bitch wouldn't let me talk to you. What you expected me to do about that? Keep callin? What my callin over and over gonna do when that heifer said I couldn't talk to you?"

"Maybe I would of answered the phone one of those times. Or Cole."

"Chile, please! I wasn't gonna get my blood pressure up foolin with that fool. I just said forget it, I'll talk to you soon enough."

"We been back with Daddy for weeks now. How come you didn't call sooner?"

"Now hold on for a minute, boy. I ain't no goddamn phone booth, you understand? I ain't gonna be callin you or nobody else on no telephone every goddamn day."

"I know what you sayin, Mama. But since you ain't got no phone, and since Miss Cency's own got disconnected, I don't have no way to get in touch with y'all. I wanna make sure you all right."

"Oh Bay, you're so sweet. You still worry about yo ole mama, bless yo heart. But I'm fine, chile. Don't worry about me."

"I can't help it."

"Oh, I'm doin good, Bay. Got me a new sugar daddy, matter of fact."

"Another new one?"

"But he ain't like Dow Jones."

"What happened to Dow Jones?"

"Dow Jones ain't bout nothin. I kicked his ass out fast as it got in here. But Wennie somethin else, Bay."

"Wennie? Is that his name?"

"Wendall Washington. But I call him Wennie. He sells insurance. A real job! Chile, we might get married, that's how serious it is."

"I thought you and Dow Jones was gonna get married."

"I told you Dow Jones full of shit. I wouldn't marry that motherfucker if he was the last fool on earth. What you keep bringin him up for?"

"I don't keep bringin him up. I just thought—"

"You just thought what?"

"I just... nothin, Mama, all right? Nothin. How's Miss Cency?"

"Bump Cency! I wanna tell you about Wennie. Guess who he look like?"

"Who?"

"Guess?"

"Mama, who?"

"Denzel, Denzel, Denzel! I mean down to the eyelashes, Bay. Oh he's fine. He's fine. No doubt about that."

"He asked you to marry him?"

"Not yet, but we been talkin about it. He says he gonna buy me a house with three bedrooms and a real live garden in the back. Imagine me with a garden, Bay. It'll be like a dream comin true."

"Why ain't he asked you to marry him yet?"

"He will, Bay, okay? Soons he gets his divorce."

"Divorce? He's married, Mama?"

"Yeah, but ain't nothin to that. It's been over between them for years."

"Oh, Mama!"

"It has! They don't even sleep in the same bed together."

"How you know?"

"He told me, Bay. And I know he can be lyin, but he ain't like that. He didn't even have to tell me he was married, but he told me. And he's so good to me, Bay. He brings me flowers, boy! Flowers! It's been a long time since a man brought me flowers, but Wennie do it all the time."

"He's got any kids?"

"I think so."

"You *think* so?"

"I don't know, I never asked. Who the hell cares? All I know is, I got him. What he got don't matter. He's a good man, that's all I know."

"How's Miss Cency?"

"Why you keep jumpin the subject?"

"It's long distance, Mama."

"I didn't call collect. I'm usin Mo Jack phone. You remember Mo Jack, boy, don't you?"

"Yes Mama, but it's still long distance."

"You're a nervous chile, you know that? Always worryin about somethin. I know it's long distance, boy. I can afford it, okay?"

"Okay, okay. How's Miss Cency?"

"Ha! You somethin else. She fine, boy, fine. Just as crazy as ever."

"She still datin that mailman?"

"Hell no! He left her ass a week after she met him good. Cency don't know how to hold on to no man. I told her she might as well become a bull dagger the way she luck out with men. But what woman gonna want her?"

"Just tell her I said hey."

"Still got that crush on that crazy woman, don't you?"

"What crush? I ain't got no crush on nobody."

"Oh yes you do. Baby Boy's got a crush on Cency. Wait till I tell her."

"Mama, don't tell that lie on me."

"Oh boy, get a grip. She'll be tickled."

"I ain't tickled though! Mama, I mean it. Don't tell that lie on me."

"It'll cheer her up, Bay."

"But it's not true, Mama."

"Oh it's true. It's sho damn true. You can deny it all you want. But it's true. Anyway. Where's Mr. Wonderful?"

"At work, I guess."

"How's he treatin you?"
"Just like he always treated me, Mama."
"Ain't nothin changed yet?"
"Nope."
"Not even after y'all left his ass?"
"It's still the same, Mama. He still fuss a lot and act like I'm not here."
"What's wrong with his crazy butt? Why don't he spend some time with you? I never met nobody like that fool in my life."
"Mama?"
"What?"
"He my daddy for real?"
"Why you ask a fool question like that? Yes, he yo damn daddy. He said he ain't? Wait till I talk to him again. Boy, I tell you. He know he yo daddy. I ain't been with no other man but him when I had you, and his sissy ass know it! Wait till I talk to that clown again!"
"He never said nothin, Mama. I was just wonderin myself. That's all. I mean, he don't hardly say two words to me."
"Well, do you say anything to him, Bay? Or are you still too scared to talk to people?"
"I talk. But I just don't know what to say when I get around him. He just stare at me all the time."
"Oh that's just how he is, Bay. He used to stare at me like that."
"The only time he ever really say somethin to me is when I do somethin wrong."
"What you did wrong?"

"Nothin. I'm just talkin."

"You better not be down there gettin in trouble, Bay. You causin trouble?"

"No, Mama! I'm not talkin bout that. I'm talkin bout like when I got in that fight with Chinesa. Junk like that."

"Who else you been fightin?"

"Nobody!"

"Don't pull that boy scout shit on me, Bay, all right? I know yo ass."

"I ain't been fightin nobody, Mama."

"You better not be!"

"I just get tired of Daddy not sayin nothin to me, that's all."

"You want me to talk to him about it?"

"You think that'll help?"

"No. But I can do it."

"That'll probably make him mad. No, don't mention it to him. I'll be all right."

"I know you will. Cause you my baby. And my baby gon make it no matter what. Ain't that right, sugar?"

"I guess so, Mama."

"Tom Bach crazy like that, Bay, all right? He's always been crazy. He'll treat strangers like kings and his own son like a dog. You should of seen how he used to treat Wine."

"Wine?"

"Yeah! He used to beat on that boy so much he would have to stand up in class, his ass was hurtin so bad."

"How you know about Wine?"

"What you talkin about? Me and Wine the same age. We went to school together."

"How come you acted surprised when I told you Daddy had

another son? How come you acted like you never heard of Wine before?"

"I was just doin that, boy. Me and ole sleepy-eyed Wine went to school together."

"And he knew you was pregnant by his daddy?"

"Everybody in the school knew. I don't see how he couldn't."

"Damn, Mama."

"Don't you dare try to preach to me, boy. You preach to yo daddy. He was the one should of known better. I was just a stupid kid. With a capital S."

"I see why Wine hates Daddy so much. I'd hate him too."

"Oh, Tom Bach somethin else, Bay, don't fool yourself. But that wife and them boys of his love him to death. He can do anything and they'll forgive him. Anything! And he know it too. That's why his ass keep messin up."

"How old daddy is?"

"Fifty. Or he will be in a few months. Why?"

"How old he was when you got pregnant with Joe Nathan?"

"Why you wanna know that?"

"He was a full-grown man and you was a teenager."

"So? I told you I was a kid when I was fool enough to hitch up with Tom Bach. That ain't no news. And ole sleepy-eyed Wine tried to act like I was lyin about it. 'My daddy don't do such things,' he used to always go around the school sayin. 'My daddy don't fool with hoes. My daddy this, my daddy that.' He tried to make like I was some kind of nut case, so in love with his damn daddy I would make up lies on him. That's when my brother Waterman and some of his runnin partners jumped

Wine and beat him so bad they hospitalized his ass. He shut up that daddy shit after that."

"He's comin now."

"Who? Wine?"

"Daddy. He's drivin up in the driveway right now. This the earliest he's ever come home. I better get off the phone."

"Why you got to get off the phone? He don't let you talk on the phone?"

"Yes ma'am. I just like to be kind of out of his way when he comes home."

"Out of his way how?"

"Just out of his way, Mama."

"Tom Bach been beatin on you?"

"What? No, Mama."

"He's a nasty somebody when he wants to be, Bay. But he better not be layin a hand on you."

"He don't be beatin on none of us, Mama."

"Quit lyin. He just kicked his wife ass. That's how come y'all left him. Remember?"

"He didn't kick her, I mean, he didn't beat her up. He just hit her one time. That's all."

"Yeah, right."

"He did, Mama."

"Uh-huh. Whatever you say."

"I'm not lyin."

"Who said you was? Did I say you was lyin?"

"He's comin in the back way, Mama, where I am. I'll talk to you later."

"I ain't through."

"Mama, please. Call me back another time."

"I ain't stuttin you. Don't nobody care nothin bout him comin in. Let him come in! In fact, put him on the phone when he do."

"No, Mama."

"No? I know you didn't say 'no' to me!"

"Mama, he get upset when he talk to you."

"You just put his ass on that phone, boy, and I mean now."

"Okay."

"Then do it!"

"He ain't in yet."

"Soon as he get in there you put him on. I upset him. Bump him! He upset me! Everybody in that goddamn sorry-ass town let Tom Bach get away with murder. And I see you doin it too. Well, I ain't doin it! He's gonna tell me why he's mistreatin my boy. He's gonna tell me why he act like he can't talk to—"

"Daddy? Excuse me, Daddy? Um. Um. Telephone. It's for you."

"What?"

"The telephone is for you."

"Who is it? Give it here. Hello? This is Tom Bach."

"Hey."

"Oh. Hey, Juanita. How are you?"

"I ain't got no complaints. How you doin?"

"Wonderful. Listen: Is there something you wanted?"

"Boy, Tommy, you somethin else."

"I just got home from work, I am tired, I am not in the mood to listen to one of your profanity-laden sermons this evening."

"I wouldn't waste my breath preachin to yo ass. You ain't worth preachin to."

"Well, nice talking to you."

"I wanna know why you treatin Bay so bad."

"Did that boy tell you that lie?"

"My son don't lie! What he told me was the truth. He said you don't hardly say two words to him, that you treat him like he still a stranger to you."

"I talk with him, Juanita, all right? This is a non-issue as far as I'm concerned. And Ralph knows it is."

"Do you spend time with him, Tommy? You take him places?"

"I work, Juanita. All day."

"Yo work more important than your son?"

"Whatever you say."

"I'm askin you."

"No. You're attempting to accuse me."

"I just wanna make sure you and that ugly bitch you're married to treat my son right!"

"Goodbye, Juanita."

"Don't you goodbye me! You know what that horse-lookin wife of yours had the nerve to tell me?"

"No. But I'm sure you're more than willing to tell me."

"That fool actually think you love her. Can you believe that? I told her Tom Bach never loved nobody in his life—and especially her. He's incapable of love. That's what I told her."

"Well, nice chatting with you, Juanita—"

"Cause if he was capable of any feelings at all, he wouldn't of done me like he did me. He wouldn't of laid with no sixteen-year-old girl who didn't have enough sense to know that sex ain't love—"

"I don't want to listen to this, Juanita."

"You will listen! I loved you, Tommy. And you know I did.

How could you leave me like that? How could you do that to me?"

"I was married."

"Yo ass was married when you threw me on Mama's bed, but that didn't stop you then. But only after I get knocked up did you become the devoted husband who wouldn't think of cheatin on his wife. Kiss my ass, Tommy. You hear me? Kiss my motherfuckin ass, you two-bit—"

"So what happened, Juanita?"

"What?"

"Where's that fellow you were going to marry? What's his name? Wall Street or Stock Market or something?"

"Dow Jones."

"Yeah. Dow Jones. What happened to him?"

"None of your damn business!"

"Every time you start dwelling on the past it's because of one of your boyfriends leaving you."

"You don't know what the hell you're talkin bout! You the only man ever left me. And that's because I was too stupid to leave you first."

"Anyway, Juanita, I really have to go now. Goodbye."

"You just wait a good—hello? Hello? Hello?"

"Yeah, Mama, it's me."

"Where's yo daddy?"

"He's—"

"He's what?"

"He just left out of the kitchen. Why was you talkin so loud? I could hear you through the phone. Daddy was lookin at me funny too."

"Bay, you better wise up and stop bein scared of him. He

don't like weak people. You better toughen up, boy, or you're in for a miserable life there."

"Why you call his wife names like that?"

"I ain't stuttin her. I call her what I wanna call her. If she don't like it she can kiss my ass."

"Jesus, Mama, why you cuss so much?"

"What?"

"Nothin."

"All right, boy. You better not forget where you came from. You ain't never said nothin about my cussin before. When since you got religion?"

"We better hang up now, Mama."

"I guess we better, since I might say the wrong thing and all."

"I love you, Mama."

"I love you, too, baby. But you better not forget where you came from."

"I won't."

"All right now."

"Bye, Mama."

"Bye, boy."

"Bye. Call me."

Nine

I always disagreed with the way my mama went about doin things. But her way always seemed to work somehow. The way she cussed Daddy out and told him he needed to spend more time with me—he acted like he wasn't stuttin what she was sayin. But the very next morning—real early too—he woke me up and told me to get ready: I was goin to work with him.

I took a shower and got dressed so fast I was downstairs sittin on the couch almost a full hour before Daddy came down. I was real quiet too, because I didn't want to wake Cole. I mean, I like Cole and all, but he had Daddy to himself for sixteen years. It was my turn now. I felt this was my chance to get Daddy to like me. I was gonna smile a lot and compliment him a lot and make him feel like I was a good boy and nothin like he thought I was. I sat on that long couch in that Florida room plannin the shit out of how I was gonna make my Daddy love me.

I believed in my soul I couldn't go back to Harlem. I loved livin large. I loved comin home on a hot day to a house with air conditioning. Whenever I opened the front door, cold air would just hit me all in the face and make me want to drop down and go to sleep right there on that floor. I loved walkin on thick beautiful carpet instead of those ugly cement floors at my mama's house. I could walk barefoot for a month in Daddy's house and still have clean feet! I loved it, man. And I wasn't about to sit by and let nobody take all that away from me.

I jumped to my feet when Daddy came down the stairs. I felt like a little overreacting fool, but I couldn't help myself. Like always, Daddy looked good that morning with his black suit and tie on. When he motioned for me to come on, I ran up to him so fast that I tripped over my own left shoe and fell. When I got up, Daddy was shakin his head.

"Slow down, all right?" he said to me.

"Yes sir," I said.

In the car we drove slow because the traffic was so heavy. Daddy was listenin to that Frank Sinatra shit again, where he's singin about how some lady is a tramp because she wouldn't go to Harlem wearin jewelry. She wasn't no tramp. She had good sense. Some rich white woman walkin around my old hood with jewelry on? They'd strip her like they was strippin a car, man.

But Daddy, who didn't know nothin bout it neither, really dug that Sinatra stuff. He was even drummin his fingers on the steering wheel like it sounded so good to him. I wanted to laugh so bad. If those homeboys in Harlem could have seen me then. Frank Sinatra! Man, they wouldn't believe it.

I was scared to talk to Daddy during the ride to his job because he seemed so wrapped up in his music. But I had to say somethin or he would never pay attention to me.

"Is that Frank Sinatra you're listenin to?" I asked, although I knew it.

Daddy didn't say anything. I don't know if he even heard me. By this time, Frank Sinatra had stopped singin about the tramp lady and was singin about catchin a fallin star and puttin it in your pocket. Can you imagine singin a song like that? White people.

I tried again. "Is that Frank Sinatra you're listenin to, Daddy?"

He didn't look at me. "Perry Como," he said.

"That's not Frank Sinatra?"

"It was Frank Sinatra. Now it's Perry Como."

"But they sound like the same person."

"Not really."

"They do to me. Who's Perry Como anyway?"

Daddy looked at me and smiled, then he kept on strummin his fingers on the steering wheel.

We had breakfast at Burger King. We was sittin down to eat for two minutes when some woman came up to our table. She was white with long blonde hair and small, kind of greenish eyes. She had on an expensive-lookin yellow skirt suit and was holdin her pocketbook close to her chest. That purse had been clipped before and she wasn't takin no chances, I could tell.

"Hello, Tommy," she said with a big smile as she came up to us.

"Leslie, hi," Daddy said, pushin the table back a little and tryin to stand his big self up. "How are you, dear?"

"Good. Haven't seen you in a while."

"I know. I've been out of touch."

"And how. It's been three months at least."

"Yeah, it has," Daddy said on his feet. He motioned for the lady to sit down. "Join us."

"Oh no, I can't. I've got a conference at U.N.F. to get to. On 'Aging,' of all things. How's Eleanor?"

"Okay. How about Ed?"

"That's a long story, my friend. Very long. Maybe I'll tell it to you some day."

Daddy smiled. The woman smiled too and looked at me.

"This isn't Coleman, is it?"

"Oh no," Daddy said real fast. "He's Ralph. Coleman is sixteen years old."

"That's right. He's the teenage minister."

"Don't mention that. That's a very long story too."

Daddy and the white woman smiled again. They did a lot of smilin that mornin. Then they seemed to run out of things to talk about. They picked back up, talkin about the funny weather we were havin, then cooled down again. Finally the lady said she had to go, and Daddy decided to walk her to her car. For a long time they stood on the sidewalk outside Burger King talkin and laughin, with Daddy doin most of the talkin and the lady doin most of the laughin. My mama didn't trust white women. She even hated O.J. Simpson because he was married to one. She said they was always comin around and stealin black men. I don't know about that. The way Daddy was carryin on, you would of thought he wanted to be stole.

In a way, my daddy was like that with every woman he came into contact with. No matter how ugly they were, he treated them like they were queens to him. I used to think he was foolin around with all of them, but it was just too many women for that to be true. Besides, Daddy flirted with men too.

I remembered when a refrigerator repairman came to our house and Daddy was just laughin and talkin with the man like they were goin together or somethin. I never seen two men carry on like that. Joe Nathan would have thought Daddy was a fruit as sure as I'm sittin here. But Daddy was just friendly that way. And he was always misunderstood, even by me.

It was after eleven when me and Daddy got to work. A big fat man was in the office with Mr. Peete. Peete was seated behind his desk lookin over a sheet of paper, and the man was seated in front of the desk lookin at Peete. *The Price is Right* was on TV and the man was sayin "Come on down!" as me and Daddy came in the office.

"Hello, Peete," Daddy said with a big put-on smile as he headed toward his desk.

"Hello, Thomas, you're late," Peete said without lookin up.

"How can I be late?" Daddy asked, still smilin. "I own this joint."

Peete wasn't stuttin Daddy, really. He looked up at the man sittin in front of his desk. I sat up on the radiator.

"Do you pay anybody?" Peete asked the man.

"I pay my bills, man."

"Excuse me," Peete said, his hand on his heart. "That is not what this credit report says."

"Fuck that credit report, man! I pay my bills. I ain't never missed one time payin my bills."

"You had a 1989 Ford Escort repossessed. Isn't that right?"

"Naw, that ain't right. Them crackers lyin, man. I gave back that junk. Always breakin down."

"What do you mean you gave it back?"

"I gave it back! What's wrong wit you, you deef? I didn't want it no mo so I gave it back."

Peete smiled and nodded his head. He was really very gayish. "I don't know what planet you're from, but on my planet that is called repossession—albeit voluntary, but still."

"So you sayin you can't rent me one of them raggedy-ass apartments of yours cause I returned a car that I didn't want?"

"Oh, dreamboat! And they say you're too dumb? That is precisely the point. You might return our apartment before the lease is up merely because you don't want it anymore."

"So?"

"Oh darling—"

"Who the fuck you callin 'darlin'? Do I look like yo motherfuckin darlin?"

"But dear—"

"I ain't your damn dear either! Damn, man! What's yo problem? I'm gonna O.J. yo ass you keep it up!"

Peete looked my way for the first time. I guess he was gettin scared.

"Thomas," he said. Daddy, who was readin some mail, looked up. "Might you have a word with the gentleman?"

Daddy seemed a little upset that Peete bothered him, but he dropped the mail on his desk and got up anyway. He had his suit jacket off and was wearin a nice white shirt. Now that's a man, I thought.

Peete handed Daddy the sheet of paper. "He wants to rent #14 on 8th Street. But as you can see, a member of Good Credit R Us he is not."

Daddy read the sheet and then looked at the man. He held out his hand. "I'm Tom Bach, how are you? Buford Greene, is it?"

The man shook Daddy's hand. "Yes sir, I'm Buford. So you're Mr. Bach. I heard about you."

"Good stuff, I hope."

"You the man. That's all I know. You the man."

Daddy smiled. He was one of those people who wanted everybody to love him.

"So what's the problem, Peete?" Daddy asked. Peete looked at him.

"I beg your pardon?"

"Mr. Buford Greene is a good friend of mine. He won't skip out on the lease—now will you, Mr. Buford Greene?"

"No sir. I swear," Mr. Greene smiled and said.

"His word is good enough for me. Give the man what he wants," Daddy said and threw the sheet of paper back to Peete. Mr. Greene stood up and held out his hand to Daddy.

"Preciate it, man. You know how to hook a brother up."

"Keep your word, we'll be okay."

"I got yo back, my nigga. Don't worry bout that."

Daddy gave one of his half-second phony smiles and went back to his mail-readin. Peete started gettin the paperwork ready for Mr. Buford Greene to sign while Mr. Greene looked at TV. Some fat lady had just won a sewin machine or somethin and was pullin on Bob Barker's expensive suit like he bought it from off one of those picnic tables at Walmart. But that was how happy that woman was. And Mr. Buford Greene, because of my daddy, was even happier than her.

Me, Daddy, and Peete went to a downtown restaurant for lunch. They served mostly seafood but I ordered a cheeseburger. Peete and Daddy sat on one side of the table and I sat on the other. Peete talked and talked through the whole lunch. People were watchin, but he kept right on gabbin. Daddy ate his scallops and nodded, as if he agreed with everything Peete was sayin. It was too much for me to take. How could a man like my daddy let this dude hang out with him? Wasn't he scared people would think he was funny too? But Daddy acted like it was the most natural thing in the world for him and Peete to be buddies. I was embarrassed. I'm sorry. That man Peete was a total wipeout, in my opinion. Dudes like him couldn't make it in Harlem. Where I come from, if the boys even thought you had sugar in your tank they'd kick your ass to the curb so fast you could swear it was a hurricane that knocked you out.

But I wasn't in Harlem no more. I was in my daddy's world. And in my daddy's world, people like Peete were treated just like everybody else he came into contact with. I sat in that restaurant that day just watchin the way Daddy handled Peete. Never once did Daddy seem embarrassed to be around the man. People were lookin, but Daddy didn't seem to give a damn. He just kept on noddin at all that bull Peete was layin on him, and sometimes he'd say somethin like "You jivin" or "Get outta here" like he was really into what Peete was sayin.

That did somethin to me. If it wasn't botherin Daddy that Peete was like he was, why was it botherin me? I mean, I would fall out and die if I had to go out in public by myself with Peete. Even when we got out of Daddy's car and walked into the restaurant, I made it my business to walk on the side of Daddy Peete wasn't on and to even act like I had no idea who that man Peete was. But Daddy was laughin around with him even while we were waitin to be seated at a table. Daddy had to know that sissies traveled in gangs just so nobody can beat them up. People probably thought my daddy was a sissy too—and I was some kind of male prostitute of theirs or somethin. It was really very embarrassing. And seemed like every time somebody walked by, old Peete would start wavin his limp hands and sashayin his big hips and talkin like a loudmouth girl. I mean, a businessman would walk by and Peete would do his high-pitched yell-laugh and the poor man would jump like he was under attack or somethin. And Daddy would laugh at the businessman instead of laughin at Peete! It was like Daddy saw everything from Peete's point of view. It was a strange way to look at things, I thought, but that was my daddy. He was different. He was his own man kind of man.

After lunch, me, Daddy, and Peete went to check out some complaints they were gettin about bad rat and roach problems at an apartment building on Madison Street. Daddy said he bought that building over twenty years ago and one day he was gonna bulldoze it down. And it sure needed killin, man. It was a half-leanin, green wooden shack with six apartments in it. It used to be an old house, Daddy said.

We walked through the front door and found a dark hall with three apartments downstairs and three up. You could just hear the rats runnin all over the place when we walked into the hall. That rat sound more than anything reminded me of home. I'll never forget that patty-pat sound as long as I live. I remember how I used to wake up in the middle of the night and one of those damn rats would be sittin up on my bed starin me in the face! Mama used to laugh about it, sayin those Harlem rats some bold motherfuckers, but when you're a kid you can't laugh at no rats. There's somethin about rats that makes it clear just how poor you are. You're so poor even the rats have to know your business. You're so poor even the rats ain't scared of you.

Daddy and Peete knocked on a couple of doors downstairs but nobody opened up. You could hear the TVs goin or the radios playin, and in one apartment they knocked on you could hear people talkin. I guess they wasn't stuttin us. I guess they figured the only thing a rent man would want was rent, so they wasn't thinkin bout openin no doors.

"Use your key and surprise them," Peete said, but Daddy smiled and said it wasn't worth it.

He then started talkin about how messy the place was, and Peete was agreein with him. They stood in the middle of the hallway lookin at all the beer cans and garbage. They was shakin their heads like they ain't never seen such a messy place. Peete even said if the people would just clean up a little, they wouldn't have to worry about no rats.

Man, I wanted to read Peete after he said that. Those damn rats don't care nothin about no clean house! My mama kept the cleanest house in America but we still had a couple dozen rats livin with us. Rats don't search out dirty houses—they search out poor houses. They know they'd waste their time foolin around in Daddy's house, because as soon as he spotted one he'd have bombs goin off, pest control people runnin in and out, and cans of Raid sprayin everywhere. Those poor rats wouldn't stand a chance at Daddy's house. But those damn rats know about poor people. They know how poor people have to buy food and don't have no money for no critter gitters. Poor folks spot a rat, they try to run them down and catch them by the tail or fly-swat their ass to death, or do like I learned to do and just knock them off the bed and go on back to sleep.

We walked upstairs. Peete was still criticizin the garbage we passed and Daddy was still agreein with him. If I was any kind of man I would have gotten those two uppity boys straight. But I had been with Daddy the whole day and still didn't have the nerve to really talk to him. He was nice and friendly with other people, but he hardly even smiled at me. Mostly he stared at me, the way he was doin when the door to one of the upstairs apartments was opened.

Daddy smiled as soon as he saw it was a kind of pretty lady. Only she looked real young, like eighteen or somethin, and she had a sleepin baby in her arms.

"Good afternoon," Peete smiled and said, but the lady looked away from him and at Daddy.

"Hey," she said with a big smile. She was black as tar almost, with those small jet-black eyes. She was real skinny too, like she was a crackhead big time.

"We understand the tenants here have been having a problem with rodents," Peete said, but the lady wasn't stuttin him. She and Daddy just kept smilin at each other. Daddy moved up closer, to get a peep at the baby.

"What's her name?" he asked.

"Tameka," she said as she moved the covers back so Daddy could see better.

"She's beautiful," Daddy said. "Just like her mother."

Man, my daddy was smooth! That was a great line. Daddy even motioned for the lady to show Peete.

"She's a doll, isn't she, Peete?" he said. But old crazy Peete wanted to get that rat situation straight. He wasn't thinkin bout no baby.

"I'm sure she is, Thomas. But we're not here to look at babies, we're here to look at rats."

The lady looked at Peete like he was a brother from another planet. "What you talkin bout?"

"You don't have a problem with mice in your home?" Peete asked her.

"Hell no!" the lady frowned and said. "Ain't no rats runnin round my baby, and I know that's right!"

"We got numerous complaints about mice being all over this building," Daddy said.

"Yeah, Mr. Bach, they round here and junk. But they ain't in my house round my baby. But they round here."

"That's what I heard," Daddy said, then nobody said nothin.

Finally Peete asked the lady if we could go in and look around. She said okay, but you could tell she didn't want us in there.

We walked in. To our shock, her living room ain't had nothin in it. And crazy Peete said somethin about it.

"Where on earth is your furniture?" he asked.

"In storage," the lady said. Her baby woke up cryin and she started shakin the baby like she was a sack of potatoes. "I had to get the carpet cleaned so I put it all in storage."

Peete looked down at the brown carpet. It was almost black it was so dirty.

Daddy smiled and nodded, though, like he believed her, but Peete gave me one of his *is girlfriend for real?* looks that made me smile. I guess me and Peete both knew all about that lady's furniture bein in storage. Her furniture—if she ever had any—was stored in some crack dealer's living room somewhere, that's the only storage some rock star like her was gonna pay for. But Daddy acted like it made all the sense in the world what she was sayin.

After we looked in the bedroom (one mattress on the floor) and checked the dirty bathroom, we said our goodbyes and left. You could tell that lady wanted Daddy to stick around. But Daddy didn't even think twice about that. He smiled at her and treated her nice, but she was just too filthy to even flirt with too long.

The rest of my day with Daddy went pretty much the same: a tenant here and there, food, lookin at TV, talkin. Only me and Daddy didn't do much talkin—we didn't talk at all. Peete did all of the talkin. And I mean about everything. From Bill Clinton thinkin about invading Haiti (bad idea, according to Peete) to Michael Jackson marryin Elvis Presley's daughter. He cracked Daddy up when he joked about that marriage, like when he said if Lisa Marie was expectin Michael to have sex with her and junk she could forget it. "His ranch isn't called Neverland for nothing," he said.

But mostly he talked about Bill Clinton and Haiti. I fell asleep around three. When I woke up, Daddy had gone somewhere and I was in the office alone with Peete. I was scared, but he didn't do anything to me. He was too busy callin tenants on the phone and writin stuff in big thick files. By six thirty Daddy came back and then we left for the day.

It was pushin seven when we pulled out onto the highway.

The traffic was slow and boring. Frank Sinatra was singin about when he was twenty-one it was a very good year and Daddy was strummin his fingers on the steering wheel. I couldn't talk to him when he was strummin his fingers. Somethin about that music, I guess, that made him want to be left alone.

My day was a big fat flop. I had the opportunity of a lifetime—a chance to get my daddy to like me—and I blew it. When I could of talked to him, I didn't. When I could of educated him about rats and poverty and rock stars like that lady with no furniture, I didn't. I didn't smile, I didn't crack jokes, I didn't do anything you have to do to get people to like you. I was quiet all day. I was scared all day. Instead of thinkin bout ways to make my daddy happy, I was doin all I could to not make him unhappy. He hardly knew I was around. Sometimes I feel like I could fall off the face of this earth and nobody would notice. I swear to God I feel that way sometimes.

Ten

Cole preached his first sermon on a warm Sunday morning. It was a big deal to Cole and he wanted his whole family in on it. I was never much of a churchgoer, since my mama never went and the only religious people I knew were scary like Reverend Ruby, but I couldn't wait to hear Cole preach. Cole's mama, though, wasn't too excited, callin it "silly" that a boy Cole's age could even be considered a preacher, but she agreed to go anyway. So did Wine. He almost never came over, and when he did, he and Daddy usually got into it and he would just leave. But even he agreed to go. Yet the person most excited about it all wasn't me or Eleanor or Wine, but it was Daddy. He couldn't wait to go. He even bought a new suit for the occasion. Boy, did he look great. He must of been the prettiest human being I ever seen in that nice gray suit he was wearin. When Cole saw him you could tell he was proud that he was his daddy, but he didn't even say he looked good or nothin. He just said somethin about not wantin to be late and went outside to wait by the car.

"You look great!" I said to Daddy.

"Thank you," he said with a great big smile on his face. He looked at me like he was gonna say somethin nice back to me, but he only shook his head. I was wearin a blue suit he bought me that looked good on the hanger at the store. But red hair don't jive good with blue, I guess, cause it sho didn't look like nothin on me.

We got to the church early. It was an old raggedy little church that looked like a store on the outside. I smiled when we first drove up to it, cause I knew Cole's mama wouldn't go for that.

"What is this?" she asked when Daddy stopped the car.

"The church," Daddy said.

"What church?"

"My church," Cole said, openin the door to the back seat so me, him, and Wine could get out.

"Your church? *That?*"

"Yeah, Mom. Now come on, please."

"I know you don't think I'm going in there."

"Now Ellie, don't start," Daddy said. "He's not asking you to join it."

"Oh, I should have known it would look like this," she said, gettin out of her seat belt. "Leave it to Beaver. Leave it to that genius boy of yours. The boy preacher. I'm telling you."

But Daddy was feelin so good that day till he didn't even argue with her. He let her bitch and moan all by her lonesome. He even waited for me to get out the car, and he held my hand as we walked in the church. It was really a church for poor people though, and the people already in it looked all poor and ignorant like all those people I used to know in my old life. They stared at us like we was aliens. Eleanor said, underneath her breath, "What y'all fools looking at?" and I almost bust out laughin.

The older women had rags around their heads, and the men had on those cheap-lookin suits Big Ike liked to wear, with the bell-bottom legs and in loud colors like pink and green and orange. Almost everybody in the church who didn't have a rag on had a played-out jheri curl, from the little monkey-lookin children to the grownups, and you could just smell the activators and moisturizers everywhere you turned. I guess I was growin to hate everything poor, cause I hated those people. I hated their hair styles and their clothes and their looks. I hated the way they smiled and nodded at Daddy like big old Uncle Toms noddin at a white man.

Was I like that in Harlem? Did I act glad to be poor? Or did I know any better? Every day it seemed harder and harder for me to get a clear picture of my past. I even forgot how Mama's apartment used to smell, how it had that funny smell every time I came in the door. I thought I would never forget that smell, but I was forgettin it with the quickness. Daddy's life was my life now. And though I wasn't no Mr. Popular in that new world of mine, I was in it, and to stay in it I guess I felt I had to hate the old one. So I started hatin it. That was the first main thing I learned in Daddy's world: how to hate.

Cole sat all the way to the front of the church beside a tall, skinny man in a big black robe and another man in an orange suit. We sat in the third row, forcin two grinnin men to slide from chair to chair to make room for us. They was just grinnin and noddin and slidin, like they would of done anything we told them to do. Half the people in the church seemed to already know Daddy, by the way they seemed to make it a point to speak to him, but none of them said a word to Eleanor. I guess that fancy light-blue dress and big white hat she was wearin made her stand out too much to the poor women with their sheet-lookin dresses and rags thrown around their heads for hats. I could see the hurt on their faces, like all they needed was to see Daddy's well-to-do wife strut into their poor little church and remind them of what they ain't got.

Before we could sit down good the piano man started poundin on the piano, a girl not much older than me started bangin on a set of drums, and the choir, which was big and filled with a bunch of older, mostly women members, bust out singin a song that I figured had to be called "Get Right Church and Let's Go Home." A fat man holdin a towel to wipe the sweat off his face stood up to lead the song. He had the loudest voice I ever heard. It was so loud that Daddy's wife almost jumped when he opened his mouth.

He went from singin about the church needin to get right to how God didn't have to do it, but He did it, to a song about God bein a battle ax in the time of battle. I ain't never been crazy about no church songs, but I kind of liked them songs that man sang that day.

In fact, by the time he got to the song about the battle ax, the whole church (except us) were on their feet clappin and bangin tambourines. Eleanor looked at them like they was fools, but Daddy kept smilin and pattin his feet. I liked it too. That girl was killin those drums and that fat man was wipin that sweat and singin them songs like his life depended on singin them right.

But then somethin happened. The singin stopped and the people started yellin "Lord ham mercy" and "Thank you Jesus" and "Hallelujah!" Before you knew it, the girl started bangin the drums faster and the piano man started playin again. But only nobody was singin. Everybody started yellin and dancin. I couldn't believe it. It didn't look like no straight-out juke joint dancin, but it was close. Even Daddy didn't know what to make of all that, and he stopped pattin his feet and kind of started lookin around.

Eleanor bent over to his ear. "Let's get out of here now," she said, but Daddy ignored her.

Some old lady started screamin and hollerin and some other ladies rushed up to her and started fannin her. Folks in the back of the church looked to be doin flips and cartwheels, they was so carried away with their dancin. One man ran straight into a steel pole and seemed to get knocked out cold. A man on our row kept jumpin up and down so high, he would land a lot of times too close to Eleanor. You could tell she didn't like that one bit. Then he landed so close that he touched her. Why he wanna do that? She pushed him away from her so hard that he stumbled into the man next to him and both of them fell to the floor. A big fat lady was already on the floor as she kicked her feet and called for Jesus. She was kickin so hard that her dress flew up over her head. Her draws had so many holes in them that another lady had to hurry up and jump on top of her. But the kickin lady still wouldn't stop kickin. The smaller lady that jumped on top of her was just bouncin and bouncin as the big lady kept kickin.

Then Cole jumped up. First he hollered, then he jumped up. He started shakin one of his legs like a dog had hold of it, then he started turnin around in a circle. The man sittin next to Cole stood up and gave him room. Even the man in the robe stood up. You could see the veins poppin out of Eleanor's neck when Cole started dancin. She couldn't believe it.

"What in the world is that fool doing?" she asked Daddy, but he just kept starin at Cole. "He's lost his mind, Tommy. I don't believe this. Wait till I get his jumping behind home!"

The dancin and yellin went on for a long time until everybody got kind of tired and started easin up. When it finally stopped, all the church members were drippin with sweat and their jheri curls had dropped and napped up. They was all huffin and puffin and fannin like mad. They looked so run-down and tired out, you would think they'd all been fightin. I just knew church had to be over. But it wasn't near bout over. They was just beginnin good.

Next came what the man in the robe called "testimony service." The man next to Cole in the orange suit started it off, thankin God for his life, health, and salvation, for the "blood runnin warm" in his veins, for his pastor, wife, and anybody else he could think of, and he wanted us to pray for him to have strength in the Lord.

Then it was Cole's turn. He thanked the Lord for all the same things the orange man thanked Him for, except instead of sayin his wife he said his parents and brothers (me and Wine), and he ain't even mentioned thankin the pastor.

One by one the church members stood up, thankin God for the same things Cole and the orange man thanked Him for, some thankin God so fast it sounded like gibberish, others draggin it out, like they liked the attention. This didn't make no sense. Why they was doin it one by one? Why couldn't everybody just stand up at one time and say it all together? It was crazy. I mean, everybody was sayin the same thing over and over.

As it got close to our row, I got scared. Children had stood up too thankin God. Did that mean I had to stand up? I tried to ask Daddy, but he was too tight. He was lookin at those people like they had all just escaped from the crazy house. I mean, he didn't blink not one time. He later told Peete that when they started goin around sayin the same things like that, he thought Cole had took and joined some kind of "Jim Jones church."

"Givin honor to the spirit of Christ," the man next to Eleanor stood and said. "I like to thank the Lord for my life, health, and salvation, for the blood that's still runnin warm in my veins, hallelujah! I thank Him for my chirren and my mama, and I want y'all to pray my strength in the Lord."

He sat down. The whole church then looked at Eleanor cause she was supposed to be next. But she wasn't near bout gonna stand up talkin that stuff. She just kept starin forward, like she was too good for them. You could see the other women in the church givin her the eye and junk, but she wasn't stuttin them. She was Taylor King's campaign advisor! Ain't no way she was standin up and she wasn't gonna explain nothin to them either.

After a while Daddy decided to stand up. He buttoned up his suit coat and put one hand in his pants pocket. Everybody seemed to smile when he stood up. They liked him.

"Giving honor to the spirit of Jesus," he said like he had been sayin it all his life, "I wish to thank God for my life, health, salvation, family, business, friends, and all of you here today. Pray that I too have strength in the Lord." He then sat down and the church said a lot of amens and started clappin. They was poor and ugly and had jheri curls, but they really liked my daddy. That made me feel good. That made me feel like there was hope for me.

When Daddy sat down, I almost peed in my clothes, cause everybody's eyes got on me. Daddy even tugged at me and motioned for me to stand up. I did. There was this big dark man sittin directly in front of me, and when I stood up he turned all the way around, lookin me dead in the eye. I wanted to bust him in his juicy red lips.

"Givin honor to honor," I said in a voice that was so low that a few people said, "What? What did he say?" I was so nervous I sounded like I was talkin under water. "I mean God," I said. "I mean givin honor to God." For nothin in this world could I remember the rest of what I was supposed to say. They must of thought I was a nut for real, but I couldn't remember nothin. So I sat back down. Daddy took my hand and held it.

Wine, who was sittin next to me, acted like his mama and didn't budge. He even looked down at his Rolex watch, like he ain't had time for all this shit. They must of understood it though, cause the row behind us took up the testifyin.

After the testimony service, a fat high-yellar lady stood up in the front of the church and told us about what the church was gonna do in the week comin up. It all had to do with goin to this church service and that church service. Finally, when she finished readin from her piece of paper, she looked up into the sky as if she was prayin and then she looked back down at us.

"I been led by the Spirit to say this. Pastor," she said, lookin at the older man in the robe sittin by Cole, "I just want you to know that me, my brother Walter McDermott, his wife Amanda McDermott, and my sister Missionary Retha Mae Horton bought you that new pastoral robe you're wearin. *Nobody else donated a dime!* I just felt led of the Spirit to tell you that."

She then took her seat back in the audience with us. Daddy and his wife looked at each other. Then another big woman stood up, this time from the choir stand, and walked around where everybody could see her.

"I'm from Georgia," she said, "and I'm gon tell it like it *I-S* is. Sister Cooper was led to say what she said, but I ain't so sure it was the Spirit that was doin the leadin. See, I'm from Georgia. I'm from Georgia. No sir, Pastor, we ain't give no money for that there pretty robe you wearin today, cause we didn't know she was buyin you one till she just announced she bought it! But I will say this. Last month when me, my husband Eddie Lee, my daughter Mamie Sullivan, and my son-in-law Juno Sullivan bought you them shoes—I'm not sure if you wearin them today—Sister Cooper ain't give a nickel on that! See, I'm from Georgia. I wasn't gonna say nothin about it, but I just want the record to show that Sister Cooper ain't the only one to ever give somethin to our pastor. Thank you."

Soon, people were gettin up left and right to tell us about all the clothes and shoes they and they families bought the pastor. There was a line of people stretched almost out the door at one time. The pastor, who kept smilin at first, got out and out mad by the time the seventh or eighth person had said their say. The tenth person went too far—talkin about the draws she bought the pastor. He stood up then.

"I didn't ask none of y'all Negroes for none of this junk! I'm sorry. Y'all can get every ever-lovin piece of it back as far as I'm concerned! Jesus Christ! But that's all right. You know why? Cause Satan is a liar. He will not steal my joy. We will sit down, shat up, and continue our worship service. As for y'all that stood up, I'll see y'all later. I got yo gift! Yeah, uh-huh. I'll see y'all later."

Then he sat down. Wine was tryin so hard to hold in his laugh that he started lookin down and shakin and rubbin his forehead. Daddy and even Eleanor smiled too. But nobody else in the church thought it was funny. I don't know, I got the feeling they was used to it all.

After "offertorial service"—Daddy put a fifty-dollar bill in the basket!—Cole got up to preach. He looked real dignified in his suit and tie, and it was hard for me to imagine that he was the same boy shakin his feet and carryin on earlier.

"Those of you who have Bibles," Cole said to the church, "turn with me to the gospel as recorded by Paul the Apostle to the Romans. The first chapter, sixteenth and seventeenth verses."

Cole waited for people to find what he said in the Bible, although nobody seemed to have one.

"Let us read it together," he said. "Verse sixteen: 'For I am not ashamed of the gospel of Christ: for it is the power of God unto salvation to every one that believeth; to the Jew first, and also to the Greek.' Verse seventeen: 'For therein is the righteousness of God revealed from faith to faith: as it is written, the just shall live by faith.' May we bow our heads please."

Everybody did, even Eleanor. Cole went on to pray and preach like he was a professor or somethin. He didn't preach like Reverend Ruby. He never once talked about miry clays and mountaintops and lion dens. He just talked to the people, real calm, and he kept everybody's attention.

But soon as he finished his sermon, the piano started playin, the drums started bangin, and the fat man with the towel stood up singin. This time he kept singin about how everything was all right with him cause he knew he had a seat in some kingdom.

Sure enough, the song got faster and faster and soon they were dancin again. Even Cole shaked his leg a little again, and the man next to Eleanor started his jumpin up and down again. It seemed like they came to church to dance and the preachin part didn't really matter. The church service lasted four hours. Four hours! Daddy later told Peete he sat down so long that day he thought he was gettin hemorrhoids.

Cole changed after that sermon. He stopped listenin to Michael Jackson music. He stopped laughin and tellin jokes about the girls in the neighborhood. He studied his Bible all the time and talked about Jesus. I would come out of my bedroom and Cole would be in the hallway.

"Good mornin, Cole," I would say to him.

"Jesus said you must be born again, Bay," he would say back to me.

It got so bad everybody in the house started avoidin Cole. We would all be wanderin around the upstairs hallway or somethin and as soon as Cole came up, you couldn't believe how fast we all tore out of there, with one runnin in the bathroom, another in a bedroom, another in a closet just to stay out of Cole's way.

Even the kids in the neighborhood started avoidin Cole like a plague too. Cole didn't care, sayin he's gonna preach the gospel in season and out of season, when they want to hear it and when they don't want to hear it. I cared. Truth is, I had no friends of my own. All of Cole's friends were my friends. They acted like they didn't know me when Cole wasn't around. I tried to go over to their houses alone, but nobody was interested in comin out just to hang with me. It got to be very lonely after that first sermon of Cole's. He was gettin to be more and more like Reverend Ruby. This was great for Cole, since he was happier than I had ever seen him before, but it did nothin for my social life.

School was no different. From the first day Daddy took me up there to be registered, I was treated like I was different. Makin a friend was the hardest thing I ever had to do.

I did meet one boy who was willin to talk to me. His name was Armstrong Marshall. He was short like me, but only he was even more rough-talkin than I was and his mama was on welfare. They picked on him too, because he was poor and wore Salvation Army tennis shoes, but it didn't bother him none. He had no friends either, but he didn't seem to mind.

We met in History class. The teacher was also the basketball coach. Every morning he made us do situps and jumping jacks and running-in-place exercises before we even touched our history books. Those big strong sports lovers loved it. But small anti-jocks like me and Armstrong didn't dig it at all. But nobody said anything because Coach was tough.

One morning, while doin situps, some boys were laughin at me because I couldn't do them right. After class, Armstrong ran up to me. He was so rough-actin he thought he was a gangster. Whenever he talked, he would hit the palm of one of his hands with the other one. "Just kick his ass," he said to me.

I acted like I didn't know what he was talkin bout. He knew I knew. He didn't explain anything. He said it and walked away.

But Armstrong didn't understand. I was tryin to hold on to the life Daddy gave me. Fightin wasn't an option anymore. If I fought somebody, Daddy could send me back to Harlem. Those boys could pick at me until doomsday if stoppin them meant I had to fight somebody.

Armstrong didn't fight either. He just went around tellin me to do it. He had a big mouth, that's all, and everybody knew it. Man, he talked more trash than Muhammad Ali. But whenever those boys said they was gonna beat his ass, he found a way to disappear for a day or two. It was a very stupid way to be, I thought. Big Ike used to say Ali talked a lot of trash, but at least he backed it up. Armstrong talked it too, but he had no intention of backin it up.

But he was the closest thing to a friend I had in all the time I went to that school. He listened when I talked about my mama and how it was in Harlem, and I even told him a few things about my daddy, like how he drove a Jaguar and liked Frank Sinatra.

Armstrong giggled like a girl. "Frank Sinatra? He crazy!"

Armstrong talked to me about his crackhead mama and her alcoholic boyfriend. He didn't know who his daddy was and claimed he didn't care. I know he cared just like I used to care, but it's not somethin you can tell people, you know? Armstrong also told me about his dream: he was gonna be a poet someday. I laughed, but your boy was dead serious, man. He talked about how he was gonna travel all over the country recitin his poems, like some lady name Maya he was tellin me about. He even promised to show me some of his poems one day. But Armstrong the poet? It didn't make sense. And I told him so.

"But you can't even speak English right, Armstrong," I said to him one day. "How you gonna be a poet?"

He told me to just forget it and never mentioned it to me again. I felt bad that I had lost his trust that way, but I couldn't help it. A person like Armstrong Marshall don't be no poet. All he knew how to do good was cuss. Nobody was gonna pay him money to stand up on a stage cussin at them. It was too stupid.

Like all my mama's friends in Harlem. They all had stupid dreams too. They would never be realistic. It was like if they were sensible in their dreamin, it just might come true, with a little work. The problem was that none of them really wanted to work at all—so they dreamed big, man. All of them. Big Ike, for example, wanted to be a scientist who found a cure for a disease (he didn't care which) and the government gave him millions of dollars because he was so smart. Then he was gonna buy him a mansion in Nebraska, God knows why, and write books about growin up in Harlem. Miss Cency wanted to be a Whitney Houston–type singer, as she put it, and sing songs that brought people to tears. The only singin Miss Cency ever did, though, was in my mama's living room when they would get drunk and sing songs with the people on the radio, but that was what she wanted to be. Monroe Oliver had wanted to be a doctor and Joe Nathan had wanted to be a tight end for the Giants, and you see what became of them. Mama wanted to be rich, she didn't care what job she did to get there. Problem was, she didn't do any jobs—except cash her welfare check—and I don't think gettin welfare could make you rich even if you saved every check you got. Even I had a stupid dream. But nobody in this world will ever know what that is.

One day in Spanish class Armstrong whispered in my ear. "That's why they call them dreams," he said. Like always, he didn't explain what he meant, but just kept on writin those Spanish words for what time is it.

I did good in school. So good, I was on my way to makin A's and B's on my first Jacksonville report card. My favorite class was English, believe it or not, because we got to read books written by black people for a change. We read plays written by blacks too, and poems. I never thought there was so much black talent out there. We may have studied black people's writings in New York, but if we did, I wasn't payin any attention. School didn't interest me then. I sort of was sleepwalkin through school in Harlem.

In Jacksonville my whole attitude toward school was different. Every time I thought about Daddy lookin at my report card and seein all A's and B's, I worked harder. I was determined to be perfect. If Daddy saw I was smart, he would probably love me for that. He would probably brag to all his friends, and even his mean wife would have to give me credit.

And it happened. I made two A's and four B's on my first report card. The honor roll man! I even made a B in Coach's class. But like everything else I did in Jacksonville, my timing was bad. Daddy and his wife was havin some big-time problems again. He was stayin out late, but she was stayin out even later than he was. He would come in the Florida room some nights where me and Cole was watchin TV and wait up for her. It got to be a regular thing. I showed my report card to Daddy as soon as he came home from work (late) and stumbled into the room.

He looked at it, said it was nice, but his wife was on his mind. Cole tried to talk my achievement up to Daddy but it did no good. He wasn't stuttin us. He wanted his wife home. Bad.

She came, too, but it was somethin like two in the morning. Me and Cole had been in bed, but Daddy was still waitin up for her. I could just hear them hollerin and screamin like cats and dogs. Cole got so nervous that I saw him go downstairs—to help his mama, he said. And Daddy started yellin at him too. I don't know what it was all about, but it was real bad. Even Wine came over (Cole called him) and started fussin at Daddy. I was scared to death. I stood at the top of the stairs and prayed the yellin would stop. Wine was mean when he wanted to be and I didn't know what all that arguin would lead to. I remembered how it was when my mama and one of her boyfriends got into it. They would be pullin out knives and breakin Coke bottles and actin like grown-up fools. One time Mama got hold of a two-by-four and broke this man name Jesse's back.

It was hours before it all settled down. Cole and his mama packed up some clothes and left with Wine. I stayed with Daddy. Not because I wanted to, but because I had no choice. They didn't even look my way when they left. They were all so mad at Daddy they couldn't see nothin but how to get out that front door.

After everybody had left, I got kind of scared. Daddy was still in the house, but I couldn't hear nothin from him. The house was too quiet. I didn't know how bad Daddy was hurtin or if he was even hurtin at all.

I went downstairs. Only I didn't go bustin down where he could see me, but when I got to the bottom stair, I peeked around into the Florida room. Daddy was sittin in his chair starin at the TV. Somethin was on all right, but you could tell he wasn't payin it no attention. He had on a white t-shirt and blue pants and was sort of slouched down in the chair. There was smoke from the cigarette he had between his fingers but he not one time puffed on it. It was like he was in a trance and didn't care no more. If I wasn't the chump that I am, I would of went down there to Daddy and told him that I loved him. He needed somebody to love him. But I was way too shy for that.

I turned to go back to my bedroom. But when I turned, my stupid feet got all tangled up and I fell on my face. I was little so I didn't make a loud noise, but it was still loud enough for Daddy to hear it.

"Ralph?" he yelled, and I thought about actin like it wasn't me and runnin on upstairs anyway. But I couldn't do that to him. Not that time. So I inhaled, said it was me, and started walkin toward Daddy in the Florida room. When I stepped down into the room, I could see where Daddy's eyes looked like two Kennedy fifty cents. And they didn't blink. I mean the dude was shell-shocked, man. That argument with his wife had bothered him big time. It looked almost as if he could bust out cryin at any moment.

"Hey Daddy," I said like a fool and halfway raised my hand to wave.

"What are you doing up?" he asked. He was starin at me the way he stared at that TV.

I decided to try it, to say somethin personal to him for the first time in my life. "I wanted to make sure you was all right," I said.

I almost lost my balance after I said it, but I was glad I said it. At first, Daddy just kept starin at me. Then he smiled. "Come here," he said to me.

My heart started beatin fast when he said that, but I managed to get up enough nerve to walk up to his chair. When I got there he put his arms around my waist and pulled me up on his lap. He leaned my head against his chest and hugged me. He smelled great and felt warm. It was the closest we had ever been to each other. Even if I would of died right then and there I would of been happy.

We sat and watched an old movie called *Guess Who's Coming to Dinner*. An old white-haired white man was standin in a living room talkin to some other old people and Sidney Poitier. Daddy was quiet. So quiet that I got nervous. When I looked up at him, he had tears fallin down his face. My heart dropped. He was *really* hurtin. That wasn't new, I guess, him hurtin. But only I started hurtin too, and cryin just like him.

When he saw my tears he tried to smile. He started runnin his hand through my bunch of curly hair.

"They hate me, Ralph. I saw it tonight. But I'm not that bad. Am I?"

Lines came around the side of his eyes when he said that. I didn't know what to say to him. I loved him too much to lie to him. But I didn't want to hurt him either.

"You're not bad, Daddy," I said. "You just act like you is sometimes."

It threw him when I said that. A painful look came over his face. He looked like I probably looked when Sheneka Johnson told me off. It wasn't that he was mad at me for sayin it. The truth of it is what hurt.

He pulled me closer to him. The white man on TV looked up at the people in the living room and started talkin bout memories and junk.

I guess that's what was hurtin my daddy: the memories were still there. Of my mama probably, and Joe Nathan, and Wine and his girlfriend, and that Mary Wright lady, and the night he hit his wife, and the times they argued, and me. He couldn't shake his past. I remembered when Cole preached his first sermon and said we should worship the Lord in the days of our youth, and then we wouldn't have a past to run away from. But only Daddy wasn't a young man no more. He was old. And burned out. And holdin on to me the way I always dreamed he would, because I was all he had.

Eleven

"He picked me up from school, Mama."

"Who picked you up from school?"

"Daddy. And we went to the mall and the skatin place and to dinner at a restaurant on the river."

"Well damn. What brought all this on, son?"

"Daddy's wife left last night."

"Again? The bitch just got back!"

"And Cole left with her and they didn't take me with them this time. So I guess Daddy needs me now."

"Hey, not so fast, boy. This just one day. Ain't no tellin what Tom Bach'll do next. One day he can eat you up, the next day he don't know your name."

Mama was right. Daddy did have a way of changin on you. But I needed to believe he wouldn't change. I had prayed for him to love me. My prayer was bein answered, that's all.

But I changed the subject anyway. "How's Miss Cency doin?"

"Chile, please! Don't mention that heifer's name to me."

"What happened now, Mama?"

"Ain't nothin happened. That witch went around lyin on me, that's all. But I sho got her ass straight."

Nothin scared me more than when Mama and Miss Cency got into it. They were two rough ladies when they were fightin. And Mama, if you said the wrong thing or looked at her the wrong way, she would try to snatch your eyes out. I swear to God.

"You and Miss Cency was fightin, Mama?"

"She got mad at me over some nigga she thought I was tryin to take from her. She came to her senses, though, when I threw that grease on her."

"Hot grease? Mama! Is she all right?"

"Is she all right? Bump her! What about me? She started it!"

I exhaled loud, like my daddy. Mama was so tough sometimes you couldn't tell her nothin. No matter how stupid it sounded, no matter how it ain't made no kind of sense, she still acted like it made all the sense in the world to her. And she ain't changed one bit. Damn.

"Is she all right, Mama?"

"Oh stop worryin, boy. That fool too crazy to not be all right. I threw a little grease on her, I didn't kill the witch. That don't mean I shouldn't of though."

"And what good would it do?"

"She'll be dead, that's what good!"

"And you'll go to prison."

"Won't be the first time, baby. Won't be the first time."

She was right. My mama's been in jail six different times

that I at least know of. Mostly for fightin, but one time she did three months for writin a bunch of bad checks. I usually stayed with Miss Cency while she was gone, or with Big Ike. Back then, it was no big deal to me, my mama goin to jail. But now I'm ashamed of it. I didn't even tell Cole about that part of my life. I mean, how could I? The worst thing his mama ever done was cheat on his daddy, and it wasn't for sure she was doin that. What the hell he gonna know about jail and cussin and all that fightin and killin I know about? I'll sound like a fool even discussin it. I figured I was in middle-class society now. And when you're middle class, you just don't spend your time talkin bout no jail and fightin and all that gutter nigga stuff.

I told Mama I had to go. She, of course, didn't want to hang up and started cussin me out and callin me uppity and shit. It was gettin to be her theme song every time we talked. She couldn't accept that I had changed. I thought she wanted me to change. I thought she wanted me to get out of that ghetto mentality stuff she and Miss Cency was always talkin about. But I thought wrong. Mama didn't want me to change at all. Changin would somehow mean I had overcome in thirteen years the poverty and rough life she had been tryin to overcome all her life. And for some mamas, that ain't easy to take.

She kept talkin about how terrible I was becomin and how my daddy was no good. She even said sooner or later he was gonna turn on me again. Then she said her famous words again: "Don't forget where you come from, boy!"

I closed my eyes. How could I forget? Nobody, nobody will let me. "I won't, Mama," I said.

"We may be poor," she said, "but when all is said and done, Baby Boy, we all you got. Don't forget that."

"I won't, Mama."

"I know yo daddy treatin you nice now and all that, but I know Tom Bach. Don't you forget that either."

"I won't, Mama."

"He's all right sometimes, you know? I'll admit that. The man ain't all bad. But you can't trust him, Baby Boy, you hear me? You can't. He'll turn on you like he was turnin a page. Just like that."

"I know, Mama."

Like usual, she started cryin. And like always, I had no idea why. "Oh Bay," she said, "it's so hard."

"What, Mama? What's so hard?"

"He left me, Bay. Wennie left me."

"Who?"

"Wennie! He said he couldn't leave his wife."

"Ah man, Mama! You should of known not to get involved with a joker like that."

"He was good to me, Bay."

"Why you always gettin messed up with these losers?"

"I believed him. He wasn't like the rest. But when he got like the rest with that 'I can't leave my wife right now' bullshit, I betcha I treated him like the rest too. Bay, you should of seen it. Me and Mojack fucked up that brother so bad he was crawlin out of my apartment when we finished with him. It was a trip! But he sho fooled me. I thought he wasn't like the rest."

"Right, Mama. That's what you always say."

"He used to bring me flowers every day. A good-for-nothin don't be bringin you no flowers every day."

"They'll bring you anything, Mama, if they're gettin what they want."

When I said that, I felt bad. I knew Mama wasn't about to let me get away with talkin to her like that.

"What the hell did you just say?"

"Nothin, Mama. Forget it."

"You better wait a good goddamn minute! Who the fuck you think you is?"

"Mama—"

"I brought you in this world, boy, and I can sho take you out it!"

"Okay, Mama, I didn't mean—"

"Don't you ever, as long as you live, talk to me like I'm some goddamn street-corner hoe! You hear me, boy?"

"Yes ma'am."

"I'm yo mama. You'll only get one mama. Yo damn daddy—"

"He had nothin to do with it!"

"He had everything to do with it! I know Tom Bach. I know he ain't doin nothin but fillin your head with so much shit about me till it ain't funny. I ain't no damn hoe, I don't care what he told you!"

"I didn't say you was—"

"Callin me a hoe. He better be glad I'm not there now. Chile, please. I'll tell that Negro a thing or two!"

"Mama, Daddy ain't been sayin nothin bout you. I swear! He ain't had nothin to do with what I said."

"Oh, I see. So you cooked up callin me a hoe all by yourself. I see. I wasn't no damn hoe when I was feedin and clothin your ass. I wasn't no hoe then, was I?"

"But I didn't say you was a—look, Mama, I'm sorry I said

what I said, okay? I didn't mean it like that. And I'm sorry about Wennie or whatever his name is but..."

"But what?"

"We can't keep doin this. Whenever we talk now we just make each other mad. I think we oughta just... we oughta just stop talkin to each other for a little while, cause this ain't helpin neither one of us."

"Oh, now I get it. You don't wanna be bothered with yo ole mama no more. Is that is, Bay? You ain't got time to be foolin up with somebody like me. Is that what you tryin to say?"

I exhaled. There was no use. "Yeah, Mama. That's it. That's what I'm tryin to say."

Mama waited for a long time, then she hung up the phone. I guess you could say I wasn't handlin my newfound middle-class status very well, but I was tired of hearin about all that hard-luck stuff. Nothin ain't never goin right with my mama. But what can I do about it? What was she expectin me to do? That was buggin the shit out of me. I loved her, I really did, but that ghetto talk just made me crazy. And the way she blamed Daddy for everything. Man, she could keep all that. That's why I didn't mind her hangin up the phone like she did. And knowin Mama, she was probably cryin and carryin on after she did hang up. But I couldn't do nothin bout that. I was just thirteen years old, dammit. What could I do? I didn't ask to be shipped off to Jacksonville. I didn't ask to be forced onto my daddy. She had to figure I would change. For better or worse, she had to know that.

I hung up too. I couldn't deal with Mama and her problems right now. It was Daddy that worried me. I had to keep the pressure on him. We was doin good together and I wanted to keep that goin till havin me around was as natural to Daddy as havin Cole and his wife around. As soon as I hung up that phone, Mama and that mess with Wennie was off my mind. I hurried up those stairs to find Daddy. He was the one I needed. Mama was Mama. She'd be all right. Cause the way I figured it, once I got my act together with Daddy and knew he would forgive me anything, like I would do him, then I could help my mama. Then she wouldn't have to settle for jokers like Wennie and Dow Jones and all those other dream-peddlin niggas who didn't want nothin from her but whatever bed action they could get.

It was Friday night and the house was real quiet. I was scared Daddy might of gone out while I was on the phone with Mama and left me home alone. Not that I was scared to be alone, but I didn't see how him goin out and me stayin home would help our relationship. And that was my goal: to help our relationship. Nothin else mattered. I wasn't gonna blow this chance to get him to love me, the way I did when I went to work with him. I was gonna be in his way. That was my plan. I was gonna do everything in my power to get him to pay me some attention.

By the time I ran upstairs I could hear his voice. He was in his bedroom. It sounded like he was on the telephone, but I knew that couldn't be right. His bedroom door was almost closed, so I couldn't understand what he was sayin. But he was talkin and talkin. I stood in the hall and stared at the door. All my big plans and goals didn't seem so easy all of a sudden. I wasn't this tough kid who was gonna make his daddy love him and pay attention to him and all that junk I kept tellin myself.

I was nothin but a short, redheaded, funny-lookin kid who didn't have enough nerve to even say hello to his daddy.

It was like my eyes opened up. He was nice to me one day, just like Mama said. That didn't mean he wanted me to be his best friend. I had life bent! I was just blowin things all out of proportion, like I always did. But reality was a hurtin thing. I started to cry, can you believe that? I stood in that hallway of my daddy's house doin all I could not to cry. My English teacher said people who cried easy had emotional problems they needed to work out. That was me. Emotional. It got so bad that I ran in my bedroom and fell on my bed. I covered my face with a pillow and cried as softly as I could. Then I went to sleep.

It was nearly seven when I woke up. I panicked, because I didn't know if Daddy was still home or not, and ran out of my bedroom. The light was still on in his room at the end of the hall but the door was almost closed shut. Before I knew it, I was yellin out his name.

"Daddy?" I said and hunched my shoulders like the scary-cat I was.

I heard a little movin around in his room, like he was gettin out of the bed or somethin, and then he said, "Yeah, Ralph?"

I didn't know what else to say, so I got quiet.

"Come here," he told me.

I waited when he said that but then my heart raced. I nearly ran into his room. But I was nobody's fool: I opened the door slow.

Daddy was sittin on the bed with a pair of jeans and a t-shirt on. Right away I could tell he had been cryin. Only he wasn't about to let me know that. He smiled.

"Finally woke up, huh?"

"Yes sir."

"Good. Good. Well come on in, I don't bite."

He put on a real big smile when he said that, and it made me kind of smile. When I walked into the room, though, I almost stopped cold when I looked up. Peete, that's right, was sittin his fat ass in my daddy's bedroom! I don't think my mouth flew open, but it almost.

He was smilin all wide too. "Hello, Bay," he said and gave a wigglin fingers kind of wave.

"Hey," I said and tried my best to smile like them. All of that smilin though made all of us guilty as sin.

"I was just telling Peete you might sleep through the night," Daddy said. "I checked on you twice and you were well sound asleep."

"You must have been a tired little boy," Peete said. I ignored him. Man, that shit looked weird. I couldn't just act like it was nothin. Why would a man let another man come all up in his bedroom like that, especially a man like Peete? I heard of some odd shit in my day, but damn if that shit didn't look weird!

But ole Peete, naturally, didn't find a thing wrong with it. He kept right on grinnin and talkin and actin like it was as normal as could be. Daddy had his arms folded and was rockin his body a little. I could tell he wasn't as easy about it as he tried to let on. I knew he knew I couldn't believe my eyes.

Peete told me to sit down and make myself at home—can you believe that? Then he and Daddy started up this long conversation about Daddy's wife. Daddy was talkin on and on about how crazy she must of thought he was. "I might have been born at night, but it wasn't last night," he said. And Peete was talkin about how he knew Taylor King from way back and how Taylor King was, is, and always will be a dog. And a woman who wanted a man like that was nothin more than a dog catcher. "Kick her ass to the curb!" he said to Daddy and popped his fingers while wavin his arm from side to side.

I sat still next to Daddy and listened. It was kind of fun, to tell you the truth, because I was never too crazy about that wife of Daddy's anyway. She never treated me right. She could be in the Florida room or the kitchen somewhere, and every time I came into the room she'd start downin poor people.

"They make me sick," she said one time to one of her girl-friends. "They don't want to work or do anything constructive, and every time you see them in the grocery store they have the nerve to have more food in their baskets than you do! I can't stand them, girl. And those children they produce are just as bad. Ill-mannered and dirty and mean as I don't know what."

She'd look at me when she gave the line about poor people's children. I was glad she was gone, to tell you the truth. And although I loved my daddy and didn't for nothin want to see him hurt, I was prayin to Jesus she *was* makin out with Taylor King.

"She's with David?" Peete asked.

"Nope. He called me this morning. Cole's with him. Ellie's staying with some friend of hers in Argyle, according to Wine."

"Don't tell me: Taylor King lives in Argyle?"

"You got it."

Peete shook his head. "I remember when she was so insecure she wouldn't let you out of her sight. Now she's in Argyle. My my, Thomas. Whatever have you done to that woman?"

"You tell me," Daddy said sadly. He loved her still.

After that, everything just died on down. But Daddy and Peete had a way of communicating without sayin a word. They kept starin at each other until they slowly started smilin.

"Are you serious?" Daddy asked.

"As a heart attack, girlfriend," Peete said.

"But what will it do?"

"Vengeance, honey chile, vengeance!"

And before I knew it, me, Daddy, and Peete was in Daddy's car headed for Argyle. During the whole ride Peete was gettin Daddy all pumped up, talkin about how Taylor King probably had the whole thing planned out.

"What man is going to stand by and let his wife stay out to three o'clock every night? King knew you wouldn't go for that, sweetheart, he had to know!"

It was all exciting to me. Finally, finally, I was a part of Daddy's life. And although I didn't like the idea that ole Peete was taggin along (and pretty much runnin things, really), I was still happy just to be there.

The fun stopped, though, when Daddy found Taylor King's house and saw his wife's car in the man's yard. Everything got quiet when Daddy drove up in front of the house and stopped. Even Peete wasn't gung-ho no more. Daddy's feelings were deep. He slumped over his steering wheel and just stared at the house. It was like he wasn't expectin it to be true, and now that it was, he didn't know what to do. He probably wanted to cry, but me and Peete was there, so he didn't. He just sat there. Looking, and looking, and looking.

Then somethin seemed to snap in Daddy and with a serious quickness he flew out of his car and started hurryin toward the house. Peete got scared. He yelled somethin about some people name Mary, Martha, and Joseph and ran on behind Daddy. I could see him pullin on Daddy's shirt, tellin him to come on back, but Daddy wasn't turnin back. He ran up to Taylor King's steps and banged on his door like a crazy man. Peete stood behind him lookin so nervous and scared that I almost felt sorry for him. He loved Daddy, I guess. It made me sick to my stomach, but it sho looked like that to me.

Nobody never came to the door. Thank God. Daddy probably would of killed them if they had. Daddy kept on knockin until it seemed stupid. He was too old to be carryin on like this. Him and Peete were just too old. But Daddy kept on knockin. I guess somebody in that house or in that neighborhood was tired of it and called the police. That's when I got scared. I never seen a time when the police didn't come on a scene and not arrest somebody. I was scared they was gonna arrest my daddy.

But they didn't. They just told him to go on home. Daddy looked so embarrassed it was a shame. He walked back to his car almost in tears. He couldn't even look at me. Peete got in too, tellin Daddy he can't make nobody love him. I wanted to kick Peete's ass. Daddy wasn't tryin to make her love him. He just couldn't stop lovin her. That was the problem. Her lovin him ain't had nothin to do with that scene over there.

We didn't go home but we left Argyle. For a while we just wandered around Jacksonville lookin for somethin to do. Peete was all excited about seein some stupid movie, but Daddy couldn't seem to catch on to the idea of sittin through anything. I mean, you can't go from plotting to beat hell out of your wife and her lover to goin to the movies. But that was what ole Peete wanted. And for some reason, I don't know why, he always seemed to get what he wanted. In no time Daddy was pullin his

Jag into the Regency Theater parking lot, and we got out and went to the movies.

The theater was inside the Regency Square mall and it was packed with wall-to-wall teenagers. I had never seen so many kids chillin without a riot or a fight breakin out in my life. But these were well-dressed kids in hiphop clothes, and you could tell they wasn't gonna be rollin on no floor fightin in those clothes. After gettin the money from Daddy, Peete stood in the long line to buy the tickets. Me and Daddy waited over by the Burger King. Daddy was lookin hard at the people walkin around us, but I could tell his mind was a million miles away. He was worryin about his wife, that's what I think. I bet he couldn't deal with the fact that she might be makin love to some smooth-talkin tough man while he was standin in front of Burger King waitin to go see a movie with a fairy queen and a thirteen-year-old boy. I don't know to this day why he cared so much for the woman. I mean, my daddy, standin there in that mall, was a great-lookin man. Even those teenage girls were givin him second and third looks. He could of had any woman he wanted. But he wanted Eleanor. His wife. The one person I ain't never been able to get along with.

We made it into the movie theater early enough to get pretty good seats up front. We seemed like the center of attention when we walked in, mostly because Peete was with us, but also because we were the only blacks in the whole damn room. What the hell kind of movie did weirdo Peete pick for us to see, I said to myself. Probably some tribute to Elvis shit or some history of the KKK or some boring shit black people wouldn't be caught dead in.

I stayed close to Daddy. I wanted everybody in that room to

know that I wasn't really with Peete. I guess it was cold-blooded the way I treated Peete, but I was so insecure myself I couldn't help it. And when ole Peete tried to sit his ass in the middle with me and Daddy on each side of him, I moved so fast to put Daddy in the middle that some blue-haired old lady in the next row clutched her pocketbook. I knew Peete knew why I moved like that, and I was sorry. But if you're gonna prance around like some damn Tinkerbell all the time, you gotta figure not everybody's gonna be happy for you and give you high fives.

The movie Peete picked for us turned out to be too stupid for words. It was all about this retard sittin on this park bench eatin chocolate candy and tellin his life story. He went from havin to wear braces on his legs to bein the fastest man in America. Yeah, right. Like that stupid-actin white boy was gonna outrun a brother. But man did he run. All the time. He even graduated from college because he could run. I couldn't believe it. How could a retarded boy who didn't even know what to do with a football get to go to college and graduate too? I knew ten or twenty retards in Harlem and they couldn't even graduate grade school. But this boy went to college. Then he joined the army and went to Vietnam and supposedly rescued a whole company of men from the enemy. He then got to meet some old President and he bent over and showed the President where the enemy shot him in his ass. Everybody in the movie house laughed when he bent over like that, even that old President laughed, but it wasn't funny to me.

I couldn't get over the fact that they would make a movie about some retard and treat him like he's some superman or somethin. I could only think about Jawbone Mason back home, who was a retard too. Jawbone never got to meet no president or go to college, and he could outrun that white boy any day of the week. That's why I could never get off on movies, man. I could never go for that make-believe, fantasyland bullshit. How could people enjoy that stuff? Didn't they know it isn't real? Didn't they know that retarded people would give a million dollars to go to college and meet some old president? It'll never happen. That's why I can't get off on movies. They're always tellin stories that'll never come true. Life is hard. And watchin some retard white boy runnin round the country like a fool ain't gonna change one inch of that fact.

I fell asleep when your boy met up with this legless guy in a wheelchair who wanted to kill him for savin his life, but he was too busy bein a drunk and feelin sorry for hisself to do anything about it. Get real. If the guy was so mad that the retarded boy saved his life, then why didn't he just kill his own self? What's the use in all that arguin about it? And please don't give me that reverse psychology shit that he didn't really want to die, but the only way he could live as a cripple was by pretendin he wanted to die. I hate that reverse psychology shit. And that's all movies are: reverse psychology. Fantasyland.

My mama always taught me and my dead brother Joe Nathan to never believe in somethin that ain't true. Like one Christmas when I was five or six and Miss Cency told me to go to bed early or Santa Claus wouldn't come. Mama looked at Miss Cency like she was crazy.

"Don't you even think about comin round here talkin that Santa Claus shit to my children. I'm the damn Santa Claus! You think I'm gonna slave my ass off gettin them these toys and let some damn fat white man take the credit? You gots to be jivin or on dope, one."

I woke up when your boy was bein told that some goofy kid was his son and your boy got scared, like he had done somethin wrong. The mama of the son then said she had a virus (AIDS, according to Daddy) and she was gonna die soon. Tears came to my daddy's eyes when Retard backed up and asked if the boy was smart or stupid like him. From the looks of the boy I say he was stupid like him, but the woman claimed the boy was smart. But what mama wouldn't say they boy smart? Even Jawbone's mama think he got sense, when everybody in Harlem know he don't.

The movie ended with Retard sittin on a bench waitin for Retard #2 to get back home from school. All I could do was shake my head. But when the light was turned back on in the place and everybody was gettin up to go, I couldn't believe how almost everybody had been cryin. Some fools were even clappin, like they had just seen a live stage show or somethin. Afterwards, Daddy and Peete went on and on about how great that movie was and how it was the best movie they had ever seen and how so much better they felt because they went to see it. I thought they was jokin at first. I mean, I saw the same movie they saw, but the praises kept on even after we got in the car and took Peete home.

"Did you see that fireball in that Vietnam scene?" Peete asked Daddy.

"Yes Lord," Daddy said. "And the way he outran everybody. He ran past Bubba like he wasn't there."

"And those helicopters."

"Best movie I seen in a long time."

They reminded me of a couple of dizzy women who liked to talk about those people on the soaps like it's real life. But it was a good night for that movie, and I was happy Daddy was happy. I felt close to him. I decided that night that he was a good man. Joe Nathan and Miss Cency were wrong about him. He wasn't selfish and mean and didn't care who he hurt. He just wanted to be like the people in the movies. He wanted somebody to stand up sometimes and clap for him.

For five whole days we were closer than white on rice, doin everything together, even my homework. Daddy's wife called every now and then, and they talked real civilized to each other, but I could tell Daddy wouldn't of minded goin on without her. She hurt him, I guess, and he wasn't like her: he couldn't pretend to forgive and then mention what happened twenty-four seven, like ain't no way he was gonna let her forget. He had me now. And as far as he was concerned, his wife could marry Taylor King and have his babies too. Of course, Daddy never said nothin like that, he never mentioned his wife or even Cole to me at all. If he cared, he wasn't tellin.

But everything changed on the sixth day. I turned the corner on Savannah Lane where we lived and saw almost right away that somebody was sittin on our front steps. I knew it wasn't Daddy because he didn't come home from work until a couple of hours after I got home from school. The closer I walked toward the house, I realized it wasn't a man anyway, but some woman. And when I saw that she had a long ponytail goin down her back, I knew it was my mama. My *mama*? I stopped in my tracks when I realized that. The other kids who were also walkin home from school ran into me when I stopped, and some of them passed by and looked back, like they thought I was crazy or somethin.

It was my mama sittin on the steps of my daddy's house.

I couldn't believe my eyes. Was she out of her mind? How could she do this to me? I got myself so mad that I wasn't even glad to see her. I ran up to her, not to hug her like she thought, but to cuss her ass out.

"What are you doin?" I yelled before I even got up to her. "Why are you here?"

Mama was standin up, ready to hug me, but my hard tone of voice caught her off guard. She looked beautiful standin there, more like a high school girl than somebody's mama, and if it wasn't for the fact that she was bound to screw up what I had goin with my daddy by bein there, I would of been so happy to be around her.

She put her hands on her hips. "What?"

"Why you come here? You know how Daddy is!"

Mama just stared at me. Her big eyes started waterin up. Once again, I handled it wrong. I was tryin to get close to my daddy at my mama's expense. I couldn't believe it myself. And Mama, without sayin a single word to me, walked by me and to the street. I turned and yelled for her to come back, but she wasn't stuttin me. How could I do that to her? She raised me. She gave me my life. She never one time left me or disowned me or treated me bad. And I was yellin at her for comin to see about me. What was happenin to me? Why was I hurtin the only somebody who ever really loved me? And why wasn't I runnin behind her beggin her to come back?

I couldn't do it. Even when I yelled for her to come back, you could tell I didn't really mean it. She had to understand what I was tryin to do. I couldn't help her yet, and she had to understand that. But she didn't get it. By the way she looked at me when I all but told her to stay out of my life, she wasn't never gonna understand what I was up to. But what did I expect? She couldn't see how bad I needed to be with my daddy. And even though she always wanted the best for me and always said if anybody was gonna make it out of Harlem it was me, she wanted a piece of the action too, for herself.

I waited for Daddy in the kitchen, sittin at the table drinkin milk and so nervous I felt like I had glass in my throat. I wanted to tell him about my mama bein in town, but I knew that would ruin everything between us. Talk about bad timing! Of all the times Mama could of come to see about me, she picked the time when I least needed to see her. Me and Daddy were closer than we ever had been, but I wasn't on easy street yet. He still stared at me a lot and sometimes acted like he was mad I was around. My mama bein in town could destroy everything for me. My daddy was a man who didn't like memories. Anytime you tried to bring up the past around him, he changed the subject. I tried a million times to ask him about Joe Nathan, and why he didn't come to the funeral, but Daddy always cut me off and went on to talkin about somethin else. He hated that past stuff. And now Mama was in town. Damn.

Daddy came through the back door in a real good mood. He smiled when he saw me and said, "Hey, sport!" real loud, like he was enjoyin the mess out of bein a daddy. When I saw him comin through that door, smilin because he was glad to see me, I made up my mind right there and then: although I loved my mama to death and was sorry that I didn't explain the situation to her better, she was still in New York as far as I was concerned. That is, until Daddy told me his news.

"Coleman and Ellie are coming home," he said, still smilin,

his gray eyes sparklin. I almost stopped smilin I was so shocked. Cole and Eleanor's comin back? How the hell could he call that great news? Who the hell wanted them back? Not me! They were my competition. They were the last two people on the face on this earth I wanted anywhere near Savannah Lane. And that damn daddy of mine was tellin it to me like he was tellin me I'd won the lottery or somethin.

"She came by my office today and we talked for hours," Daddy said. "There was a lot we had to discuss. But at the end of the day, we both agreed we'd be better off pulling together."

Wasn't that a bitch. I dissed my own mama big time because I didn't want nothin to come between me and Daddy. And at the same time I was dissin my mama, probably to the very moment, Daddy boy was cookin up a scheme to bring Cole and Eleanor back into the picture. I couldn't win for losin. I felt like a natural fool. I felt like I had just sold my soul to the devil only to find out the devil ended up gettin it for free.

The plan was for him and me to meet Cole and his mama at David's house for dinner, and then the two of them would pile in the car with Daddy and me and we'd all live happily ever after. But it wasn't that simple for me. Daddy's wife still hated me, I was sure, and Cole was still Daddy's son years before I hit the scene. The only sure bet I had in the world was my mama, and I had told her to take a hike. I had to know that if Eleanor and Cole didn't want me around and Daddy agreed with them, I could always go home to Mama. That was why I had to get my mama back. That was also why when Daddy got out of the shower, I was sittin on his bed.

He was drippin wet and naked, and wipin his face with a big green towel. His dick was so much bigger and wider than mine that I hunched my shoulders. As soon as Daddy saw me, he slung the towel around his waist and tucked it in at the hip.

"What's the matter with you?" he snapped at me like he was embarrassed.

I wasted no time. "Mama's in town," I said. I had nothin to lose.

He waited for a while and then slumped down in the chair by the dresser. His face was serious and scared-lookin at the same time. He didn't even try to hide his shock. "Juanita's here in town?"

"Yes sir. She was waitin for me when I came home from school."

"Here? At *my* house?"

I looked down. The way he said "my" house didn't sit right with me, like he was sayin my mama wasn't good enough to come to his house. And besides that, he could of said "our" house, since I lived there too. "Yes sir," I said, too tired to even admit my feelings.

"How do you like that?" he said to the ceiling. Then he looked at me. "What did she want?"

I looked up. "She came to see about me," I said.

He shook his head, like he was beginnin to realize the burden of havin me around.

"That woman!" he said and stood up. He started walkin around the bedroom rubbin his neck with his hand.

"What's the matter, Daddy?" I asked, as if I didn't know.

"Juanita's in town and you ask me that? What if my wife was home when she decided to *drop* by? What if my children were here? But that's Juanita. Never cared about anybody but her own damn ass. I curse the day I ever got involved with that crazy bitch!"

He was walkin fast around that bedroom, back and forward, like a nut case. I've never known a man who could love like Daddy and I've never known a man who hated like him. Everything was great or everything was horrible. And my mama bein in town was horrible to him. He was actin worse than I thought he would act. He was makin like my mama comin to see me was the worst thing that could happen.

I felt I should take up for her and explain to Daddy that my mama was just doin what mamas do: she wanted to see for herself that I was all right. Why should he be mad about that? I thought for a moment it could be for the same reason I was mad, that he didn't want her to come between us, but I wasn't born yesterday either. Daddy's anger had nothin at all to do with me. That was some old shit he was mad about. I could tell it by the way he moved back and forward, like every time he thought hard about it, it made him change directions.

I decided to tell him everything: how I didn't want her to come between us and how I caused her to run away cryin. My honesty slowed him down, and for a little while it seemed like he was finally thinkin about the effect my mama bein in town had on me rather than just on him. He even sat down and stopped callin her names.

"Before we go to Wine's house," I said, "will you take me to apologize to her?"

He couldn't believe I asked him that. "Take you where? Where is she?"

"At Grandmama's house, I think."

"And you want me to take you... You don't know what you're asking me, Ralph. Your mother and I don't get along. I can't. No, I can't."

"But you should of seen her, Daddy. I think I broke her heart."

I had a way of fixin my face until I looked real sad and pitiful to people, and when I gave that *I think I broke her heart* line, I laid the pity act on thick. Daddy fell for it. I thought he was gonna cry he was so touched by me.

He drove me to Grandmama's house. It was the first time I went on the east side since Daddy picked me up from there that windy night and took me to his house to live. We didn't talk during the ride, and Daddy listened to those Frank Sinatra songs without drummin his fingers. Our relationship was changin already.

Chinesa and some of her drinkin buddies were sittin on Grandmama's porch when Daddy's Jaguar drove up. Chinesa was still mad at me for jumpin on her, and I could tell she was ready to start somethin when I stepped out of the car. She had on one of her too-tight joggin suits and had a can of Colt 45 beer in her hand. And she was loud, as usual.

"Well. If it ain't Sugar Ray Chump and his daddy," she said, and her friends—three goofy fat ladies—started laughin.

"That's the boy what jumped on you, Nesa?" one lady asked.

"That's the one," Chinesa said. "Hey, Baby Boy. Wanna try it again?"

Daddy ignored Chinesa's showboating and put on a big smile.

"How y'all ladies doing?" he asked. The ladies, who probably wasn't used to a handsome man speakin to them, was all too happy to answer back that they were doin good. Even Chinesa spoke and tried to smile.

"How you doin, Mr. Bach?"

"I can't complain, Chinesa. My back's been trying to give me trouble but it's still manageable."

"That back pain somethin else when it wanna be."

"You telling me. My back used to bother me so bad that I could hardly stand up. But that's been years ago."

Chinesa's friends were smilin and lookin Daddy up and down, like he was a piece of meat or somethin. Daddy just stood up there in his sparklin brown suit, smellin good and lookin good, and acted like those fat ladies didn't exist. Not because of anything they did, but because every time Daddy visited the east side he was in a hurry to take care of his business and leave.

"Bessie home?" he asked Chinesa.

"Yes sir."

"Is Ralph's mother here?"

"You mean Nita?"

Chinesa's stupid question caused Daddy to exhale like he was gettin mad. It was like he was sayin "Who you think?" and Chinesa understood that's what he was sayin.

"She's in there too," she said. "You can go on in."

Daddy buttoned his suit coat and started walkin slowly up the steps.

"How you doin, O.J.?" Chinesa said to me when I walked past her, and her girlfriends laughed. I ignored them. I had more important things on my mind.

Daddy knocked on the raggedy door but didn't walk in until Grandmama said for him to come in. Grandmama was sittin on the sunk-in couch in the living room shellin peas. She looked fatter and older than I remembered her, and her house smelled, as always, like a cheap liquor joint.

"Well hello there, Tommy," she said to Daddy.

"Well hello yourself. How're you doing?"

"I seen better days. But I thank God things are as well as they are."

"That's a good attitude."

"I try to be positive. I always said ain't no use groanin and moanin. Nobody wanna hear that wang."

Daddy smiled and started lookin around. In a hurry once again.

"Hey, Baby Boy!" Grandmama said to me.

"Hey, Grandmama."

"Come and give yo old Grandmammy some sugar."

Grandmama hugged me tight and whispered that she loved me in my ear. She smelled pretty awful, like a combination of snuff and beer, but I sat down beside her anyway. I loved her. She was a good person. When I grow up, I said to myself, I'm gonna take care of that lady.

"Sit down, Tommy," she said to Daddy. "Waterman, come and get these clothes out the way so's Mr. Bach can sit down!"

"This is fine, Bessie, I can sit right here." Daddy sat down next to me. The couch didn't have many springs, and his butt was nearly sunk down to the floor. Daddy looked at me and smiled.

Waterman came in from the back room to get the pile of old clothes out of the chair. He said "hey" to me but acted all nervous around Daddy. He got the clothes and went on back into the back room. That's when Daddy asked Grandmama if Mama was there.

"She's here, Tommy, I ain't gon lie to you," Grandmama said. "She just wanted to check on Baby Boy, that's all. She's goin back home tomorrow. She was worried about Baby Boy, that's all."

I felt bad for Grandmama. She was actin like she had to apologize to Daddy for her own daughter comin to town. She was actin as bad as I did. I don't think my daddy ever understood how special he was, how people always made excuses for him, how people care about what he thought. And it wasn't like he did anything to make people treat him good, because he didn't. He was just blessed that way. Some people got all the luck.

"Where is she?" Daddy asked Grandmama.

"In the back yard," Grandmama said. "She went off and came back and been in that back yard since."

I stood up to go see Mama. I had it all planned out what I was gonna say to her. I only prayed it was enough.

She was sittin in a chair under the big oak tree in Grandmama's back yard. Man, was she young-lookin and pretty. She had on a pair of jeans and a white shirt with no sleeves. Her little arms were light brown and muscular-lookin and her big eyes were dancin. She didn't realize I was out there until I was almost standin right in front of her.

"Hello, Bay," she said with no emotion, like we barely knew each other. That's the way she acted when she was sad.

"Hey, Mama."

"How you get all the way out here?"

"Daddy brought me."

"Oh, did he now?" Mama said, suddenly gettin hot. "My my. The mighty Bach among the peasants. Ain't that some shit?"

Every time I heard my mama cuss, I cringed. It just didn't seem right no more for a mama to be talkin like that.

"I came to apologize, Mama. I didn't mean to act so stupid like that."

"So you admit you acted stupid? Well, that's a start."

"I been tryin so hard to get along with Daddy that I forgot about everything else. But I didn't mean it, Mama."

I put on my pitiful look, although Mama could see through it. But she still smiled and pinched my cheek.

"You're cute, you know that?"

"Yeah, right."

"You *are* cute. With all them fancy clothes on. You look like new money, boy!"

Daddy made me shower and put on a suit so I could be presentable at David's house. Mama thought I had dressed up for her. That made her happy.

"I guess I forgive you, boy," she said, smilin. "I know how hard it is to get Tom Bach's attention. Lord knows I been tryin for years! But you keep the pressure on his ass, you hear me? It just might work for you."

We stared into each other's eyes, and then she gave me a great bear hug and rocked me side to side. I couldn't help gigglin at the way she was slingin me around, but then all of a sudden she stopped. When I looked at her she was starin at the back door.

"Jesus Christ, he's still gorgeous," she said almost under her breath. I turned around and saw Daddy standin on the back porch starin at Mama. He had a cigarette between his fingers and his suit coat was unbuttoned. He looked big with his almost pot belly, and even from a distance you could tell he wasn't young. But Mama was right: he was gorgeous. And when he started walkin toward us, Mama squeezed my hand. She still loved him.

Daddy put on his big phony smile like he ain't never in his life thought nothin bad about her. I guess he forgot he was callin her a bitch when we was home.

"Hello there," he said like he was meetin up with a good old friend of his.

"Hi," Mama said. You could tell she wanted to smile but was too scared to. I had never seen her so nervous.

"How long has it been, Juanita?"

"A long time."

"Absolutely. And you haven't aged a bit, young lady."

That line brought the smile out of Mama. That made Daddy smile even more, if that was possible. It was as if he forgot she looked so good.

"Bay told me you were in town. I couldn't believe it."

Yeah, he couldn't believe it all right, I wanted to say. He almost stroked out.

"I missed Bay. I had to see his face again."

Mama pinched my cheek when she said that. Daddy put his hands in his pockets and started lookin at Mama's breasts, which were real big. Mama seemed to like it, though, because she sat up straight and stuck her chest out further. Daddy rattled the change in his pockets when she did that.

"I was hopin he's been a good boy. I sho tried to teach him right. But I had to see it for myself."

"He's all right," Daddy said without takin his eyes off Mama. "How's that singing career of yours going?"

Mama waited, then bust out laughin. "You remember that?"

"Sure I remember it. You were going to be the next Gladys Knight. All you needed were three Pips, you used to tell me."

Mama laughed. "You remember that for real," she said.

"Oh girlfriend!" Daddy said like Peete. "Why wouldn't I remember it?"

It was great the way they carried on. They were actin like good friends, not like two people who hated each other. I laughed with them, even though it wasn't all that funny, and for a long time they were talkin about everything from afros to platform shoes. I went inside the house when Grandmama called me in to eat dinner, but when I said no and headed back out the door, she stopped me.

"They need to talk, Baby Boy," she said.

I went to the back bedroom window and looked out. Daddy had pulled up a chair next to Mama and they were talkin their heads off. For nearly an hour they talked. Then Mama came into the house, said she and Daddy would be back, and before I could ask if I could go, they was gone.

Me, Grandmama, Peanut, Waterman, and Chinesa spent the evening in the front room watchin a tape on Waterman's new VCR. He got it from some rent-to-own store that let you get anything you want even if you have real bad credit. Waterman said he only have to pay fifty dollars a month for almost two years, and that, according to Waterman, was the "deal of the century!" He planned to get him an entertainment center next.

We watched this Spike Lee movie about a black family in Brooklyn who liked to yell and dance and watch *The Brady Bunch* on TV. We all laughed when some old lady in the movie started runnin around her yard cryin for her dog to come home, only to find the dog dead in the rollaway bed. By the time the movie was over and Waterman was slidin a tape called *The Inkwell* into the VCR, Mama came home happy, but by herself.

I jumped up. "Where's my daddy?" I asked and Mama laughed.

"He gone, Bay."

"Gone? Why didn't he wait on me? Why didn't you make him wait on me, Mama?"

Mama laughed again and ran her head through my curly hair. I was about to start cryin.

"He's outside waitin on you, boy. Stop gettin yoself so worked up."

I hugged and kissed Mama and flew out that house like I was leavin hell. I guess I should of spent more time with my mama since it was her first night in town, but I had a lifetime to spend with her. I had to be with Daddy.

He was sittin in his car all hunched up like. He looked tired out, and not happy like my Mama was. His suit was all wrinkled and his Smokey Robinson eyes looked bloodshot. He didn't say a word to me when I got in the car, and he drove off like he was suddenly in a hurry. I wanted to ask him where did he and Mama go, but he was in the kind of mood that didn't take too well to questions. They had been to a motel, I decided.

It was after ten p.m. when we got to Wine's apartment. I was surprised we went at all. Daddy stood outside the car straightenin his clothes and rubbin his hair in place. He was actin like some nerd goin to pick up a girl or somethin. He kept fumblin with his tie and pullin up on his belt buckle and feelin around to make sure his fly was zipped. And when he did start walkin he walked fast, causin me to almost run to keep up. I was expectin him to tell me not to tell his wife where we had been, but he didn't say a word to me. I guess he knew I wouldn't tell. I guess he knew I wasn't about to let the world know that my mama went to a motel with somebody's husband like a common street-corner trash-barrel hoe would do.

Daddy rang the doorbell twice. He kept fumblin with his clothes and movin around. And when the door was opened by David, you should of seen the smile my daddy slapped on his face. You would of thought he was the nicest man alive the way he put on that grin.

"Hi there, David!" he said loudly like he was actin on a stage, or drunk. "How are you?"

One thing about David, he was consistent. He chilled Daddy when I first met him and he was still cold toward him. Daddy could smile like a fool for all David cared. Cole said David never forgave Daddy for sleepin with his girlfriend, and you could tell in David's eyes that was true. "You're late," he said to Daddy and walked away from the door.

Daddy's smile didn't let up though, and he busted on into David's apartment like David had just told him he was a wonderful man.

Cole was sittin in the living room pretendin to watch some junk on TV. When he looked up, he acted like he was just noticin that me and Daddy had arrived.

"Hey, Daddy," he said with a small smile. Cole didn't know it, but he was a lot like Daddy. Cole was a preacher and Daddy was no Christian man, but they had those ways about them, the smilin and carryin on, that made it clear they were related.

Daddy started movin toward Cole. "Hello, sport! How's it going?"

"Good. Where have you been?"

"I had to take care of some business. Where's your mother?"

"She's lying down. She didn't think you were coming."

"Of course I was coming," Daddy said, suddenly gettin angry. "I said I was coming, didn't I?"

"You said you were coming hours ago," David said and fell down in the chair. He was a pretty boy with pretty, droopy eyes, and if you didn't know him you'd think he was gay.

"I'm not that late."

"You are that late."

"That's your opinion."

"That's a fact, jack."

"Your fact."

"Ah c'mon, Dad," David said. "Who do you think you're fooling? Gimme a break! If I was Mom I wouldn't give your butt the time of day."

"Fuck you!" Daddy said so loud that it startled Cole. "Where the hell do you get off judging me?"

"I do anything I want to do in my own house."

"You just get your sorry ass up and get your mother—that's what you do. All right?"

David was tough, but he wasn't tough enough to buck Daddy. He waited, to let us know he was his own man, but then he got his sorry ass on up and went to get his mama—like Daddy ordered him to.

Daddy put his hands in his pockets and started walkin around the room. I sat next to Cole.

"Long time no see," I said to him. He was still starin at Daddy.

"How are you, Bay?"

"I'm good. What about you? Still preachin?"

Cole looked at me. Suddenly he turned mad. "Of course I'm still preaching. What kind of stupid question is that?"

Me and Cole stared at each other for a couple seconds, then he stared back at Daddy. I guess he knew me and Daddy were gettin close and he was kind of jealous about it. I looked at the TV. A commercial was on showin a rabbit beatin a drum. That was when Eleanor came stompin into the living room, with David stompin behind her. Daddy turned toward her. He smiled again.

Eleanor was wearin some big blue shift-lookin dress and bedroom shoes. She looked like a weather witch. But Daddy wanted her, veins and all.

"There she is!" he said, like she was Miss America. Yeah, right.

"Well, what happened to you?" she said as she kept walkin toward him.

"Oh nothing," Daddy said. "I had a few things to finish up at the office."

"I called the office," she said. "Nobody answered."

"I know. But I was in and out, you must have missed me."

"What do you mean in and out?"

"I had to get some work orders ready for a few of my properties, Ellie, that's all."

Daddy was a good liar. He looked her straight in the eye when he lied like that. He must of forgot I knew better.

Eleanor and Daddy went around and around about why he was late. Then Daddy smiled. That made his wife smile. Then they stared into each other's eyes like they always do before they kiss. Daddy pulled her to him and French-kissed her. Man, was he horny! I thought he was gonna do her right there in the living room in front of all of us. I think Daddy came on strong to stop her from askin questions, but that didn't stop her from fallin for the act and actin hornier than him.

We didn't have dinner at David's house since they had already ate, and the question of Taylor King and Argyle never did come up. Ever since that night Cole tried his best to get me to admit that Daddy was late because he had been with another woman. But I never told. I guess I felt good that me and Daddy had a secret. I guess in a small-time way I finally felt that I had the goods on him.

As for my mama, she tried to get back together with Daddy, but he gave her the chill. I begged her not to make a scene about it, since it was clear he didn't want her, and it worked. She was embarrassed that she let Daddy use her again. She was embarrassed that after all the big talk about how independent she was, she fell for Daddy as quick as lookin at him. She went back to New York. We cried and hugged and she got on the bus. I wasn't sad that she was leavin. I was sad that she had come. And slept with Daddy. And lost the right to call him names like horny dog because, when it came down to it, she was no better than him.

Twelve

The return of Eleanor meant the return of my old self again. I tried to be bold and talk up around her, but somethin about that witch scared the shit out of me. Words wouldn't come to me, and when they did come, they didn't make sense. Daddy went back to ignorin me, and Cole was still caught up in his Jesus stuff. Eleanor told me I looked different the first day she came back, and then she didn't say another word to me. Daddy started his comin home late from work routine, causin him and Eleanor (who stopped havin anything to do with Taylor King) to start their all-night arguments again. Boy, was their honeymoon short! Within a week of Eleanor's return, they was at each other's throat. I didn't know the real reason for the arguments, if it was because Daddy was stayin out late or if it was what he was doin while he was out there, but I did know Daddy didn't have time to be botherin with me. So no matter how you looked at it, the return of Eleanor made it clear: I was on my own again.

I didn't mind bein left alone again because I appreciated the time I did spend with my daddy, but as the weeks and months came and went, I found myself hating like mad the way my life was goin. I thought me and Daddy had connected, but months later, I found myself no closer to Daddy than when I first met him. I gave it my best shot when Eleanor was out of the way, but my best wasn't good enough. I guess that made me wonder if there was anything I could do to win Daddy's love. Good grades didn't do it; stickin by him didn't do it; even knowin he humped my mama and not tellin his wife didn't do it. I gave up. I didn't know it at the time, but now it's as clear as day to me: I made it up in my mind that if they didn't care about me, then fuck them! I wasn't playin that Mr. Nice Guy shit no more.

I even changed at school. I used to love makin good grades and hopin that would mean somethin to Daddy. But after he started ignorin me when Eleanor came back I couldn't care no more. What makin good grades was gonna do for a hard-luck joker like me anyway? Man. I was wastin my time. I went from makin the honor roll one semester to barely passin the next semester. Even in English, where people said I was smart, I couldn't keep my act together. I remember one time when the teacher, a nice lady to tell you the truth, kept askin me to tell the class what some T.S. Eliot poem meant. I kept tellin that crazy lady I didn't know or want to know what "Prufrock's motivation" was, but she wouldn't let up.

"Oh c'mon, Ralph. Your paper was superb. I loved reading it. Give the class a sampling of what you wrote."

"I don't want to, Miss Sullivan."

"Please, Ralph, it's a wonderful interpretation. Just give them an overview."

"I don't want to, Miss Sullivan."

"But, Ralph. Please."

"No."

"Ralph."

"Ma'am?"

"Pretty please. With sugar on top."

"No."

"Please."

"No, Miss Sullivan," I said for the hundredth time. But damn if that lady didn't stop messin with me. She even had the nerve to threaten to read my stupid paper out loud if I didn't fess up and let the class in on this great work I was supposed to of wrote. But why she wanna threaten me? I jumped up mad.

"Leave me alone, Miss Sullivan, all right? I don't give a shit about no damn Prufrock! It was a stupid poem, that's my interpretation! Stupid! Got it, class? That's my interpretation!"

The class was rollin in laughter, mostly because they didn't like the poem either, but also because they thought Miss Sullivan was buggin a brother too hard. She got the last laugh, though, cause I was kicked out of her class for talkin back and cussin.

I felt bad because Miss Sullivan was really the best teacher at Stuart and the best teacher I ever had, but it was like I couldn't help myself. It was like people were always messin with me just when I decided I didn't wanna be bothered. I was mad all the time. I was doin everything I knew I shouldn't do, but it was like I had to do it. I felt like I was on the edge, you know? I felt like it was just a matter of time before somebody said somethin wrong to me and I was gonna go off.

Bein picked at in gym class didn't help. Those so-called athletic guys kept downin me and Armstrong because we couldn't climb the rope as fast or as pretty as they could. Them pickin at us was nothin new, but for some reason, I wasn't in the mood for it one particular day. This dude name Dwayne Rodgerson got the naggin goin that day. At one point he called me a sissy and said the reason my sissy ass couldn't climb was because I was a woman trapped in a boy's body. They all laughed real good at that line. Armstrong kept tellin me under his breath to kick Dwayne's ass.

"You gonna take that shit?" he asked. "If that was me I'd kick his ass past Jupiter, man!"

So I did it. Not because Armstrong told me to—Armstrong was always tellin me to—but because I was tired of bein messed with. I went at Dwayne like I was a bull. I rammed my head into his stomach and knocked him off his feet. He wasn't expectin the hit so he fell to the ground hard. And I didn't let up either. I dropped my little body on top of him and kept beatin him in the face. His homeboys were cheerin me on too. It took Coach Reed and two other coaches to finally pull us apart. Dwayne got in a few licks (he split my lip) but I kicked his ass. His ass looked like Rocky when I finished with him.

They couldn't find Daddy, so Eleanor came to school to get me. I like to died when she walked in Dean Myers' office.

"What the fuck she want?" I said as she walked in. She quickly slapped my face.

"Excuse me?" she said. "I know you're not talking to me."

I was hot and mad and wasn't stuttin her at that point. So I let her slap me and get away with it. But she had better not try it again, I thought.

"Hello, Mrs. Bach," Dean Myers said and rushed to offer her a chair. "I'm so sorry to bring you down here under such trying circumstances."

Myers was a baldheaded white man with flunky in his bones. He butt-kissed to parents so bad that a lot of the students called him Dean Bow Down. And man was he scrapin the floor when Eleanor came in.

"I understand he was fighting," Eleanor said, sittin her high behind down next to me.

"Yes ma'am," Bow Down said. "And of course you know, Mrs. Bach, we are absolutely opposed to violence."

Eleanor looked at the dean funny. "And I'm not?" she asked.

"Oh, of course you are. I didn't mean it that way, Mrs. Bach."

"Yes you did. Because I'm black I'm supposed to be in favor of violence, is that it?"

"No ma'am, not at—"

"Telling me you're opposed to violence. Well, who the hell isn't? Have you ever met anyone who was in support of violence, because if you did, I sure would like to meet him."

And on and on it went. Old Bow Down lowered his head and listened to her craziness with more patience than I had. After about three or four minutes of this, she finally shut up. He then told her exactly what happened.

"It wasn't my fault!" I yelled at Bow Down.

"You shut up," Eleanor said to me.

"We have ten witnesses, Mrs. Bach, and all ten declare it was Ralph who charged at the Rodgerson boy first."

"It ain't happened like that though," I said.

Eleanor started lookin at me like she couldn't believe I could talk, let alone talk tough.

"Everybody's not going to lie, Ralph," Bow Down said.

"Did they tell you they was messin with me, did they tell you that part?" I was a snap from cryin like a baby. I held it in, but they could tell I wanted to cry.

"Did someone hit you, Ralph?" Bow Down asked me.

"They was messin with me," I said. "What you think?"

"I think they may have exchanged words with you and you were rightly upset about that, but instead of going to Coach Reed you took matters into your own hands and initiated contact."

"Coach Reed? He be eggin Dwayne on! Man, please! Coach Reed worse than all of 'em."

"In any event, Mrs. Bach, that is what I was told happened."

"Were you there?" I asked Bow Down.

"I didn't have to be there. There were witnesses—"

"Naw, man. Fuck all that shit. I want to know if yo ass was there!"

Eleanor turned completely around toward me when I started cussin. I never ceased to amaze that bitch that day.

"Aren't you Mr. Hot Stuff all of a sudden," she said. "All of this gutter profanity. What's the matter with you?"

I ignored the shit out of her. Gutter profanity. What the hell she meant? I wanted to bust her up right then and there. Every chance she got she was throwin up the fact that I'm poor. Bitch.

She started tellin Dean Myers all about how she didn't realize what kind of child I was. "You ought to know," she said to him like tellin my business wasn't nothin to her, "he's actually not my son."

I shook my head. She was too much. "No shit, Sherlock," I said. She looked at me then, like she suddenly realized what I had just said, and hit me upside my head with her purse. She stood up. She wanted to make certain I understood every word she was about to say.

"Oh, now you wait one good goddamn minute," she said. "You will not sit up here and disrespect me, oh no sir. You can forget that notion right here and now. You think you're bad and from Harlem but wait—"

"Harlem?" I said. "What Harlem got to do with this?"

"You may be from Harlem and think you're bad and rough and tough, but wait until I get through with you. I am not the one to play with, and you'll do well to realize that!"

While she talked I shuffled around in my chair and did everything in my power to let her know I wasn't stuttin her. But she kept on yappin. I was a disgrace, she said. A savage. A ghetto wild boy. And old man Myers agreed with all of it. And as if they weren't enough, Daddy came. And he looked madder than his wife!

"Mr. Bach!" Myers said and stood to his feet. "Come in, please."

Daddy walked over by me. He was the tallest person in the room. He put my chin in his big hand and lifted my face up toward him. He was checkin out my cut lip.

"What happened to you?" he asked me. Naturally, Eleanor jumped in.

"He decides to brutally—"

"Let him answer," Daddy said to her without takin his eyes off me. I tried to explain it, includin how they was messin with me, but the more I talked the more I felt my goose was cooked. Daddy wasn't buyin it. I was wastin my time.

Daddy looked at Bow Down before I finished tellin my side of things. "Is he being suspended?" he asked him.

"Oh, yes sir. We have a strict policy—"

"How long?"

"Ah, ten days, sir."

Daddy looked back at me. "Get your things and let's go," he said.

I had the nerve to move slow gettin up, because I was in that kind of mood, but Daddy wasn't the one to play with either. He grabbed me by my shirt collar and pulled me up. Then he slung me out the door. If I had some kind of crazy notion that my tough-guy behavior was somehow gonna win him over, I was dreamin.

The Rodgerson incident never came up again. Eleanor tried to bring it up, but Daddy wasn't interested. He didn't even talk to me about it. I couldn't help but wonder if he would of acted the same way if Cole was the one suspended. Cole said that Daddy would of knocked him out if that was him, and I guess he was right. Daddy loved Cole, I was sure of that.

But those ten days came and went fast and before I knew it, I was back in school. Armstrong treated me like a hero, sayin Dwayne won't be messin with me no more, but most everybody else continued to give me the chill. My smart-boy image disappeared like magic, like people started figurin that ain't no way some wild joker like me could have brains. I got into fights and arguments most every day. I got suspended three more times. Daddy tried to talk to me, to tell me I was headed for danger, but you could tell his heart wasn't in it. He had other things on his mind. Me headin for danger wasn't nowhere on his agenda, really.

Even Cole tried to play that big brother shit with me. One day, while we walked to the 7-Eleven together, he talked about Jesus and gettin saved like he was scared he had to hurry up and let me know, for the thousandth time, before I died or somethin.

"Why don't you give your heart to God, Bay?"

I smiled. "What He want with my heart?"

"He can change your heart. And that's what you need. He can give you a change of heart."

"Yeah, Cole. Sure He can. But I'll think about it, all right?"

"You have an emptiness inside of you, Bay, that nothing's going to fill. Only Jesus can fill you. Besides, you don't really have nothing to lose and everything to gain."

"Gain? Like what? Goin to church every night? Listenin to that dull ass gospel music? No thanks!"

"You gain eternal life, Bay. You'll gain a place in heaven. This world won't have the same meaning it once had. You'll feel like a stranger just passing through on your way to your long home on high. Believe that, Bay. It's the truth."

It probably was true, the way Cole told it anyway, but I didn't have the right frame of mind for gettin saved. I felt like the world had screwed me over. I tried to go along with it like it wasn't so, but it was so. And before I found Jesus, God, or anybody else, I had to get back at that mean, cold world. I had to let them know it was my time to screw.

The baddest boy at Stuart was a big Barry White–lookin joker name Rory Long. Rory was a trip, man. He had knives and guns and once slashed up Dean Myers' tires. He and his brothers loved to go around braggin about how many times they been in jail. One of his brothers, Mike Long, had been in the Duval

Detention Center so many times that everybody called him DDC. Rory was the only one of those Long brothers who halfway came to school, but that was mainly because he sold crack and all of his customers were at school.

Rory and me was cool because I did everything in my power to stay out of his way. Then one day Rory was questioned by police about his drug dealin and, although he was let go, he made it his business to find out what dude set him up. Dwayne Rodgerson put the bug out that I was seen talkin with the cops, which was a lie, but Rory decided I had to be the one that busted him. I knew he suspected me, because Armstrong kept me informed, but I acted like I didn't know a damn thing. Rory was gonna jack me, I knew it, and I was ready for him. Me bein ready and him not knowin I was ready gave me the edge. He wouldn't try to knife me or shoot me because he knew that would put too much heat on him, but nobody that we knew of never went to jail for beatin shit out of somebody. His plan was to beat shit out of me.

It happened in the hallway after lunch. Rory and his boys came up to me real friendly. Then big Rory closed his brass-knuckled fist and slammed me in the stomach. I bent down and fell to my knees. I was hurtin for real, but I fell on my knees as a shield to pull out an iron crowbar I had cut down to fit underneath my shirt. When Rory grabbed me by the shirt to pull me up and give me some more, I slung out my crowbar and rammed it upside his head. The blood flew out like ketchup. His homeboys scattered, scared the blood would touch them and they would catch AIDS or somethin. Rory stumbled but he stayed on his feet. But I was a crazy man by then and I kept hittin him. I didn't stop until he was on the ground and stopped movin. By that time blood was all over him and me. I was breathin so hard I thought my heart was gonna tear out of my chest. Cole said God could change my heart. I wondered if that still was true.

By the time the ambulance came, Rory was awake and cussin me out. While I was beatin on Rory with my crowbar I was so crazy that I didn't even realize he was beatin the shit out of me with his knuckles. We was both taken to the hospital. The cops questioned both of us, but neither one of us would admit to nothin. I figured Daddy had connections, though, cause by the time I got out of the hospital the cops left me alone. Rory recovered too, but he stayed in the hospital longer. I guess you could say I got the better of that fight, I don't know. But the word that came down from the school board was tough: I was expelled and would not be allowed ever again to attend a Duval County public school.

Eleanor wanted me back in Harlem as fast as my ass could get there. Daddy stood by me, tellin that wife of his it would be over his dead body if I go anywhere. Even Cole was agreein with his mama, sayin I wasn't even tryin to do right no more. And David, who liked me in a way and hated me in another because I was Daddy's son, was tellin him to ditch me too.

But Daddy hung on. He listened to all the talk and all the doom and gloom and stood by me. I guess he was actin the way I had always dreamed he would: against the world he was standin by me. But it wasn't the same no more. The timing was wrong. It was as if he was standin by me because he felt guilty or somethin. It was like he wanted to prove to people that he could stand for somethin, and I guess I was all he had at the time.

Besides, we didn't get closer or nothin. He brought me home from the hospital, told me he hoped I had learned my lesson, and I was the invisible child again. Instead of feelin better about my relationship with Daddy, I was feelin worse. He didn't care nothin bout me. I nearly died in that fight (at least I felt like I was dyin), and he still was dissin me. The only personal thing he said to me was when he asked me if I wanted to call my mama. I told him no—I didn't want to worry her—and that was as far as he went.

Things changed forever for me one Saturday night, about a week after I got out of the hospital. Eleanor was goin on and on about kickin me out and Daddy was goin on and on tellin her no way. But you know what happened to me that Saturday night? I stopped carin about it. Nothin mattered no more. I felt powerful for the first time in my life. I felt like Michael Jordan must of felt when he scored all those points against the Knicks, man, cause I was in the zone too. They couldn't hurt me no more. They could kick me out, not kick me out, treat me bad, treat me good, love me, hate me. I didn't give a shit. Givin up felt good. It was the only thing I hadn't tried.

It took almost two weeks for Daddy to find a private school that would accept me. It was called Reese Academy and it was a trip and a half. All the guys had to wear these Scotland-lookin skirts. You couldn't talk loud in the hallway, and if you was caught cussin they sent you home. I got sent home a lot. And when I was there I didn't learn a damn thing because all the teachers were scared of me. They took my daddy's money and gave me a pass, man. I would sit in their cute little classes and go to sleep, and they would act like they didn't notice. One teacher, a nice young black lady, tried to notice and to talk to me and set me straight, but I cussed her out one day and that took care of that.

My life was upside down if you wanna know the truth. I couldn't see nothin. I knew I was hurtin people and ruinin my life but I couldn't stop it. It was like I had no control over what I did. I didn't even think about no consequences. Not until December 2, 1994. That was the day my shit caught up with me.

Me, Cole, and a boy name Hakeem, Cole's friend, was walkin to the 7-Eleven after shootin hoops at Rodney's house. Cole was talkin bout Jesus, naturally, and me and Hakeem were talkin bout girls (also naturally). I had Hakeem rollin when I described the girls at Reese.

I saw the car slow down behind us, but I didn't think nothin of it. The windows were all tinted so I couldn't tell who was inside. It wasn't until we had gone into the store and was walkin back home that I noticed the car was followin us. I didn't say nothin though, because Cole and Hakeem were too busy arguin about angels and shit. Then the electric window rolled down and I saw DDC. I knew right away he and his brothers had come to roll me.

I yelled for Cole and Hakeem to run and I took off runnin myself. DDC, Hipster, and some other boy jumped out of the car and took off behind us. That stupid ass Cole wouldn't run until he saw the danger, but by then it was too late. Hakeem was already gone and I was jumpin the fence when I heard the gunshot. I looked back as Cole was fallin down. He looked like a feather when he fell, like he was grabbin for the air to hold him up. Monroe Oliver's arched back flashed through my mind when Cole fell down. I was over the fence but I could see his body lyin in a curl on that ground. But almost by reflex, I kept on runnin.

The funeral was sadder than Joe Nathan's. Eleanor cried so much they had to take her out of the church. Daddy didn't cry, not even when he viewed the body in the casket, but he carried on like a baby when a big fat woman started singin a song about walkin the last mile of the way. It was a song about a man goin to heaven when he died. Cole went to heaven. I knew it. If anybody was goin, he went. That's what kept me goin. That's what kept me from snatchin all my clothes off and runnin and screamin from the top of my lungs.

David was there too, with some new girlfriend of his, and every now and then you could see him wipe a tear or two from his sleepy eyes. It was sad. Cole's church members were hollerin and jumpin up and down and Cole's pastor kept tellin us not to cry, that we should be rejoicin right now. "This ain't Brother Coleman's funeral," he said. "This his home-goin. And ain't no need of cryin when somebody goin home."

I told Mama over the phone that Cole got shot. She couldn't believe it could happen in a neighborhood like Daddy's. I didn't tell her why he got shot. I didn't tell her the bullet was aimed at me and Cole just got in the crossfire. She was sad that Cole was dead, and she asked how Daddy was takin it, but she was thankin Jesus it wasn't me. I wanted to throw the phone through the wall when she told God that.

Before Cole's accident I was tough. I didn't care about nothin. But after the shot was fired I went numb. I felt like I was in a trance. I felt like I was watchin a movie, and I was in it, and what I wanted to do didn't matter cause the movie was already wrote. And Mama was cryin and thankin God that it was Cole in that box and not me. And I didn't tell her nothin. I couldn't.

Eleanor left Daddy after the funeral. She blamed me for Cole's death. She said if Daddy didn't send me packin now, she would leave him. Daddy didn't make me go, and she left. He probably wanted her to go anyway. She liked people to feel guilty all the time. She wouldn't let Daddy forget that he should of never brought me near her house. Now Cole was dead. Who can live with that kind of shit over their head?

The house got quiet after she left. No more arguments, slammin doors, ringin telephones. Even the television never came on. I guess we didn't see the point no more. Daddy went to work and came home. I went to school and came home. And DDC got away with murder cause I didn't tell the cops nothin. I couldn't. It wasn't me no more.

The nightmares started almost right away. Daddy would run into my room if I screamed loud enough, and some nights he slept in a chair beside my bed. It was too much for him. He wasn't used to this kind of life. He lost his wife, his son, and probably David forever because of me. *Me!* I wasn't worth it. I could see it in his eyes. One night I told him. I told him everything I was feelin. I told him how he didn't never love me and how he was a nothin for a father and how he didn't even come to Joe Nathan's funeral. I was yellin and screamin at him before I was through. I didn't care that my yellin was a nail in my coffin for sure. I had to say it. It wasn't like I had somethin to lose.

Daddy listened to me go on and on, but he ain't said nothin back. He sat quietly in that little chair by my big bed and let me do my thing. It was late, almost after midnight, and he looked like he didn't have no energy to be arguin with me.

He got up to leave when I couldn't find nothin else to blame him for. He put his hands in his pockets and looked down at me. He was worn out. I did that to him. Him and his family was probably happy and satisfied before I came along. Now they wasn't even a family no more. All because of me. All because of some stupid dream I had that any fool could have seen wasn't about to come true.

He turned to leave but then he turned back toward me. He had one of those stunned looks on his face, as if he couldn't believe what was happenin in his life. He started to say somethin. I could see his lips part as he started to tell me somethin. But he didn't. He just turned back around and walked out of my room. We didn't have hardly nothin in common, me and my daddy. Except maybe how good we were at givin up.

Thirteen

I left Florida on a rainy December morning. Me and Daddy stood outside that station and waited for the bus to come like we was two people that didn't know each other. I didn't look at him and he didn't look at me. We didn't even try to talk or smile or even pretend that we was gonna stay in touch with each other. Some things was never meant to be, like me and my daddy.

The bus drove up and an old, short man started loadin people on it. Daddy told me goodbye and tried to hug me. He tried to anyway. I pulled away from him and reached out my hand. He looked at me hard at first, like he couldn't understand what was goin on, but then he stopped tryin to act like he was somebody's concerned daddy and shook my hand instead. I trembled. I wanted to cry so bad but I didn't. I ain't cryin no more. It took me a long time to figure it out, but tears don't get nobody like me nowhere in this world. People don't treat you right when they think you're weak. You show them the first sign of emotion cause you can't help how you feel, and they treat you like somethin wrong with you. Uh-uh. I wasn't thinkin bout cryin no more.

When I let Daddy's hand go I turned and got on the bus. I didn't turn back around to see him wave or smile or do what all those other people were doin when their loved ones got on the bus. I tried everything I knew how to get him to love me but he wouldn't do it. I'd understand it better if I had asked him for a lot of money or a lot of fancy clothes or somethin like that. But all I wanted was his love. I ain't gonna never understand why he wouldn't even give me that. Then when I gave up too and stopped givin a damn just like him, Cole got killed. That was on me. That was my fault. That's why I got on that bus in Jacksonville, Florida and didn't look back. What I'm gon look back for?

So I left the sunshine state on that rainy December day. I left slumped down in my seat on the back of the bus. The rain was beatin hard against the window like it was darin me to look outside, but I didn't. I was glad to be leavin Florida. What Florida ever done for me except tear my dream apart? I folded my arms and closed my eyes. The bus driver announced we was enterin Georgia, the peach state. And I said amen. I finally felt like I was gettin somewhere.

I was gettin far away from my daddy and I was feelin better the farther I got. There was a time when I could forgive my daddy for anything. And I mean *anything*! But I can't forgive him no more. Even if he had ran up on that bus and begged me to come back to him, it wouldn't of changed nothin. I would of just turned my head away and acted like I didn't know him. That's what Tom Bach and Florida did for me. And if anybody ask me ever again to tell them about my daddy and what kind of man he is, I'll look them dead in the eye and tell them like it is. *My daddy ain't shit*, I'm gonna say.

But Mama want me to tell her more. She think Daddy took his grief over Cole dyin out on me and that's why it didn't work out in Florida. She think it's as simple as that. And she want me to tell her what happened. Dr. Dan told me to tell *him* what happened. I'll tell them all right. They tried to put a tuxedo on a rattlesnake and pretend it wasn't so. That's what happened. And when the rattlesnake started rattlin, which is what it's supposed to do, they started pointin fingers and yellin, "I told you so! I told you so!" That's what happened.

But Mama still don't get it. She believe in happy endings. She won't accept the fact that ain't no happy endings in this world for me. From the day I was born I been behind the eight ball. That's a stone cold fact. Mama thinks talkin bout it is gonna change that fact. Then I can be happy, she thinks. She's dreamin big time. How the hell my talkin is gonna change the fact that Cole is dead and my own daddy hate me? What my talkin gonna do about that? My dumb ass got a good boy like Cole killed. I can't change that. I've gotta live with that for the rest of my life, and I can talk till I can't talk no more and I still gotta live with it.

But that's old news now. That's in the past, and I can't deal with that past shit right now. I thought I was livin large, that's all. I thought there was plenty good room in that world of Daddy's and I was gonna fit right in.

But I didn't. How could I? He dangled that good life at me like it was as simple as danglin a carrot, and as quick as I reached for it he snatched it right back. That's too much to deal with. Cause it ain't right for somebody like me to get peeps at paradise. I don't know how to handle peeps. I start gettin all personal, like maybe that world I'm lookin at is meant for me, and soon as I start dreamin bout it, soon as I start believin that it might can happen, somebody always makes a point of tappin me on the shoulder and closin up all the peepholes.

Teresa McClain-Watson has been writing books, plays, and poems since the age of nine. A lifelong resident of Florida, she received her Bachelor's degree from Florida State University and her Master's degree in History and Education from Florida A&M University. Currently she is employed by the State of Florida as a social services counselor. In her spare time she enjoys viewing foreign-language films with her husband John. *Plenty Good Room* is her first published work.

Other selected fiction from Fjord Press

Love Like Gumbo
by Nancy Rawles
$14.00 paperback

The Five Thousand and One Nights
by Penelope Lively
$12.00 paperback

Runemaker
by Tiina Nunnally
$12.00 paperback

Maija
by Tiina Nunnally
$12.00 paperback

Niels Lyhne
by Jens Peter Jacobsen
Translated from the Danish by Tiina Nunnally
$14.00 paperback

Mogens and Other Stories
by Jens Peter Jacobsen
Translated from the Danish by Tiina Nunnally
$12.00 paperback, $24.00 cloth

Please write, fax, or email for a free catalog:
Fjord Press, PO Box 16349, Seattle, WA 98116
fax (206) 938-1991 / email fjord@halcyon.com
Visit our web site at http://www.fjordpress.com/fjord
for more information and reading samples